Private Classes

By NatLJohns

DEDICATIONS

To my family and friends for their love and support.

ACKNOWLDGMENTS

I would like to thank God for giving me so many gifts and talents. I do believe in the saying "If you don't use what God has given you, He will take it away." If this isn't the truth, I don't know what is. Within this statement, I want to thank my mother. Well, I was the youngest of three with eight and twelve years being the difference in our ages. That meant, I basically grew up as an "only" child. I had plenty of time to daydream, imagine, and create scenes and stories in my head to keep me busy and be preoccupied. That creativity never decreased as years went by. It increased with age and the stories advanced with circumstances, life, and education. It made the creativity stronger, broader, and relatable. So I thank you both.

First, I would like to thank my family. I appreciate the patience you have exhibited with me for not only getting the first book done and published, but for the second book to be done, while I am working on the third book. I know there may have been some missed dinners, phone calls, interactions yet again, and sports games (basketball, football, and track). I appreciate that you kept your frustrations to yourself (or away from me). Some of you may have thought this was a hobby since I have had the love for writing for so long but as you see, it is not just a hobby. I love writing just as any other author, poet, storyteller, activist, speech teacher, blogger, etc. It is a passion of mine and I really do believe I should have started publishing my works many years ago. However, maybe it wasn't my time and there is no time like the present. It was a joy for me to see your wide smiles when I showed you the beautiful book cover. Thank you for sharing it with your friends. It warmed my heart to see your excitement when I showed you *Private Classes* was now on Amazon and your daughter, mother, sister, aunt, cousin, social club member, and co-worker is now a published author. Hey, what can I say? I took some time out for me. Thank you Che'la, Che'Nay, Zachary, Mama Katie, Mama Neicy, Kevin, Korin, Kordell, Kayla, Ka'Mya, Tierra, Breona, Marlee Rose, Phillip, and Jace. I love you all dearly!

Secondly, I would like to thank my friends. Those who saw the very first draft of my creation when we were on that plane headed for Las Vegas. I was nervous as heck but I had several glasses of wine while y'all read it (thank you). I know both of you thought I was writing about you and your steamy sexcapades … wrong (lol). Strictly from my creative imaginary house. Thank you Jackie and Arlette. Those who read it and didn't falter in suggesting that I needed to hurry up and share my gift with the world. Those who proudly broadcasted on our bus trips about my venture. Thank you Brenda, Michelle W., Angie Ang, Ree, Verna, Kathy, Darlene, and Linda M. You are very dear to my heart. Those who took the time to talk about it with me and others as if they were in a book club. Maybe we should have some sessions and create a blog, what you think, lol? Those who shared and participated in the advertising of birth *Private Classes*. To my Facebook family, friends, and the groups I belong to, thank you for being so loyal. You know I will need you for Book 2 also, right? I'm just keeping it real. Much love to you!

Thirdly, my loving pets. Now, I know you wait for me to put that special ingredient in your food when I get home. I apologize for it was being missing. Your mama was on a mission and she made the first step in completing it. I might be on Book 3 right now, but I promise that I will make sure you get your rice, grits, oatmeal, or potatoes mixed up in your dry food. Love you Rambo and Javier.

Renee and Daddy, I know both of you are looking down on me smiling. Renee you always were proud of me no matter what I did. You may have been my big sister but you were definitely my other mother. I love you and miss you so much. Daddy, you always bragged about your "L'il Girl" and how she was great at whatever she put her mind too. I thank you for that. I know you are up there bragging right now and I have a wide smile on my face. Can you believe that Grandma is about to turn 101 this year? She is still going strong. I promise I will get down to West Palm Beach to see her and Aunt Lucy, okay? Love you Daddy.

Oh "NL," I want to thank you for taking the time to further edit this novel. You saw the errors and corrected them. Many of which were not made by me. What would I do without you and your proofreading skills? I have so much love for you. Muah!!

Hey Momma, I know I frustrated you through my many talents of Gloria Baker's School of Dance (ballet, modern, tap, and, point), DC Youth Orchestra (clarinet, flute, saxophone, and HARP (yes readers, I said HARP), knitting, crocheting, sewing, drawing, pattern designer; college, grad school (I won't be going for my Doctorate lol). I was trying to see where I fit in. I know I did them all well, and you would always say I was a "Jack of All Trades and a Master of None." Not anymore. I believe I am where I need to be. Love you Mommy (and she's 79 years YOUNG)!!

Many thanks to you all.

Chapter One

1

Mmm, what time is it? Yuck, I have an awful taste in my mouth and it is dry. The sun is shining too damn bright through the window this morning. What happened to my sleeping mask? Shit, I didn't wrap my hair last night. I hope it isn't messed up. I just got it done yesterday. I must've come home and crashed hard. How many apple martinis did I have? I lost count after the fourth glass. Oooh, I have to pee but I can't move. Oh my goodness!! What is that ... is there a dick behind me? I'm scared to turn around. Let me turn around slowly so I won't alarm him too much before I start swinging.

Colleen begins to turn over slowly. At first the body behind her holds on as if it doesn't want her to move. She is persistent though. Colleen has to see who is in her bed. Then again ... wait a minute. As she looks around at the room scene in front of her,

Colleen realizes she isn't at her home. The bedroom she is in now is the same size as her grand Master bathroom. Plus her bedroom is paprika, gold, and olive with hints of warm browns. This room is navy and burgundy with white dingy walls. None of this looks familiar to her. It is apparent that she hasn't been here before. Enough of the damn suspense. Colleen needs to know where she is and with whom. She turns over to see whose bed she is sleeping in.

"Good morning Colleen," the sexy voice says as she's turning around to see whose body the dick is attached to.

"Devin? *What?!* How did I get here? This isn't your place, right? Is this your place?" Colleen is confused to be waking up to this scene.

"Yes, this is my place Colleen. You were pretty drunk last night. I wasn't about to have you drive home in that condition. I drove your car here, and my cousin has mine."

Colleen looks at him still trying to process what is going on. Looking at herself, she asks, "How did I get out of my clothes and what's this I have on?" She rubs on the strange garment.

"The jersey belongs to me. I helped you take off your clothes before you threw up all over my floor. I didn't want to get it on your clothes. It's not like you have a change of clothes here."

"Threw up?! Shit! I *knew* I shouldn't have had more than four martinis. Devin, I am *sooo* sorry. Did I mess up anything? I'll pay for it." Colleen is truly embarrassed. She has never gotten that drunk before. Especially to the point that she doesn't know what is going on.

"No, you're all right. Don't worry about it. I don't have carpet. My floors won't be buffed until next week."

"Devin … did we …?" Curiosity is killing her. Even though he has never tried anything before and she knows they are just friends, she just wants to make sure. Besides, if Colleen is going to get filled-up, she wants to be coherent enough to experience the fill-up moment.

"Nooo, we did not. We're friends but not those *kinds* of friends, remember?" Devin smiles at Colleen. His teeth are so perfect and white sitting behind his full lips. Colleen is looking at Devin a little.

"I know that, but it doesn't hurt to ask, right" Colleen says smiling back. "What do you have for a headache? My head is banging!"

"I have ginger-ale and a bed for plenty of rest. I don't drink like that so hangovers are not one of my specialties. If there is a hangover in this house, it's doesn't belong to me. Are you hungry? I can cook you some breakfast."

"Oh, no thank you. I would take a ginger-ale though, thank you. The thought of breakfast is making me nauseous right now," Colleen is rubbing her head and stomach trying to calm down the ache and the queasiness.

"Okay, I'll be back in a minute with that for you. You can rest here until you are ready to go. No rush. Take your time. I hung your clothes up in the closet."

"Okay. And Devin … thank you," Colleen says discomfited.

"You're welcome. Sometimes, we all need real friends of the opposite sex." Devin winks at her and turns around to walk out of the bedroom.

Colleen gives Devin a faint smile, gets up slowly to go in the bathroom.

Devin's bathroom is really nice. His trash can, soap dish, toothbrush holder, tissue box and a strange looking bowl with potpourri in it all match. Everything is beautiful and the potpourri smells good too. *Hmmp, two toothbrushes? I wonder who the other one belongs to? These sconces are beautiful and different. Mmm, candles to match the decoration, huh? You go boy! Where did he get this wall border? I need to shop where he is shopping. This bathroom definitely has a woman's touch. I wonder who she is,* Colleen says to herself looking around the bathroom and touching the decor.

Looking in the mirror, Colleen's hair is a mess. She quickly wraps it and puts a few bobby pins in it so it would stay up. If she doesn't carry any other hair products, bobby pins and a hair band are two items she makes sure are in her handbag at all times. They will always come in handy. Colleen notices her make-up is gone. At first she thinks maybe it is all over the pillowcase. She looks again at the younger version of Wendy Racquel Robinson - from the *Steve Harvey Show* - staring back at her and realizes her face has been cleaned. She still has on her panties but the bra is gone. She really couldn't believe she was that drunk. She doesn't remember a damn thing. Devin has seen her body without her really knowing and respected her enough not to try anything. Colleen smiles at the thought of how reverential her friend is.

Walking back into the room, Colleen realizes the room isn't bad at all. It looks nothing like it did when she first woke up. She looks back at the bathroom to see if she came out a different door than the one she entered through. Nope, one way in and one way out. Holding her head she says, *Those martinis really got me trippin'.*

Actually, the room is comparatively nice and has a feminine touch to it as well. It isn't even navy and burgundy. The bedroom is a combination of ivory, mocha, and sage with hints of rust. Colleen nods her head in approval of what she is observing. *Very niiice Devin. Nicely done. I didn't know you had it in you. Where did I get those other colors from?* Peace Lilies, Rhododendron Hopes, and Mother-in-Laws plants are all around the room. It seems like they are evenly distanced apart as if the space is measured.

"I am positive Devin had help from the opposite sex with his place. He must be in a serious relationship. Which explains why he didn't touch me last night. He's never mentioned a woman to me but that will be asked soon." Colleen said out loud to herself.

Colleen lies back down on the bed. She notices it is a plush queen size with a very expensive king size comforter on it. She moves her arms up and down as if making an angel in the snow. "Hmmp, dry clean only, huh? I think I better fold this back out of my way. Don't want to mess anything up. Devin, boy ... I didn't know you had this type of taste. Or maybe someone helped you get this taste. But still a man after my own heart."

Devin comes back in the room with the ginger-ale, a glass of ice, a plate of *Nabisco Premium Cheddar* crackers, and *Jif* peanut butter with a butter knife in it on a tray. He carefully sits the tray on the night stand. As he walks over to sit down on the tapestry covered ottoman, he asks Colleen, "Sooo, how do you feel? You're looking quite beautiful regardless. Is there anything I can do for you?"

Colleen blushes and runs her hand across her hair to assure it is still wrapped. *He always says the nicest things and treats me like a lady. That's good home training right there. His Mama raised him right.*

"Aren't you so *sweeeeet*? Thank you, Devin. Now that I have gotten up and moved around, I don't feel too bad at all. I went in the bathroom to wash my face but I see that's already been done.

Do I need to thank you for that too? I mean, I've never had to say 'thank you' to any man so many times. Especially in one day."

"I gave you a facial, no big deal. No need for a thank you. Besides, I didn't want that make-up all over my sheets." Devin smiles and gets up to kiss her on the forehead. Colleen laughs and pushes his arm.

A facial? I knew my face was feeling extra clean and soft but, a facial? What in the world? Where has this man been all my life? I guess he's been too busy being my "friend." Damn! Too bad I was too drunk to enjoy anything he did to and for me.

"Okay, wait a minute … hold up. This is too much to absorb all at once. You did all this for *me*? And you were willing to cook me breakfast *too*? All for me and you didn't ask or want anything from me in return. Why? What's your angle?" Colleen pours the ginger-ale into the glass of ice.

"What's my angle? What are you insinuating? Excuse me? What are you talking about? Colleen, what type of men have you been seeing? Never mind, I already know that," Devin waves Colleen off and goes to lean up against the wall with his arm folded.

"Now, what is meant by that Mr. Maddock? There is nothing wrong with any of the men I am dating or have dated." She is getting very defensive at what she is hearing.

"Yeah, if you say so. I guess that's why you're not used to telling men 'thank you' so often in a day. Or ever for that matter. That is what you said, right," Devin sarcastically says.

"So you did all of this for me to try and prove a point?" Colleen snaps at Devin. She is not feeling all that great about herself right now. She knows Devin is right. It just didn't sound all that great when he said it. Yet the words rolled out of his mouth so easily.

"All of what Colleen," Devin's eyebrows crease into a confused frown. "I didn't do anything for you that I wouldn't do for any other friend. And I expect my friends to do the same for me."

"Devin, not today, please. You've treated me so nice and I love you for it. Please don't bring me down." She takes another sip of her soda and leans back on the bed.

"That's not what I'm tryin' to do. Does that sound like me? It just bothers me to see you settle for less because ..."

"Because you want us to be together?" Colleen knows the answer. She just wants to see if he'll say it. She knows Devin wants to be with her but he has never said it or tried anything. Maybe her behavior scares him.

"Colleen ..."

"Never mind, Devin. Don't say it. Don't even worry about it. Again, I'm just trying to enjoy the pampering." Colleen starts realizing some things are better left unsaid. Besides, what if he really doesn't want to be with her? She is not too keen on rejection ... that'll be a new one for her. Colleen rolls over on the bed so her back is to Devin. She doesn't want him seeing her pouting, yet, she doesn't know what she is pouting about.

"Okay, if that's the way you want it," Devin says throwing his arms up. "This is your moment. I won't say anything else. I'll be downstairs in the sunroom having a little breakfast. You can join me if you like."

Colleen abruptly rolls over. "A s*unroom*? You have a sunroom? This is a house? You live in a house?!" Colleen is about sick of the surprises. It's apparent she knows very little about her friend. *I guess what he lives in never came up in our conversations. He's been over my house plenty of times and never mentioned it.*

Devin looks at Colleen and shakes his head in amazement. "You may not have been here before but you have been told where I live and what I live in. Feel free to look around. I have nothing to hide. My house is open to my friends."

"I'll look around later. I want to rest up for another hour or two." *Why does the word "friend" keep coming up?*

Colleen watches Devin leave the room. She never realized before how sexy Devin is. Or maybe it has something to do with waking up feeling his dick on her ass. Right now, feeling it inside a part of her body is what she wants. Like men wake up in the morning with a hard on, Colleen wakes up with a moist pussy ready to roll around in the sheets. That's why she has never stayed over any of male friends' place. She will be willing to screw anybody in the morning.

Colleen knows she and Devin are just friends and it seems as if he is adamant about remaining strictly platonic friends. That's cool though. So at this time, she'll just fantasize about his hardness. Colleen starts thinking about Devin in a way she never has. She is so horny she'll fuck a nineteen year old and wouldn't be ashamed either.

Colleen starts squeezing her breasts and bringing them to her mouth for nibbling and sucking on her nipples. She moves her hands slowly down to her moistness. Colleen softly rubs her inner thighs with her right hand while the left hand rubs softly through her well manicured pubic hairs. Colleen imagines Devin's hands are doing this instead of hers. As she starts imagining Devin's balls smacking against her ass, she couldn't take it anymore. Colleen inserts her middle finger while playing with her clit. She is soak and wet. She could feel her juices running down her butt cheeks. How she longs for the juices to be mixed with Devin's cum, running down his balls, her butt, and onto the sheets. Oh, how she loves a messy fuck.

Colleen's fingers aren't doing it for her. They are too skinny and aren't long enough to hit the right spots. She is trying to figure out what can she use instead. She remembers she has a perfume bottle in her purse that is shaped like a silo. Colleen hurries to get it and inserts it in her wetness. She didn't want to mess up her rhythm. Aaah, this is perfect. It is going as deep as she wants it and thick enough to do for the moment. She lifts a breast to her mouth again. She is in another world. Completely forgetting she isn't at her home. It doesn't matter anymore. She needs to get off. The bottle is the closest she'll get to a dick right now.

It is feeling so good. The bottle is covered with her juices, which makes it glide in and out easily. Colleen is moaning and moving against the bottle to help with clitoral friction. Still imagining it is Devin's dick and hands, something strange happens. Colleen feels a warm hand touch hers, helping to glide the bottle in and out her drenched pussy. Is she imagining this? No.

Colleen opens her eyes to see Devin on the side of her, looking into her eyes, then at her pussy, as he continues to help her glide the bottle. She moves her hand and goes back to sucking on her nipples, hoping he'll help out there too. Instead, Devin guides her hand to rub his erection through his sweat pants. She could see little wet spots on his pants. Colleen decides to free his dick from being cramped inside his pants. *Oooh*, Devin isn't wearing any underwear. This is making Colleen hotter and hotter.

When she frees his dick, it is fully erect and standing at attention. She and dick are staring at each other. It is huge and dripping pre-cum. *Did he want her to suck it? It is too big.* She has never seen anything like it. She knows she will get lock-jaw in ten seconds. Colleen rises anyway to taste it. Devin closes his eyes, shakes his head "no" to stop her. Maybe he knows better. He takes her hand and start moving it up and down on the shaft. Colleen decides to rub her thumb on the head spreading the pre-cum all over the head. This makes Devin lean back to further enjoy, watching and moaning.

Both Colleen and Devin are working their hands on each other in a frenzy. Neither can stand it any longer. Colleen raises her legs and spreads them as wide as she can, screaming, "Move it hard baby! Move it deeper!" Her body starts trembling uncontrollably. Her orgasm is hard. Devin has his teeth and jaws clenched tight together and he's rubbing on his balls while Colleen is still stroking his pre-cum soaked manhood.

Watching Colleen's swollen clit and wet pubic hairs, Devin removes the bottle and inserts three fingers moving them in different directions while using his thumb to play with her clit. Colleen never had this before. She moans out loud, arches her back, and grabs one of her legs raising it to her breast.

She wants Devin's fingers to get in as far as they could go. She explodes all over his fingers and hands. Devin can feel her inner walls contracting on his fingers. Devin is about to go crazy. His dick is getting harder by the second. Colleen watches on ready to have her fourth orgasm. She didn't think he could get any harder. With a trembling voice, Devin says, "Damn your pussy looks so good. I just wanna … *aaaagh*!" Devin explodes all over Colleen's hand, his stomach, the bed, and the nightstand. Colleen puts her soaked fingers in her mouth lapping it up like it is homemade gravy.

She is ready for the real thing but slightly afraid. Of all the dicks she's had, she has never even come close to one with the length and mass of Devin's. It is almost as if he is deformed but it is so beautiful. *We need to be careful for what we wish for. We might get a Devin. He puts Mandingo to shame.*

Colleen doesn't know whether to be embarrassed or thankful Devin joined her. Devin has his eyes close still enjoying Colleen rubbing his manhood.

"Devin, how long was you watching me? I thought you were eating breakfast. I really didn't mean to be doing that."

"I did eat breakfast. All I had was two slices of wheat toast, a fruit bowl, and a glass of orange juice. You didn't want anything so there was no need to cook. I thought you were going to look around. When you didn't, I came to see if you were sleep. If you were, I was going to close the door. I didn't want my video game to disturb you. However, when I got to the door … I was shocked to see you busy at pleasing yourself. I have never actually seen a woman masturbate. Many men have told me they love watching and I see why. The closer I got, I saw you were improvising. I'm sorry, but it was really turning me on. I didn't mess up our friendship, did I?"

"No, you didn't do anything wrong. I really shouldn't have been doing that here. But, I did want you to do more. I wanted to do more but I know you would have been uncomfortable."

"Oh, I wasn't uncomfortable but you would have been. I didn't want to start something we wouldn't have been able to finish. I've been down that road plenty of times."

"What do you mean by that? How would I have been uncomfortable? You think I wouldn't have been able to still be friends?" Colleen is playing coy. She knows exactly what he is talking about.

"No, it's not that. I know I am extremely large. There hasn't been a woman yet that can handle me. That's not me sounding arrogant either. Plus, I have a freaky side and it's hard to be me when the woman is in pain."

"Damn … freaky, huh? I mean you are large and no I haven't seen one like it before, but …" she hesitates looking at his limp phallus.

"But what?" Devin asked, wanting to know what she really has to say.

"But, if you don't mind me asking … what do you do for sex?"

"I'd like to call it intimacy. However, I have had encounters like we just had. It's been a while because that's a tease for me. I'm a man. I want to feel the warmth and wetness inside of a woman like any other man and not just with my fingers and tongue. However, I think I just woke up that feeling. It has been sleep for a minute."

Tongue? Why didn't he use that today? I mean, since he was all out to help a sista.

"I can tell it's been a while," Colleen is laughing hard. "Cum is all over the place. You had a serious back-up. How long has it been for real Devin?"

"Let's just change the subject. I'd rather not answer your question. We are friends and I know we just had a sexual moment but my sex life is private. You don't talk about yours with me, do you? Besides, I don't need any of your friends secretly laughing at me when I'm in their presence."

Colleen throws her hands up as if to surrender. *Secretly laughing? My friends? Hmmp. Hell, they'd be more apt to jump his bones*, Colleen said in her mind.

"Hey, you got it. I will say no more. When you're ready to talk, I'll listen. I'm about to take a shower. May I have a wash cloth and towel please?"

"Sure you may. Sooo, what do you have planned for today? No clients?" Devin goes outside of the room to the linen closet.

"There are a few people I need to see before I go to the Spa this evening with the girls. Other than that, my day is free."

Devin comes back in the room with the softest, thickest gold towel and matching wash cloth Colleen has ever seen. They are beautiful, rich in color, and smell good too.

"These are beautiful. My goodness, you are really full of surprises. Every time I ask something, your response or presentation leaves me in awe."

"Surprises?! I don't think so. You still talking about the wrong man, I see. I am for real … every inch of me. Nothing about me is fake."

In her mind, Colleen says, *"You got that right."* Looking down at his almighty limpness, she smiles and asks, "Do you want to join me, my non-fake friend?"

"I'll take a rain check. I don't want to run you away. Now, you go take a shower in there and I'll shower in my bathroom downstairs."

"Your bathroom? Downstairs? Dammit Devin, I said no more surprises. So this isn't your room?" *I can't take too much more of this. Maybe he needed to have written me a newsletter or something and gave it to me to read before I got out the bed.*

"It's my room because it's in my house. This isn't where I sleep. You thought this was the Master bedroom? Umm, no. I will remind you again, we are friends. So the guest room is where you'd stay when you are here. I mean, even though we have just crossed the line a little bit, this is one of my guest rooms."

"One of? Well, how many guest rooms do you have Mr. Maddock? I mean can I get a floor plan please? I'm not trying to get lost in here." Colleen is really paying attention to Devin now. *I have really missed a lot about my friend all of this time.*

"On this floor, there are three. Oh and there are two toothbrushes in this bathroom. Unless you carry a one in your purse, help yourself. They're new. "

"This floor? How many rooms and floors are there? I surely do not remember any of this. Oh, and I'm glad you cleared up the toothbrush matter. When I thought this was your Master bedroom, I thought the second toothbrush represented a mysterious woman."

"Well, for one our conversations are always about you, your girlfriends, some man you met, or one of your clients. I would ask how was your day and 'your day' would be the entire conversation. That's until some man ask you to dance or buy you a drink. Then there is the matter of you actually coming to my house last night and you were pissy drunk. Oh and if there is a mysterious woman, you will be the first to know and see. I do value what you think and feel."

Colleen didn't realize how much she talks about herself. Nor did she realize how much she meant to Devin. *Have I really been self-centered? Have I been taking my friendship with Devin for granted always demanding to be the focus? I've been told by several that I am selfish and I just have never understood what they meant by that. Maybe I just wasn't listening. But what Devin has said to me today was well listened to.*

"Oh Devin, I'm sorry. I don't even know what to say. I never meant to be selfish. But just within this little bit of time, I really see what I have missed. I will work on that. I will add it to my New Year's resolution. Today will be all about you. I promise. I will take the personal tour of your place now. After that, I will wash every muscle … and I do mean *every* muscle … hard and soft."

They both laugh. Devin motions for her to follow him. When she gets close to him, he grabs her hand saying, "Your new year's resolution? Oh, you're gonna wait that long before you start working on it, huh?" They both continue having a "laughing friends" moment. "At least being your friend, I know what to expect from you. But I told you don't start something I know we won't be able to finish … *friend.*"

Hmmp, but I wouldn't mind having fun trying. Putting all of what I learned in class to practice, Colleen says to herself swinging Devin's hand in hers.

Chapter Two

2

Regina sits up on her plush king size sleigh bed trying to wake up. Her eyes are still tightly closed refusing to let the day in. It is seven o'clock in the morning and she is feeling like Annie Lee's painting *Blue Monday* even though it is more like blue Thursday. The radio alarm clock goes off again. Regina has already hit the snooze button three times. She knows she really has to get up now. There is a list of things she needs to get done before tomorrow.

This time, WHUR is playing a song she likes. She forgot she changed the radio to that station last night to listen to The Quiet Storm. Now, she's listening to The Real DC Morning Show. Regina starts moving her head and humming to the beat forcing her to open her eyes. By the time the song gets to *"In the morning, the sun's gonna shine,"* Regina is up off the bed heading to the bathroom dancing as if she doesn't want to wake anyone in the house. However, she knows better than that. The only other person in the house is Maria and she hasn't been sleep since five this morning.

A nice warm shower was just what Regina needed to help her wake up. She doesn't know why she'd feeling tired since she was in the house all day yesterday. The not too hot stream made just enough mist inside the frosted glass doors to awaken her slowly. As she steps out of the shower, closing the shower doors, she grabs her plush slate blue towel to wrap it around her and walks over to the marbled top double sink.

Regina looks at her face in the mirror and smiles. She knows she looks young for her age and her mocha skin is beautifully glowing. It is truly flawless. Regina wonders how long will it last. Regina always gets compliments on her skin. Men have always thought she look like Cindy Herron from En Vogue. Women will ask her what kind of foundation she uses. They always think she is lying when she says she doesn't use any foundation. Some of them even get mad at her as if she is being secretive. That always tickles her. Regina closes her eyes and laughs to herself at what she is thinking about.

Since Regina is admiring herself, she takes off her robe and looks at her body from the front, back, left, and right side views. Walking over to the two matching lemon sherbet painted doors, she opens the door to the Hygiene Closet, reaching for a jar of La Mer moisturizing cream to apply to her skin. Gathering cream in her hands, sitting the jar on the sink, Regina begins applying cream to her body as she studies it.

She examines her breasts and thinks they can stand to be a little bigger. Well, at least the next cup size. When she was growing up, the older girls used to say they would get bigger when they start getting sucked on a lot. That definitely had to be a myth because

Regina's have been played with, sucked on, as well as pulled and massaged quite often after she heard that. Yet, her breasts never got any bigger than an "A" cup. However, she has never been teased or got any complaints. They are more than a mouth full so that's definitely a plus.

Moving down to her stomach and turning around to check out her back, Regina rubs her skin softly, slowly massaging it with the moisturizing cream. The weightless cream has her skin so smooth that it feels good even to her touch. She is imagining being watched while she does this. So her moves become a little more sensuous. Still looking at her body in the mirror, she says to herself, *No rolls or love handles. No blemishes or acne on the back or at the waist side. I can still see the signs of a four pack appearing in my stomach.* Regina was trying for a six pack but she had to let the trainer go. Found out he was a little on the crazy side. It was imperative for me to evict him from my life.

Looking at the curve in her hips, they aren't too small or too large. Regina's hips are just the right size and they help to accentuate her ass, which looks like two cantaloupes attached to her lower back. Rubbing on her thighs and legs, she thinks they are just the way a man wants them, firm enough not to shake but soft to the touch. Once she gets to her feet, she makes sure her heels are well lubed and she gets lotion in between each toe. Regina has the perfect toes. They look like stair steps and she keeps them done with either a French manicure or cotton candy nail polish. Getting a little tickled, she smiles. She loves getting her feet massaged and her toes sucked. Just the thought right now makes her shiver.

Putting back the body cream, she retrieves the Avon cleanser, toner, and moisturizer for her face. Regina begins cleansing her face while going over in her mind what she needs to get done today. She is going to *The Poconos* with her husband Stan for the weekend. They have never been to *The Poconos* before and she doesn't know what to expect. She has an idea what it is going to be like but she just wants everything to be perfect. She has some surprises for Stan and is hoping he has some surprises for her too. Just thinking about the weekend makes her feel like a cheerleader at a football game and her team is winning. She really enjoys spending time with her husband even if it just means sitting in the same room with him while he is working. Just to be near him is enough to satisfy her at times.

Sometimes when Stan is in his office preparing a presentation for an upcoming meeting, Regina will come in quietly, sit down on the leather chaise lounge and read one of E. Lynn Harris book or thumb through a *Shape* or *Fitness* magazine. Periodically, she will look up at him and smile. Nothing warms her heart more than to see her husband seriously at work for his job. Regina knows Stan literally earns every cent of his six figures salary. There are times when he doesn't get but two hours of sleep before it is time for him to go back to work or jump on a plane.

That is one of the reasons why Regina doesn't waste or blow money on anything. It just never made sense to her to blow away money on meaningless things. Regina doesn't want to take her husband's experience and job for granted. She doesn't want him to feel like she is using him. Especially since Regina doesn't work. She never has worked even a part-time job during their marriage. However, they did get together when Stan had nothing. She was right by his side as he climbed the corporate ladder … and then moved on to having his own business. Now he has two businesses.

The smell of food brings Regina out of her daydream. Her stomach is growling and she knows for sure she isn't thirsty. Some nutritionists have said that sometimes when your stomach growls, you could actually be thirsty instead. However, this is not one of those times. Regina is in fact hungry this morning and has the hunger pangs to prove it. She opens the bathroom door and gets a better whiff of the food.

Imagining she is walking around the kitchen looking at the meal, she says in her mind, *Mmm, I can smell the coffee brewing, the maple sausage has been cooked and warming in the oven, scrambled eggs with cheddar cheese are finished with the top on the pan, and buttermilk biscuits with sweet grape jelly are piping hot on the pan. Damn that smells and looks sooo good. Maria is doing it up this morning.*

Maria has been their housekeeper for nearly four years. Not once has she disappointed them with anything. She is always on time and stays later if she has too. For her late nights, she stays at the Wootens' house in the Maid's Suite. Her cooking, cleaning and manners are just how Regina and Stan like them … clean and on point.

Regina walks out of the bathroom smiling with her eyes closed still taking in the aroma when all of a sudden, she is lifted off her feet and twirled around. She opens her eyes to see her husband Stan playfully smiling at her as he is spinning around with her in his arms. She loves being wrapped in his big muscular arms. She grabs him around his neck to hold on.

Regina is surprised to see Stan. He isn't supposed to be home until later tonight. He must've gotten home early this morning because he has been home long enough to have on his sexy pajamas pants. Regina loves when her husband walks around the house like that. His body is off the chain and with the pajama pants on someone would think he is getting ready for a photo shoot. She knows she has seen Maria taking her little peeks. Maria may be twenty or more years older than she is but she is a woman and she ain't dead.

"My baby's home," Regina shouts, wraps her arms around his neck tighter and plants a big juicy kiss on his lips. She pushes her tongue into his mouth and he responds by giving her his tongue back. "When did you get here? I didn't hear you come in." She has missed her husband and is glad to see him back home. Stan has been away on travel for business for the past four days. It's been somewhat lonely in the big house all by herself.

"*That's riiight.* Your baby is home and he has cooked breakfast just for his woman. I got here around the time Maria normally arrives, slipped into something comfortable and started throwing down. Since you were sleep, I just chilled in my office," Stan said rubbing on his wife's ass as he puts her back on the floor slowly, making sure she slides against his dick. Then he plants a kiss on her lips that is juicier than the one she just gave him, sharing his tongue. Regina accepts it with full force. She has just put conditioner on her lips but it is okay because she has enough on her lips to condition his too. So she can kiss her man all morning.

"It was you coming in and not Maria," Regina asks Stan leaning back to look up at him. "You cooked breakfast for me, huh? Who helped you? Where is Maria anyway? I bet you she cooked and you told her to let you pretend you cooked it for me." Regina smiles and gives Stan the side-eye trying to see if he is joking about cooking her breakfast.

"Maria isn't here babe, for real. I called her at home yesterday and told her to take the day off. So I cooked the entire meal for you all by myself. Oh, don't act like your man can't get busy in the kitchen." Stan has a devilish grin on his face as if he is up to something. Then he peeks in Regina's towel as if he is playing a private game of peek-a-boo. She watches what he is doing for a few seconds, then joins in on the peek-a-boo game by helping to open and close her towel for him.

Winking at Stan, she asks, "Oh really, you gave her the day off? Well, am I the only one that's going to be eating this breakfast this morning? It seems like you're hungry for something else. What are you doing with my towel?"

Regina smiles noticing Stan is rising to the occasion. She knows her husband like the back of her hand. He has been gone for four days and it had been two days prior to him leaving since their last escapade. He has never given Maria the day off. That is definitely something new for him. *What is Stan really up to?* Regina still has a list of things she needs to get done and she doesn't want Stan tagging along. At least not today. That will spoil her surprises and plans. Plus, she has some *"ME TIME"* things to do and all he would be doing is getting antsy and rushing her.

To keep Stan out of her way, at least for a few hours, she decides to participate in what they both want … a quick fuck. Regina drops her towel and her nipples harden from the chill in the air. Stan moans from the stimulation from the sight his wife is giving him. He firmly massages the right breast and bends down to take the nipple of the left breast in his mouth. Regina moans from his touch, slowly unties Stan's pajama pants and watches them fall around his ankles. His dick is bouncing as he steps out of the pants. She eagerly watches his semi-hardness as if she is being hypnotized by it.

Oh, Regina is very much wide-awake now. *Such a beautiful sight to see early in the morning,* she says to herself. She wants to put all of it in her mouth but doesn't have time for that this morning. This is supposed to be a quickie and that is what it is going to be. When it comes to tasting her husband, Regina likes to savor the moment as if it is a roast with all the trimmings in a crock pot. That is some good eating right there and there won't be any rushing with that.

Stan takes her by her waist and guides her backwards towards the bed. He is a tall man and doesn't like his bed too low to the floor, hurting his knees. So Regina has a step stool for the bed to help her get on and off of it. She takes the two steps up to get on the bed and starts to lay on her back. Stan smiles and shakes his head "No" turning her over instead. He wants it from the back this morning. Her pussy juices are flowing now. He starts kissing down her back slowly and around her waist side. Once he moves down to her butt, Regina pokes it out hoping he will eat her out from behind. Stan inserts two fingers in her instead. He watches as her juices spill all over his fingers and then puts them in his mouth to taste. The sweetness of her juices turns Stan on and his dick is harder than concrete now.

Regina looks behind her to see what he is doing since she no longer feels his fingers sliding around in her. He is just standing there staring at her well trimmed pussy, smiling. She smiles back at him, takes her left foot and starts rubbing it up and down on his massive dick and balls. He leans his chest back and his hips forward assuring that her foot can reach him with no problem, taking pleasure in the moment.

Regina wants to swallow his pre-cum but he has her so wet, she really wants to feel his tongue in her instead. Since Stan has a front row seat to her performance, Regina reaches underneath and starts playing with her pussy. She is balanced on her right knee and left hand while the left foot is playing with dick and the right hand is playing with pussy. Thank goodness for those abdominal exercises in class. Stan seems to be unable to handle the excitement any longer once he sees her fingers start shining from her juices.

He grabs Regina's hips and enters her with so much force she screams a mixture of pain and pleasure. There is no warning to Regina that this is the next move. The sound of his wife turns Stan's ego up a few notches. He stands there for a few seconds feeling the bottom of his shaft meet her pussy lips. She is hot, tight, and soaking wet. He closes his eyes and begins moving slow just to get a feel of how wet Regina is. Her pussy is making slurping sounds up and down his stiffness. Stan pulls out for a few seconds trying to slow down his mounting nut.

Entering Regina again but slowly this time, Stan picks up the pace while looking at his dick get sucked by her second set of lips. That sends him over the edge. He starts concentrating on his authoritative thrusts like a lion observing his prey. Deep ... strong ... and hungry. Regina can't take all the force at first. She grabs a handful of the luxurious navy Duvet cover and buries her face in it concealing the screams of pain and pleasure. It seems like it is taking forever for it be over but she doesn't want Stan to stop. He quickens his pace again to a banging rhythm. He is going extremely deep but Regina likes deep hard thrusts when it is a quickie. She seems to get extra wet with every thrust.

Stan feels his balls getting slippery. He looks down watching his dick go in and out of Regina's hot wetness ... thick, hard, and soaked with her juices running all the way down to his balls. A sight he loves to see while giving both of them pleasure. Stan starts to feel his nut build up again and can't hold back this time. He doesn't even want to. At this very moment, Regina's walls begin to throb, engulfing Stan in extreme hotness. The sensation creates moans and growls within Stan. With one more thrust, they both moan and yell in pure ecstasy.

Regina's pussy is contracting hard around Stan's dick. It grips him tight as if to never let go forcing him to grab her ass and jerk forward going as deep as he can. She remains motionless - still on all fours - enjoying the feeling of her pussy still contracting and throbbing around his dick. Then she slowly slides her legs down on the bed to allow Stan to slowly lay slumped over her. Both of them are panting and sweating as if they just got finished thirty minutes of

The Firm Cardio Sculpt video. After a few seconds, Stan rolls over onto the bed with both of their juices shining on him and touches Regina on her waist. They kiss, smile at each other, and lay there for a few minutes to catch their breath.

Twenty minutes later, Stan gets up to turn on the television. He is hoping to catch *Martin* or *The Cosby Show* but he is too late. Then he turns to *The Maury Show* and doesn't want to watch that either. *The same old crap. Women returning to the show with three more guys trying to find their baby's daddy.* He says to himself. So he decides to put the Jamie Foxx *"Might Need Security"* video in the VCR. Whenever Stan wants a good laugh he watches this video.

"Babeee, I wanna watch *Maury*. Why did you put in Jamie? Me and the girls watched that the other night after our class. I'm sure by now you probably can perform the entire stand-up word for word. Why not watch something else like *All About the Andersons* or *All of Us*? I do record those and they're new," Regina says as she lays her leg across Stan's thigh.

"It's the same 'ol mess on that show. Maury really needs to find new topics. It's either Baby Mamas tryin' to figure out which of the twenty guys tested is the daddy. Or it is the lying, cheating mate sleeping with a friend or relative. After being on travel for four days, *Maury* is the last show I wanna fall asleep to. And I haven't watched any of the new black shows yet. So I wanna go with what I know right now."

"Oh, aight then. I have to get up anyway. Enjoy Jamie *again*. I'ma have to find you a new video. This one is going to get stuck in the VCR as much as you watch it." Regina gets up and heads toward the bathroom for a quick wash of the coochie and other important parts. She doesn't mind smelling like sex but not when she is going out into the public. Plus, cum was running down her legs and she just moisturized her entire body.

"Hey, where are you going Mrs. Wooten? What is on your agenda for the day? What were you gonna to get into while I was supposed to still be on travel? You don't wanna change your plans and spend the day with big and little Stan instead? After we done flew *all* the way back home early and cooked you breakfast?" Stan gives Regina a playful pout then tries to catch her before she disappears into the bathroom. His fingers tips brushes against her left butt cheek.

He is smiling at her round melons jiggling as she runs from his grasp. Regina is too quick for him though. She knows what he is trying to do and she runs closer to the bathroom. Regina turns around smiling and licks her tongue out at him. She knows he is trying to get another round in but she has things to do. All that back to back action would wear her out and she wouldn't get anything done today. Time is of the essence and Stan is going to have to wait to get round two later. Much later.

"Babe, I have things to do today and you can't tag along. I really appreciate you coming home early, really, I do. But if I don't get these things done today, then it won't get done. That is not an option. I am gonna spend time with you tonight, I promise. Sorry if I am messing up your surprise plans. You know I'll make it up to you. Cross my heart," Regina takes her finger and crosses an "X" on her chest. "Now may I have my breakfast please?"

Stan gets off the bed rubbing his abs as if he just got finished working them at the gym. Yawning and stretching, he heads to the stairs to go down to the kitchen, not bothering to put on his pajama pants. He hasn't been able to do that during the day in a long time. His semi – hardness is swinging around and Regina is watching the handsome sight. Stan notices and smirks to himself. "Yea, okay, I hope you are really enjoying what you see. You know we need to start working on that baby too. It's time for us to have some little

Reginas and Stans running around here. Those hips are ready to carry my seed."

Regina stops in her tracks, turns around to look at Stan taken aback by what she just heard him say and walks towards him. "Excuse me? Oh it's time, huh? I hear you talking Big Man. You know damn well twins run in both of our families so you just make sure you clear your traveling schedule to be on hand to help take care of all of these children. Maria and I won't be able to handle all of that responsibility by ourselves." She turns back around heading towards the bedroom and toots her ass out at him. Regina walks back into the bedroom to the bathroom, over to the glass shower doors opening them to start the shower water. Returning to the hallway she says, "But I promise, I will be back home before you know it."

"What you got planned for today anyway that's sooo important that you have to get up right now? You never told me when I asked a few minutes ago," Stan asks looking up at her from the steps. "Maria isn't here. We got the whole house to ourselves. We can do some loud moaning in a few of the rooms and she will never know that we have christened them again," he says winking at her with that sexy devilish grin. She loves his smile. She smiles back at him shaking his head.

"None ... of ... your ... business, Mr. Wooten. Stop being so nosey. If I tell you, then I would have to kill you and since we have plans for this weekend, I don't plan on that happening," Regina chuckles. "So go on downstairs and fix my plate. Let me check out your cooking skills. You haven't cooked me anything in about seven or eight years. Let me see if your cooking skills have gotten rusty. Then while I'm gone, you can just chill, watch your little stinking video, and sleep off that jet lag. I know you gotta be tired. I really do thank you for surprising me though. That was very sweet and spontaneous of you baby. I can get used to that. I got you when

I get back from the Spa, okay? I promise." Regina is leaning over the mahogany wood banister watching Stan jog down the stairs. His biceps are flexing, his pecks are twitching, and his dick is swaying. *Damn my man is sexy. Look at all of that and it belongs to me.*

Stan stops in mid jog on the mid landing of the stairs. "Whoa, whoa, whoa. You wanna see if my cooking skills have gotten rusty? Go on with that. Stan Wooten ain't rusty with shit. It could have been twelve years since I've been in the kitchen and my shit will still be on point," he laughs looking up at her admiring her firm perky breasts. He gets a twitch in his groin and grabs his dick to adjust it. Regina notices the movement and playfully tries to cover up her nakedness.

"Will you stop? Go get my breakfast please, Mr. Nasty. I'll bring all of this back with me from the Spa. This ain't going nowhere," she moves her hands around her body in a displaying motion.

"Yea, okay Mrs. Wooten. We're gonna hold you to that promise. We'll be right here waiting ... big *and* little Stan," he yells once he lands at the bottom of the stairs. He turns left to walk down the hall towards the sunken kitchen.

Regina turns around walking back into the bedroom to enter the bathroom. *Oh, I am quite sure the both of you will be waiting. That's one thing I don't have to worry about*, she says to herself out loud adjusting the water in the shower.

"Did I hear you say something," Stan yells up to her as he continues walking down the long hallway.

"Nope, your ears are playing tricks on you. I've not said a thing. I'm getting in the shower boy," Regina says smiling as she steps into the shower, closes the door, and grabs the raw Shea butter soap. *Here goes shower number two for the day but it was worth getting sweaty,* she says to herself.

"Yea, okay sexy. I know I heard you say something," Stan says as he finally steps into the sunken kitchen walking to the right over to the stove. He heard what Regina said. He just wanted to see if she was going to repeat it. That's his baby. " ... And you are absolutely right about that. You definitely do not have to worry because we *will* be waiting," he says out loud to himself trying to make sure he is loud enough for Regina to hear him all the way upstairs in the shower.

Stan opens a chestnut wood kitchen cabinet to retrieve an everyday china plate and begins fixing Regina's plate. Smiling, admiring the meal he has prepared, he opens a drawer to get a fork, knife, and a burgundy linen napkin. He walks over to the stainless steel refrigerator to take out the carafe filled with Mimosa he had made while Regina was sleep. Stan pours some into a champagne flute and places everything on a mahogany wood tray to take upstairs to Regina. Even though he fixed a pot of coffee, he drinks it and she only likes the smell of it.

He places the tray on the night stand on her side of the bed. Regina is still in the shower and he hears her singing Chapter 8's *I Just Wanna Be Your Girl* with Anita Baker on lead vocals. Stan walks over to the bathroom entryway to hear her better. He leans up against the door, folding his arms across his chest, smiling with his eyes closed listening. *Damn my baby can sing her ass off. I can't wait until she is singing like that to our babies.*

Walking away from the bathroom door, Stan puts his pajama pants back on, while waiting for Regina to finish in the bathroom. He lays across the bed and pushes the "play" arrow on the VCR remote control to begin the video. He yawns putting his hand inside his pants, playing with his dick and balls, getting comfortable, relaxed, and in position to fall asleep. He really wishes he could be relaxed in Regina's pussy right now. *Damn!! She just has to be going somewhere today. Oh, it's on when her ass comes back!!*

The jet lag combined with the draining of his tool has Stan's eyelids getting real heavy. He is jolted by the ringing of the house phone. *Sigh!! I already know who it is.*

Chapter Three

3

"Good morning, this is BeLynda Giles. How can I help you today? Are you calling to place an order or find out about the business?"

"Good morning to you too Ms. Giles. This is Cheryl, Cheryl Smith."

"Cheryl, how are you today? What you sounding all professional for? How long we been knowing each other? Now, what can I do for you?"

"Well, you answering the phone all professional, so I put on my professional hat too," Cheryl laughs. "Honey, I'm okay. But I'll be just wonderful once I get some bubble bath. I am completely out and need a rush order. Is that possible? If not, how long do I have to wait before your next order comes back? I will come and get it instead of you dropping it off."

"Bubble bath? Now how did you run out of that and already? You normally stock up when there is a sale. You got about four bottles a month ago. And if you check the number you dialed, you'll see that you did call the office phone. So how am I supposed to sound Lady?"

"Girlfriend, I couldn't tell you. Maybe my sister took a few bottles instead of ordering her own. Or maybe the children are pouring too much in the damn water. They like a lot of bubbles but, you know what? I got something for their asses this time. I will be hiding some of these bottles and they will have to come to me for it every time they need it. Money don't grow on trees and if it did, I wasn't fortunate enough to be to plant one in my yard."

"Ha, ha, ha I know that's right. I can't fault you on that one. What kind did you need this time? I do have 'Kids,' 'Vanilla for Dry Skin,' and 'Sensitive Skin' here at the house. Did you want your regular order? Or do you want to try something new?"

"Nothing new, chiile. If it ain't broke I won't try to fix it. The normal order will be just fine. Hell, if I did try something new that might just disappear too. Oh yeah, go ahead and add two bottles of Moisture Therapy Lotion to my order too, please. Those little knuckleheads have some dry ashy skin. It seems like their skin drinks up the lotion as soon as I put it on them." BeLynda and Cheryl laugh.

"Girl you know you need to cut that out. Stop talkin' about your kids like that. They can't help it. They had to have gotten that ashy-ness from somewhere. And if I am not mistaken, you were buying Moisture Therapy lotion long before you were a mother." BeLynda is laughing so hard, she almost falls out of the chair.

"That's true but I'm serious. I can tell you I really don't know who they take skin after. It surely isn't from me for real. My skins healed in ten days. It's been a few years since I've been using that on them."

"Okay, I'll add the lotion to your order. I will have everything to you no later than Saturday at two o'clock. Is that all right? Or do you want to come by today and get it? I'll be here until twelve thirty."

"Oh, no that's all right. I know you're busy with the school fund-raisers. Saturday at two o'clock is fine."

"All right Cheryl. See you Saturday." They end the call.

BeLynda finishes writing the order and lays it in her In Box. She doesn't have to get this one together until Saturday.

BeLynda smiles to herself and starts thinking. She can't believe it! Her current fund-raiser order is huge. Seventy-five orders and none of them under a hundred dollars. With a fifty percent profit, she will be able to put three months of mortgage, car notes, as well as money for a nice vacation into her personal account. She has a separate account for only business matters so there won't be any confusion. BeLynda has been working so hard.

It's been two years since she has taken a break from managing her business. Everyone is always telling her, *"BeLynda, you work too much. Take a break ... slow down."* Managing a business means serious time and hard work dedicated to it. She knows that being lazy and not putting her all into her business would not have worked. It wouldn't have been prosperous. There wouldn't have been a business or any of the rewards or accomplishments that come from a prosperous business had she'd been lackadaisical.

She has so much work ahead of her. She has to sort the seventy-five orders, which are packed in a hundred boxes and sitting in her morning room. She had the delivery man to stack them no higher than five boxes each so she can reach them. Plus, some of them may be too heavy to lift if they are stacked any higher. Thank goodness BeLynda doesn't have to sort each individual order. She would be there all night. She will be providing the correct size and amount of bags so the parents will help their children.

Along with the bags, brochures and samples will be provided as well. These are just in case someone decides to become a customer at a later time and want to see what else she sells. Then the orders have to be delivered to the school. BeLynda doesn't have a personal deliveryman but she was able to buy a delivery truck just for her business. She knows owning her business at times mean she has to do all the work. When her business is where she wants it, then maybe she can afford to hire an assistant.

BeLynda does a lot of fund-raisers with the schools and church organizations. She does have individual customers but fund-raisers are where she makes eighty percent of her money. However during October – December, business is really up due to the customers buying Christmas gifts.

Ring! Ring!

Shit, the phone is ringing again. That's the fifth time this morning. I have to get started on these orders. I am supposed to have the orders at the school by 1:00pm today. The school told the parents they could pick-up orders between 3:00pm – 5:00pm. If I get there by 1:00pm, that gives me two hours to unload the truck, sort by classroom, and go over money matters with the PTA President and Treasurer. I need to turn on my answering machine now. I am sure they will leave their orders on the machine.

Ring! Ring!

Who in the world is calling me on my cell? That's probably whoever called the house first. I have got to get these damn orders sorted. I don't have time to talk right now. Sorry, but you're going to have to leave a message there too. BeLynda says to herself. She doesn't even bother to look at her cell to see who it is. It doesn't even matter. What she is doing now needs to take precedence over this call. *As soon as they leave a message, I will cut that off as well. I have a 5:30pm Spa appointment and I refuse to be late.*

No matter what, that's one appointment I always keep. This is Thursday. I don't care what I do and do not have planned on Thursdays my ass is at The Galleria Spa by five fifteen waiting to be seen. This is the closest I get to a vacation and my weekly appointment to get The Retreat that is a two hours special will not be disturbed. As hard as I work, I deserve and enjoy every minute, rub, and squeeze placed on my body.

Besides, Marcus is working today. Or at least he better be. No one but Marcus can work on me. Those big firm hands and his deep voice talking to me while I am deep into the moment ... whew, gives me chills as I think about it. I used to always request a female but when I saw his muscular body come into the Tranquil Area that time as a fill-in for my normal, I knew that he would be the only one working on me at every visit.

With his Arnold Schwarzenegger body and his Michael Jai White face, I was in heaven. When his deep voice sounding like a Goddess mixed with the tone of Barry White, I was almost creaming in my panties. But after that, I made sure I didn't have on panties anymore. If he wanted to take a peak, his wish would have been my command. One day I am going to get up enough nerve to step to his ass though. As my Mama would say "grow some damn ovaries and say what you mean and mean what you say."

The only thing that has been missing is Marcus locking the door, dropping his pants, letting me see the full package and giving me a real orgasm. I know that body has to be a sight for sore eyes. Hell, I would even take one of his damn fingers as big as they are. When he tells me to turn over onto my stomach, with my face resting in the hollow pillow, he's standing in front of me working on my shoulders and upper back. I just want to raise my head and watch the pulsating bulge in his pants. It surely be looking like he doesn't have on any drawers. Like he knows I am watching his crotch.

But he stays so professional. I wonder what his dick looks like. Is it straight or have a curve to it? Is it thick or slender, long or short? I would take it no matter what the length or girth is. I wonder if he has an idea that is what I am thinking. I wonder how many does he work on in a day? In a week? In a month? I wonder if he has approached any of his clients. Am I his type? Hell, how many women have had my same thoughts about him .... BeLynda's thoughts are interrupted by the doorbell.

"Who in the hell is at my fucking door? Done messed up my damn groove. I was about to give Marcus some in my thoughts." BeLynda isn't happy about that at all. She goes to the door to see who it is. It is Colleen. *Dammit!!*

Leaning up against the door with her eyes closed, she says in her mind, *Not now. What does she want? I don't have time to deal with Colleen and her drama. I do not feel like hearing about any soap opera type crap she is going through with some ghetto client of hers. I will see her at the spa this evening. Dammit!! I am gonna have to open the door anyway. She knows I am in here because both the truck and the Avalon are parked outside. Shit, I should have had the car parked in the garage. But, as persistent as Colleen is, she would have looked in the garage window. Well, that's okay because I am about to put her ass to work. The next time, she'll let me finish day dreaming in peace about Marcus' sexy ass.*

BeLynda opens the door. Actually all she did is turn the knob and Colleen bursts in the house as if she is Miss Marvelous on a catwalk. BeLynda always know when Colleen has something new on. She struts around as if she has on an original. She shakes her head and says to herself while looking at Colleen, *Look at her sauntering around my damn living-room as if she is the shit. She does look nice though but fuck, I'm her girl. Do I have to feed into her wanting a compliment all the damn time? When is she going to realize that if they made one, there is going to be a two, three, and a four to follow? Especially, since she shops in department stores like the rest of us. You don't have a personal tailor Colleen, so quit while you're ahead with the fucking show. 'Colleen' is not the only one with money. Today it must be your entire ensemble that you want me to see.*

BeLynda notices Colleen's cinnamon brown streaks have been touched-up, blending in nicely with her natural dark brown shoulder length hair and is styled in a bone straight wrap. Normally, Colleen has a roller wrap but from time-to-time she does change it up.

Colleen resembles Cindy from the group *En Vogue*. She is wearing a red luxurious wool/cashmere mink trim Ruana. It has to be over four hundred dollars. Colleen swings around as she takes off her wrap. She is really performing for BeLynda now. Colleen has on a Patrick Christopher outfit. It is a red silk Carmeuse wrap blouse and a matching silk twill skirt. To finish the ensemble, she has on black mink trimmed boots with the matching mink purse. *Oh, it must be the shoes and the purse she is advertising for me today.* BeLynda realizes she has seen the rest before. BeLynda looks at Colleen, waiting for her to finish.

"Well, hello to you too Missy. Don't come busting all up in my house like you're Miss America or somebody," says BeLynda with her hands on her hips.

"Mmmp, hey girl, what's up? What are you in here doing," Colleen asks looking around BeLynda's house. She is trying to see what was taking her so long to come to the door. "I knew you were in here. I thought I was gonna have to start yelling your name or something. You tryin' to duck a sista?" Colleen looks BeLynda up and down with one hand on her hip and the other swinging her purse. She is popping and chewing her gum like a cow grazing in the grass. BeLynda just looks at her in astonishment.

"I am in here working, why? What do you want or need? I have to be done by twelve thirty so I can pack up the truck and get over to Middleton Valley by one o'clock. I wasn't expecting anyone, especially you. What brings you out so early Ms. Jeffries? Oh and … do I need to thank or applaud you for that imposing entrance? I mean, you were working it. That was quite a show, I'll give you that."

Ignoring BeLynda's statement, Colleen says, "Oh. Damn Bee, you're always working. I get tired of only seeing you at the Spa. Why do I have to drive to The Galleria Spa all the way down in Waldorf just to see you? Why don't you live a little? Fuck, why don't you live A LOT!! There's more to life than trying to make another dollar. You have plenty of those. You're starting to become boring Bee! We used to hang out all the time. Now, all you do is sit in this house and place orders." Colleen rolls her eyes at BeLynda hard and sashays into the morning-room to look out into the backyard. *Yea, I'm giving a show winch. That's how I roll. I know damn well I look good and you need to see all of it.*

"Boring?! Oh, because I don't spend all my time shopping, picking up men, and getting into other's business? Well, I will remain boring. As long as I have you, I will always know where the men hang out, what's on sale, and who did what. Yea, I know we used to hang out ... ALL THE TIME but I have a business to run just like you. As we BOTH know, we cannot afford these houses, cars, or the maintenance on them, our bills cannot be paid, we cannot shop the way want we to, go to the Spa every week, and have hefty bank accounts if we are not running our businesses to the fullest. And how do you know how many dollars I have? Now, since you're in the morning-room, pick up a box, open it and start sorting the items according to that invoice on the table. I can be finish that much faster."

Colleen turns around putting both of her hands on her hips responding, "Ummm, I didn't come over here to work. Since you weren't answering either of your damn phones, I decided to drive over. I knew you weren't in here doing anything but working. Surely I knew I wouldn't find a man in here ... Old Lady. But it sure would have been a nice shocker had a man came down those stairs in a towel. Anyhew, I am going down to the Zanzibar Saturday night. I want you to go too. Are you interested? I don't want to go by myself. Let it be like old times. Are we on for Saturday?"

"Yea, we are on. Old times? I'm not a Stick-in-the-Mud Colleen. But, the *Zanzibar*? Why there? What is that? Some secret male strip joint," BeLynda asks with a smirk on her face.

"*What is that?* You haven't heard of the Zanzibar? Damn Bee!! It's a fucking club and restaurant. Do you want to go or not? We will have a lot of fun. I promise you will not be disappointed. We can have some fun together for a change."

"Ha, ha, ha girl shut up. I know what the fuck the Zanzibar is. I was just playing with you. You really believe that I am that lost about the happenings, huh? I see I got you all revved up ready to educate. News Flash … take your glasses off and pull your hair out of the bun, Bee don't need no teaching today. I've been to the damn place before."

"Okay, good. You had me nervous there for a minute. It has been a minute for you Ms. Work-A-Holic. You can be in denial all you want but I know how much we don't hang out. And it irks me that every time I turn around Regina and Sandy are always doing something together. Doesn't it bother you?"

"I'm not a workaholic and I'm not in denial either. I know I've not hung out much but it hasn't been that long. And, I'm not worried about Dee Dee and Regina anymore than they are sitting around pouting about us. We are all friends Colleen. Cut out the jealous shit. Sooo is it just going to be us? Or are you going to invite some of your tack heads to meet us?"

"Tack heads," Colleen has to laugh from getting in her feelings. "I don't know any tack heads and if I did, guess what? They all have money and we wouldn't be spending a motherfuckin' *DIME*. But no winch, no niggas will be tagging along. I am actually hoping Regina and Sandy will go too. I haven't spoken with them today. Have you? I called them but Stan said Regina wasn't home and Sandy wasn't at her desk. I've not called either of them on their cell phones. So I decided to wait until I see them at the Spa."

"Well, Regina won't be here this weekend, remember? She and Stan are going out of town. Girl, where is your memory? Keep your focus on what's going on with your girls and stop worrying about what tack head has money," BeLynda laughs because she knows Colleen really wants to curse her ass out.

"Girl will you shut that trap, damn!! You just all mouth today. I didn't forget they were going to the Poconos. But hell, the Poconos thing is this weekend? Shit! Do they ever stay home?

Every time I turn around they are going somewhere. It seems as if I only see Regina at the Spa too."

"'The Poconos thing'? Why is it a 'thing'? Oh and you did forget about them being out of town this weekend heifer. And why do they have to stay home? They have no children, grandchildren, or pets. So if Regina's husband wants her to tag along from time-to-time when he goes out of town, then she should go. Do you ever stop shopping? HELL NO! So don't start hating Missy. Or are you mad it ain't you and some man going out of town somewhere?"

Colleen rolls her eyes at BeLynda and pulls out a cigarette. "Yea, well, you *mean* they don't have any children *yet*. I didn't say I had a problem with her traveling with her man. It just seems so damn often. She misses out on some good girlfriend time, you know? And, for the record, I don't shop that much. At least no more than any of the rest of y'all chicks. We are in the stores the same amount of time. I don't want to be at the damn Poconos with no damn man. That's for couples and I am not coupled up with no one. I like my options. When one *neegro* gets on my nerves, I have others I can call. I like it like that." Colleen rolls her eyes and continues taking items out of the box, placing them on the table.

BeLynda rolls her eyes and shakes her head at Colleen's response. "Yea, yea, yea … I'm not playing the violins for you. I don't know why you keep putting on an act for me. I'm your girl … Bee, remember? But okay Ms. Options. Do your thing. No one is hatin'. One day you gone look up and realize that you will be forty years old still calling on 'options' and the rest of us will have husbands or potential husbands and a few children. Hell, come to think about it two us have gone down that aisle already."

Colleen looks at her as if her head just turned around like Linda Blair's did in *The Exorcist*. "Fuck you Bee. I will do me and keep my options. You are right. Two of us have walked down that aisle but … how many of us are still married? Don't be throwing jabs at me. I didn't come over here for that. But, fuck it, hell. It'll just be the three of us then. We can tell Regina all about it when she gets back. Just say 'yes' and find something whore-ish to put on. Don't put on none of that 'Do-you-want-to-place-an-order-or-know-about-the-business' crap. This is the girls' night out and I expect you to dress like it."

"'Whore-ish'? 'Do-you-want-to-place-an-order-or-know-about-the-business crap'? Did you just say that?" BeLynda laughs at Colleen. "No, I must be hearing things. You must be in your feelings over what I just said. Whatever!! You are really full of yourself today, huh? Don't get choked with that red riding hood cape of yours. Maybe you should have waited until you saw me at the spa to ask me too. I will not be that desperate or degrade myself. I have plenty of male friends and none of them are attracted to me because of what I did or didn't have on."

Yeah ... I know, Colleen mumbles to herself. She could tell BeLynda is getting mad. BeLynda knows Colleen doesn't bite her tongue. *Maybe I hit a nerve on that one. Hell, BeLynda wasn't thinking about nerves when she said that shit about me and marriage.* This conversation can turn sour real fast.

"Whatever snob, you just be ready at nine o'clock. You're riding with me. I'll see you at the Spa." Colleen gets up, grabs her purse preparing to leave.

"Hold up. Wait a minute. You really came *all* the way over here getting on my damn nerves just to ask me to go out with you to the Zanzibar this weekend? What happened? No meetings with clients today? I actually really could have been in here with a man, you know." BeLynda can't believe Colleen. Then again, yes she can. She is dealing with Colleen, who does strange things when she is bored and can be very selfish majority of the time.

"Nooo that is not the only reason why I came by here, Bee. I just wanted to see you, that's all. Can't I come see how my Chica is doing? Gosh." BeLynda thinks Colleen is lying but she is not. "I do have appointments with two clients today though. I'll see Miss Dina at one fifteen to go over her menu. Miss Lisa is coming by around three o'clock to pay her deposit on the limos. She better not try to reschedule either. I have plans for that damn deposit. What do you have to drink? Do you have a Diet Sprite?"

"Oh my, clients got you riled up today, huh? I told you to stop dealing with the ghetto, non-class category. You walking around here with an elegant business and leaving the 'tacky' to advertise for you.   Yeah, I have Diet Sprite. You want it with ice? Hell, do you want something stronger? I got some Cognac and Maker's Mark. What you want?"

Colleen leans back and looks BeLynda up and down, shocked and smiling. "Damn!! Bee got Yak up in the house? Maker's Mark? What the fuck is going on? Oh, I forgot. That young ass nigga you fucking with probably drinks those, right?"

BeLynda, waves Colleen off laughing. "Girl, what you talking about? I drink Maker's Mark. That's my shit. It's nice and smooth, leaves no hangover in the morning. Mix it with some Diet Cranberry juice, and it's all good. *Siiike*, nah I'm just kidding. Ain't neither of those liquors in here. Khalil brings his own drinks when he comes. He knows it's BYOL up in here," BeLynda lies with a straight face.

She has more than brandy and whiskey in her house. Since she hasn't been out to the club in a minute, she has to make her own drinks at home now. So she makes sure she has the ingredients on hand for French Martinis and Tequila Sunrises. Colleen looks at her side-eyed saying in her mind, *Who you think you fooling? I bet you got all kinds of liquor up in here. Trying to keep the loose side of your ass hidden, huh? You ain't taking these classes with us just to be a part of the group.* BeLynda notices how Colleen is looking at her, so she tries to keep the topic on track. "Fuck it, I'ma get you that Diet Sprite. Do you want it or not?"

"Yes please, thank you. That would be great. Do you have any limes on hand?"

"Winch, you are not at your house. Nor are you at the club. Sprite on the rocks with no lime is what you get here. You will have to wait until get home or Saturday night at the Zanzibar to get accessories for your drink." They both have to laugh.

To help soften the mood a little more, Colleen gets up and starts working on another box. BeLynda is happy to see Colleen's attitude has changed and she is helping with the orders. She smiles at Colleen and says, "Let's start over, okay? Some of this moment got out of hand and I am sorry. I didn't mean to step on your feelings. That wasn't my intentions at all. Sooo ... Good morning Colleen, how are you today?"

"Good morning to you too, Ms. Giles. I am sorry too. I didn't mean to be too harsh ... or harsh at all. I got in my feelings because I miss you. May I have a hug and a kiss?" BeLynda isn't going to admit that she got in her feelings on the marriage topic.

"You most certainly can." They give each other a very intense loving hug and a kiss on both cheeks and continue working on the orders. BeLynda tries to have the last word though.

"Hand me one of those cigarettes. And I got your 'Old Lady,' heifer."

"Mmm-hmmm, just like I got your 'forty and options.' Oh, you ain't getting the last word winch. You know I'm ready at all times for yapping females."

They fall out on the floor laughing like two girlfriends at a slumber party.

Chapter Four

4

It is such a beautiful day outside. Sixty degree weather and it is November. Indian Summer was last month yet Mother Nature decides to give me a little bit of it today. I hope this isn't a sign of some damn snow is coming. I better hurry and find a way to enjoy this weather though. I shouldn't be all cooped up in this damn office looking at the people below down on the ground just walking around looking so happy and free. There has got to be something else better out there for me to do today. Something has to be better than me sitting in here all day and leaving when it gets dark. If it is going to snow, I will be in the house. So I need take advantages of this pretty day if we are going to get that type of precipitation soon," Sandy thinks to herself leaning back in her seat swiveling it around with her feet propped up on the leg base.

While in a meeting, she is supposed to be listening to her supervisor discuss the Travel and Contract budgets. She can care less about what she is talking about. Her mind is on what she prefers to be doing rather than what she is supposed to be doing. Right now, Sandy would rather be at the Spa sipping on a glass of Robert Mondavi Merlot while her temples and feet are being massaged. However she needs money for that and payday isn't for another four days. It's not like she has a man she can ask for the money for the Spa.

She has already splurged on the winter white Via Spiga boots sitting in the trunk of her car. She saw them in Bloomingdales and they kept calling her name. She could hear them loud and clear. So Sandy answered the call by buying them. Now she is done spending with this check. More than likely though, she will be at the Spa this evening with her girls but using her credit card instead of cash. Maybe someone will give her a few gift certificates for the spa as a Christmas gift. *Yeah, right ... wishful thinking Sandy.*

Sandy sits attentively knowing damn well she wants to forget about the budget. Sometimes she thinks her supervisor just likes to hear herself talk. It is not like the meeting is going to solve something that needs to be fixed. Sandy can really do without this face-to-face right now. She starts thinking about other tasks she needs to handle later on in the day. She has to meet with Clarice at nine-thirty to discuss one of the contracts. She can do without that meeting too. *Meeting with all these people that like to feel important and don't know shit*, she says to herself.

Clarice is a bitch and thinks she's better than everybody in the office. She also thinks she knows everything yet she shouldn't be in the position she is getting paid for. Half of the time Sandy has to recalculate the woman's figures before the supervisor can approve the contract. That's why Sandy has to meet with her today. The math is always jacked up. Sandy would love to just slap her ass a few times. However, no matter how much she hates working, she needs her job, like most of the workforce. So slapping Clarice is wishful thinking … for the time being anyway. *I have to figure out a way to meet with that bitch early and fast to get that shit over with.*

Then there is the management meeting at eleven thirty. Sandy already knows how the day is going to go already. It is the same every Thursday. It's going to take all morning to get Clarice to understand how screwed up her contract is. Then Sandy and Clarice are going to have to settle it in the supervisor's office before it gets too heated. That will leave only an hour for Sandy to prepare and process it for the management meeting. Hopefully that won't mean she ends up sitting in the meeting with the managers all because she didn't get it to the supervisor in time to explain it first. *I want to leave at three o'clock, not four- fifteen. Why won't Clarice stop trying to prove me wrong and just listen for a change?*

Sandy can't believe her supervisor is still yapping. She is going on and on and Sandy has no idea exactly how much or what she has missed. "Who cares anyway about this shit? Nobody but your ditzy ass," she mumbles under her breath.

"Excuse me? Did you say something Sandra," Mrs. Winston asks. Mrs. Winston is Sandy's supervisor. Sandy hates when she calls her "Sandra." She is so professional all the time. She is very sweet and really knows her stuff too but sometimes Mrs. Winston can be too sweet. This makes Sandy wonder at times who her supervisor knew in order to get the job. Sandy always thought supervisors were supposed to be firm yet demanding when they need to be. Not Mrs. Winston … she just goes with the flow. However, it does make a better working environment.

"Oh, I'm sorry. Don't mind me Mrs. Winston. I was just thinking out loud about what I need to do today," Sandy responds. She didn't want to tell her what she actually was saying. It might have broken Mrs. Winston's heart to know that she isn't taking the meeting seriously. When the supervisor looks down at her notes, Sandy sarcastically grins back at her like she is in second grade saying "cheese" for the photographer, then rolls her eyes.

Sandy actually likes her supervisor but she can really irk Sandy's nerves with these damn meetings that go over the same stuff and never accomplishes anything. She thinks the meetings are redundant and Sandy wants to move forward with matters that are actually moving. Sandy doesn't care about the budget. It's not like they are paying for her to travel and she doesn't manage any part of the budget, type the reports, or watch the budget get spent. They need to give her some of this money. She can show them how to spend it all right. Every last dollar.

It is only eight-thirty in the morning. Sandy has been at work since six-thirty so she could get off at three o'clock. She likes getting off early so she can do some of the things that make her not want to be at work in the first place. However, this morning is really dragging. It seems like it should be lunchtime by now but lunch isn't for another three and a half hours. Not that she has anything to do during lunch. She just wants the day to go faster than it is going.

Sandy has no problem admitting that she really hates getting up to go to work. She hates it with a passion. She knows she needs to be thankful for her job because there are many that will love to have her job. Plus, it does pay the bills and allows her to satisfy some of her wants. *If only I could hit the lottery for about four million dollars. That's all I really need. I swear I won't be too greedy,* Sandy says to herself smiling. She still isn't paying Mrs. Winston any attention. She looks up at the clock watching the second hand slowly go around the face a few times before she gets back to her thinking.

Then I can live like my friends. Sandy really envies them. They live the way she surely wouldn't mind living. One has a man that supports her and the other two have their own businesses so they answer to themselves. None of that over-sleeping and panicking about what the supervisor might have to say. One can get up when she feels like it, or just lay around in the bed if she wants to. The other two can get up and walk around in their pajamas to do their jobs. Well, until it is time to show their face to a client, but there is no rush because they are the boss and they set their schedules for the day.

Now, Regina ... she and Sandy go way back. Way back to seventh grade in junior high school. They are real close. They might even be best friends but no one has ever said that to the other. Sandy guesses it is because something like that should already be known. They were in the same homeroom, took the same classes, shared lockers, dressed alike on Fridays and even lived in the same apartment building. Sandy lived in #204 and Regina lived in #301. They saw each other every day, all day and most nights. Sandy was the one that always talked about getting married to a man with a six figures salary and Regina was just wanting to have a job to help get out of the ghetto. It just didn't work out the way. Regina got the man and Sandy got the job.

"Okay, well I think that is all for this meeting Sandy. What do you think? Should we take ten minutes to go over what the meeting with Clarice might cover?" Sandy doesn't know what Mrs. Winston has said in the past fifteen minutes but sure is happy that it is over.

"Oh, no, we don't have to do that Mrs. Winston. There shouldn't be any problems making sure everything adds up. Everything will be just fine. I still have a few things I need to get ready before I meet with her to assure that it won't take longer than it should. We can just wait until after I meet with Clarice. I will prepare something for the Management Meeting."

"Okay then that sounds good to me. I have a few calls I need to return. I knew you would have it all under control. I know how Clarice can sometimes have the data a little wrong. I was just checking. I wouldn't be manager if I didn't." *Isn't she being so nice?* Sandy thought to herself. *Why not just say that the bitch wasn't the smartest in her math class. And I know she didn't just throw her job title at me. What is she trying to say?* Sandy just looks at Mrs. Winston with a smile on her face, playing the Work Face Game.

After about ten minutes, Sandy leaves Mrs. Winston's office and plops down in her chair in her cubicle, rolling her eyes, and letting out a big sigh. Time is still passing by very slow. *I sooo not want to be here.* She is twirling her Dr. Grip pen between her fingers looking around her space at the pictures she have posted of her and her friends. Sandy isn't doing anything pressing at this time. She really didn't have anything to get prepare for the meeting with Clarice. She just said that to get out Mrs. Winston's office.

However, having Regina on her mind, she decides to call her to see what she's up to. She knows Stan is out of town and Regina gets up early as if she has somewhere to go. Well, sometimes she does but most of the time she doesn't. *She probably gets up just to take a shower and put on fresh loungewear. Damn!! Such good living,* Sandy says as she dials Regina's number.

Stan was just about to dose off when the ringing of the phone startled him. "Hello Sandeee," Stan drags out her name, sounding tired. He knew it was Sandy from the caller ID. However, even if he hadn't looked at the caller ID, he would have bet money that it was Sandy calling for Regina.

"Hey, Stan, good morning. What's up? Why are you answering the phone? Where's Maria? When did you get back in town? I thought you were coming back later tonight. Is Regina home? Or is she busy?" Sandy has to giggle after she asks the last question. Regina has told her a few stories in confidence that she hasn't even told the others.

Stan laughs sleepily at Sandy. "Lady, one question at a time, aiight? Let's see … good morning to you too. I am answering the phone because I do live here, remember? Maria isn't working today. I caught a redeye flight back so I could surprise Regina when she got up this morning. Yes, she is home and she isn't busy anymore. Did I answer all your questions?"

"Look, don't get smart with me *neegro*. Anyway, sooo … is she busy? Did I interrupt something? I mean, I can call back so you may continue licking, sucking, and spanking each other." Sandy has to catch herself from saying too much more. She doesn't want Stan to start getting suspicious or irritated by her comments. Plus, she is getting hot and moist just by saying the little bit she has already said. Lord knows it has been a few weeks since she has seen or touched a man, a dick, or any part of a male's anatomy.

"Only Sandy Robertson would be so explicit. I'll hand the phone to Regina now. And don't ask her about anything we just did either. That's private marriage bedroom shit, you feel me? You shouldn't be living through our sex life anyway. Make some stories of your own. Now let me go cleanse my virgin ears." Stan laughs at what he is saying to Sandy.

"Oh so now you got jokes? You think you are sooo funny this morning, huh? For your information, I got plenty of men. I don't need to hear about your tired ass little bedroom games. That's aight though. I'll get your ass back and when I do, we'll see who's laughing then. Just put Regina on the phone fool."

"Awww, somebody is getting in their feelings? I'm sure you'll get over it. So wipe those fucking tears. Hah!! Whoosh!! Two points for Team Wooten ... Zero points for Team Robertson!!"

"Fuck you Stan. You don't get any points for that." Sandy is getting pissed.

"Aight, aight. Hey, you know I am just playing with you, right?" Stan hears silence. He opens his eyes and is fully awake now. "Hello? Sandy?!" Stan is making sure Sandy is still on the other end of the phone. "Sandy!! Hello?!"

"I'm here. I heard you. I know your ass is playing. I was actually reading an email that my supervisor had just sent out," Sandy lies. "Boy please. I know you are playing. Ain't nobody thinking about your LL Cool J looking ass. Now, if you don't mind, would you *please* put your wife, my friend, on the damn phone? Go take a nap or something. You sound sleepy anyway." Sandy rolls her eyes at the phone.

Sandy and Stan are like brothers and sisters and they always joke around but today it isn't funny. She already doesn't want to be at work and to know that Regina is at home with her man is getting to her right now. She definitely wants and needs a man from time to time too. If she had a man, she would love to be home with him on this lovely day. The lonely women are always saying, "Chile, you don't need no man. They just give you mo drama."

Fuck what they are saying. They probably just tryin' to justify why they don't have a man. I mean what about companionship and love? Who doesn't want or need that? What about conversations, excursions, being wined and dined, and gifts? Ain't nothing like romance when it is mixed with some adult talking, a trip, dinner, date, or affectionately wrapped packages.

Hell, what about SEX? I have plenty of toys but sometimes I need the real thing. I need to be able to grab onto something, scratch a back, grab a butt, wrap my legs around, and bounce up and down on a male body. I damn sure can't do that with toys or kicking it with my girlfriends. I know one day my prince charming with a six figures salary will come along. Heck at this point, a five figure salary starting with the number seven would be just fine for a beginning. Sandy is deep in thought while she waits for Regina to come to the phone.

Regina comes out the bathroom giving Stan the "who is this" look. She really needs to get going. All of these interruptions are cutting into her schedule. Stan hands her the phone responding with the look of "you know who it is." She smiles at his look, takes the phone from him, speaking into it.

"Hey girlie" Regina says into the phone. She already knows it is Sandy because she heard the conversation from the bathroom. Even if she hadn't heard the conversation, Stan's look told it all. She just gets a kick out of seeing the facial expressions he makes when it is Sandy on the phone. He will always say, "I bet you when she gets a man, she is going to take your number off of speed dial. You won't hear from her for days. And I won't have to worry about her still thinking you're single living alone."

"Hey yourself Mama. What's up? What's going on with you this morning? I knew you would be up but I had no idea that Stan was going to surprise you with an early flight. Now you gotta whisper don't you," Sandy asks and laughs.

"Nothing much right now. I just came out of the bathroom. Now I am about to eat my breakfast that my baby cooked for me this morning. Yea, he came home and surprised me. But after I eat, I am going to get dressed for the day."

"Just coming out the bathroom, huh? Unh-huh, washing Stan off your ass? He answering the phone and spends a few minutes talking to me … and you're coming out of the bathroom? Sounds like some mornin' fucking to me." Sandy laughs.

"Shut your face Dee Dee! I don't think I asked you to investigate the scene over here. Close your legs. So, what's going on with you," Regina smiles trying to change the subject. She doesn't want Sandy getting too comfortable with her "sex" comments. Especially with Stan's ears sitting so close by. She knows that she has told Sandy some "private" things but the last thing she needs is for Stan to start asking her about what exactly is it she tells Sandy about them. *Sigh, either me or her have to find her a damn man fast. She probably using the stories I told her as mental porn images while she is using her toys.*

"Okay, wait. Did I hear you say that Stan cooked you breakfast this morning?! Stop playing!! For real?! Okay, what's going on, really? That nigga ain't stepped in that kitchen he got custom built for you since y'all been there. What is he trying to do? What is he up to," Sandy laughs.

"You heard what I said. So no, I'm not playing and yes, I am for real!! Yea, it has been a minute since he has cracked an egg or flipped a sausage patty unless it was on the end of a damn fork and he's putting in his mouth," Regina looks over her shoulder to see where Stan is so he won't be frowning at what she is saying. He has his eyes closed, letting the video watch him instead. "But what's up with you Girlie? How's work going so far? Either someone pissed you off already or you're not wanting to be there. Which one is it?" Regina laughs. She knows her friend all too well.

"Girl, I'm bored," Sandy whines into the phone. "I wanna *do* something else today. I wanna *be* somewhere else today. I'm *sooo* not feeling work today. It is sixty degrees outside … in

NOVEMBER!! Can you believe it? If I didn't know better, I would think that I am in Georgia. But, why am I in this damn office Gee Gee? What do you have planned for today? Hanging out with Stan? Or are you chilling in the house until it's time to go to the Spa?"

"Nah, I've got some other stuff to do. Stan is staying home. I already told him that he can't roll with me today. Plus, he's already falling asleep, thank goodness. But yea it is pretty outside. I hope it is still like this where we are going this weekend." Regina smiles at Stan, while looking down at him on the bed. "You know he would have jumped up off the bed if he heard me talking about him. He would have been staring right in my face." They both laugh. "Anyway, I will be solo today unless you are able to leave work. Would you be able leave early? If this is a busy day, I do understand. But if you can, do you want me to come get you? Or do you have your car – you can meet me if you want. I'm going out to White Flint Mall. My first stop is Victoria's Secret."

"Naw, I drove today. Didn't feel like being bothered with that damn subway. This way, when I am ready to go, I can go downstairs, get in my car and roll out. So I can drive to your house and we can leave together. Oh, you're going to Vicky's? *Damn* Gee Gee, I don't have any money. I'm done with this paycheck. You know that's my store. I mean, not that I need to be buying a damn thing but I'm gonna have to be in there with my eyes closed. Or maybe I can make note of what I might want to get next payday. What are you going in there for anyway? You probably have every style bra and panty in every color already, don't you?"

"Girl shut up. Don't be ridiculous. They come out with a new damn bra or panty almost every day. How can I have them all? And you know I don't buy anything from that pink line. That's for teenagers, if you ask me," Regina says laughing at Sandy's comment. "I'm not going for everyday bras and panties today anyway. I'm going to get some things to take with me this weekend.

It would be nice to have you there to tell me what you think. C'mon, I'll treat you to lunch."

"Gee Gee! Stop it!! C'mon now, Vicky's *and* lunch? I hate when you do that. But I love you for it at the same time. And you know damn well you don't need to get new stuff for this weekend." They both laugh again.

"I know you do Sandy-Dandy. Just say 'yes.' No need to get all mushy and shit. It's only lunch with your friend of twenty years. And even though I have some sexy shit here, I want some new sexy shit he ain't seen before."

"I know that's right!! Get ready for your man. But umm … let me make a correction! It has only been eighteen years. I'm only thirty-one. Don't get it twisted! Don't be trying to push my age up."

"Ah, yeah … right. And I no longer wear Burberry cologne. You know damn well I know how old *WE* are and *you* have a birthday coming up in a few months!" They both are laughing hysterically now. Sandy looks around to see if anyone is watching or listening to her conversation. She needs to keep it down since she is at work on a personal call. Those nosey ass bitches that make up a complete square connected to her cubicle are always listening to her phone calls.

"Girl, forget you. Okay look, our first stop is Vicky's. Where else are we going? I'm getting real excited about leaving this damn place." Sandy stands up pretending to stretch but she is actually trying to see if the nosey trio is in their cubicles at their desks. Two are missing and one is at her desk with her headphones on. *Hmmp, she probably ain't listening to a damn thing but my conversation.*

"Oh, so you *are* going with me today?! Good!" Regina looks back at Stan to make sure she hasn't disturbed him and walks in her closet, shuts the door for more privacy and starts picking out an outfit. "Okay, first we'll hit Vicky's. Then we'll move over to Bloomies. From there, we will head out to Bethesda to eat at Ruth Chris and then stop in Nails R Us. That will give us about an hour to get over to the spa by five-fifteen."

"Damn girl!! You're spending some money today, huh? I'ma be just like you when I grow up. Hell, after all that walking, shopping, and eating, I will definitely be ready for the Spa when we get there for sure."

"You know when I have something planned I'm on a serious mission. Regina Wooten doesn't play around. My To-Do list is all mapped out. Hey, have you heard from the others today? I mean it is still early for Colleen, but I was just asking."

"Are you kidding me? They've been M.I.A. since we left your house Monday night. One probably got her head stuck so deep into work trying to keep busy to forget that little episode in class. My heart goes out to Bee though. I'm gonna have to treat her to dinner or something. Then the other one probably has her head stuck up some man's ass … literally. I'm sure she will have a damn story to tell us when we see her this evening. Sometimes I be wondering if she is making that shit up like niggas do."

Sandy is checking her caller ID to see who called her while she was in the meeting with her supervisor. "Hey, maybe they've been practicing what we learned in one of the classes and are going to tell us all about it this evening at the spa. I do see that Colleen called me earlier while I was in the meeting. That's strange. Normally it is BeLynda that calls me at work. Colleen usually calls me on my cell. I wonder what she wants. I mean, she *rarely* calls me at work. You know I am not in the mood for her mess. I refuse to talk to her right now. All she is going to do is give me a headache and I don't feel like talking about her foolery to you on our drive to

White Flint or over lunch. I meant it when I said I want to enjoy this day, for real."

"Girl, you are so terrible but so right. You know them like you know your skin. I'm sure Colleen is going come in there with a story about something. BeLynda is already gonna be there flipping through magazines like she is actually reading it but only praying that Marcus is at work," Regina couldn't stop laughing. Her stomach is hurting now. "Woo girl, our friends. They are something else. We gotta love them though."

"Hmmp, no, we must love them to be putting up with those two characters. Sometimes they act just like Frick 'n Frack."

"Yea, and other times, they act like they belong on the *Tom and Jerry* cartoon. But I feel you on Bee's episode in class Monday. She was right beside me too. I peeped a little bit to make sure she was okay but the instructor had her. So she was in good hands. I'm sure in that type of class the instructor sees stuff like that all the time." Regina sighs.

"Aight girlie. My breakfast is cold now. Let me go warm it up so I can at least eat half of it before I leave. I'm gonna need some energy for the mall. I'll see you in an hour. That gives you enough time to lie your way out of the office. Be ready Sandy. I'm serious … don't have me waiting. We are on a tight schedule today. I should have already been gone. Sitting here talking to your ass on the damn phone and already had established fifteen minutes ago that you were going. I still have to get dressed too. You know White Flint is not around the corner and all it takes is for us to be deep in conversation and I miss my damn exit." Sandy laughs at Regina's statement because Regina is telling nothing but the truth. Regina's sense of direction is way off.

"Lady, look … I'll be ready. Forget Mrs. Winston's silly ass meeting. Clarice can kiss my smooth ass too. I'm about to have fun. Which car are we riding in today?"

"I haven't figured that out yet. I might sport the Suburban since we are going shopping. We need enough room to hold all our bags." They both laugh at Regina's response. Sandy is too excited.

"I know that's right!! Girl, you are too crazy. Okay, see you in an hour." Sandy hangs up the phone. *Damn, what am I gonna say to this bitch … how am I gonna get out of work today?!*

Chapter Five

5

Monday, three days ago ...

"Good evening ladies," Kelly, the instructor says walking into the room. She lays her bags down on a few of the chairs situated on the other side of the room. She looks around to see if everyone has in fact actually made it to this evening's class.

"I am glad that all of you could make it today. This evening's class will cover the importance of breathing properly during sex. I know you are probably saying that breathing is the last thing you are thinking about in the heat of the moment. Trust me, it is more important than you can envision.

We usually take – or suppose to take – several breaths a minute twenty-four hours a day. The correct breathing delivers the oxygen needed to our cells and our emotions and sensuality are therefore liberated. Most women do not breathe deeply enough on a daily basis just to experience a better life. So it is not surprising for me to see I am getting these strange looks from each of you, wondering how it is connected to great sex and intimacy. FYI Ladies, it can lead to ecstasy and even orgasms. Is everyone following me so far," the instructor asks the ladies with a little smirk on her face, tickled inside at how they are looking at her.

How in the fuck is breathing going to lead to a damn orgasm? A better one at that. That would take a lot of practicing because right now all I can see is me drying up fast like a damn prune from putting all of my concentration and energy into another area that I shouldn't be focusing on at that time, says Colleen to herself.

Kelly starts walking around the room moving in between the Ladies giving them all eye contact as she approaches and passes each of them. However, she sees Colleen is looking a little perplexed about what is coming out of her mouth.

"I see you are deep in thought Colleen. I think I have somewhat of an idea of what you are thinking. As a matter of fact, many of you may be thinking the same thing Colleen is thinking. Okay, let me see if what I am about to say will answer any of the thoughts floating around in here, okay?" Many of the Ladies in the class nod their heads in an up and down "yes" motion.

"Now, the breath is the key to us lasting longer during sex, having more passionate orgasms, and feeling more intimacy during lovemaking sessions. Did I answer at least some of your thoughts Ladies?" Many of the Ladies in the class nod their heads again in an up and down "yes" motion. Colleen hasn't responded yet.

"Colleen? What about you? Is there anything else I need to explain?" Colleen shakes her head from side to side in a "no" motion saying, "Oh, no, I am fine. You answered it for me, thanks Kelly."

Regina and Sandy are paying close attention to what the instructor is saying. Regina knows this will probably help her when she is tired and Stan wants to do an all-nighter. Sandy is listening attentively so she can go home and practice with her little friend in the box. BeLynda is just trying to connect this class with the rest of the classes so she won't be all over the place come time for her to get some dick.

"Now, what all of you probably haven't realized is that the majority of the time, you are actually holding your breath. That means you are showing evidence of shallow breathing, especially those of us who have a tendency to hold the abdomen in for a flatter appearance to enhance a leaner look. Holding it in may give the impression of being flatter and yes, it may even be attractive mentally or even to that man but that is not necessarily healthy. And I am sure all of us would love to live a lot longer with breathing right as oppose to living shorter trying to impress a man, right?" Kelly looks around the class at the Ladies trying to see if she gave some very important food for thought that warranted some positive head shakes. There are a few of those but more deep in thought looks is what she is getting.

"Hell, I thought it also helped to tighten the stomach muscles. At least that's what that damn trainer told me. Now, she's telling me I shouldn't be doing that. Ugh!! I can't win for losing," Regina whispers to her crew.

"I know Girl! It's amazing how every time we come to these damn classes we learn that something we are used to doing shouldn't be done or is somehow fucking with our health or sex life. I guess it pays to really do our research instead of listening to what 'they' been saying all this time," BeLynda whispers back to Regina.

The instructor continues. "While many women have no problem having orgasms, some women struggle a little with having them all the time and some have never had the orgasm experience with or without a partner. I can almost bet that there are a few of you here right now and no one has a clue as to where you actually are right now. For whatever reason, you have made a decision to let this be your own personal accomplishment and that is fine. I'm not knocking anyone. Let's just make the best of the time you are here, all right Ladies? So listen up!! Even though it may not seem very sexy to appear to be breathing, the proper breathing is the main ingredient to orgasmic fulfillment and self-empowerment for all of us. It also helps us with lasting much longer for our man ... or shall I say "men," for some of you," Kelly gives a wink and a smirk to the snickers she receives in the room. "They will love you for the increased stamina Ladies. They wouldn't even know that all it came from was you practicing to breathe right and understanding the importance of it goes a long way.

But breathing right isn't just for sex Ladies. It has healthy benefits too. Many use it in yoga and other exercises as well as meditation and I can say I am speaking from experience. If any of you workout or take exercise classes, I am sure you have heard over and over again about breathing right. Now if any of you are into tantric sex, breathing properly is an absolute must. But that is another class so that's all I am going to say about that."

Oooh, tantric sex? I wonder if we will be having that topic in one of our classes. I need to check the listing, Colleen said to herself.

"Deeply breathing into your abdomen improves relaxation, while reducing stress and strains. I'm sure we all can appreciate relaxation in this hectic way of expected living. If we would get into the routine of doing this on a regular and daily basis, we will see that it is the entrance to primordial intimate feelings and more physically powerful feelings of peaks of bliss along with the improved relaxation. Now, ladies, let the class begin ...

BeLynda looks at the instructor as if it has just been revealed to her that she has three heads and is out to get them. She raises her hand saying, "Excuse me, um, Kelly," clearing her throat. "May you back up a little bit please?" Kelly is smiling, with her hands clasps together and turns to face BeLynda saying to herself, *Oh goodness, here she goes.* "Yes, Bee, what can I help you with?" Looking down at her notes, BeLynda says "Um, you just said 'the entrance to primordial intimate feelings and more physically powerful feelings of peaks of bliss along with the improved relaxation.' What in the world does that mean? I mean, can you break it down a little simpler than that?"

Kelly smiles and puts her hands behind her back and starts walking around the room giving everyone eye to eye contact but always ending up back at BeLynda's eyes. "Okay, let's take the term 'primordial intimate feelings' ... let's look at this phrase. When I said this a few minutes ago, what I meant is there is an erotic energy in all of us. Some of us just don't know it yet. Some of us do know it but refuse to let it show for fear of losing control or giving in too much to something or someone.

However, with this energy, we can create anything we want. It can be a new book, song, life, or class ... *anything* we want. This primordial energy is really the driving force behind many things we do *BUT* ... it remains hidden in the subconscious. Is that where it should be? Is that where it should stay? Many here in this class have either suffered with their sex drive and sexual expectations whether it is from within or from their mate. Come out of your mind, let go of the ego, bring it down to an id sometimes. Ignore what you have heard and what you may have been taught. Some of the things we may have heard could have been from those who were uncomfortable with themselves. I'm sure they meant well but many have no idea that they are being negative. They confused it with reality. Stop hearing those things over and over in your head. Take control of your mind, body, and soul. Whether you know it or not, there is a separation between the conscious sense of self and the hidden sexual drive."

All of the Ladies are really listening to what Kelly has to say to them. BeLynda is writing away in her notepad. *This is great!! I will be using this as one of my motivational speeches when I am getting in tune with myself. All that bullshit my grandmother used to say to me about being a "Fast-Ass" when I wasn't even out there trying to be fresh with the boys. Yet, my mother was forever coming to the house with a new handsome man with money on her arm. She may not have been setting a positive example but she apparently wasn't shallow breathing and had entered 'primordial intimate feelings' long before I even paid attention to her "Fast-Ass" behaviors.*

BeLynda was all in her mind of the past figuring out where her negative triggers were. She was no longer listening to Kelly even though she knows she is still providing some very enlightening, uplifting, motivational words. The instructor had told enough to get BeLynda to understand what the phrase meant and how she had been depriving herself of a more free spirited enjoyable life. She continues digging deeper to understand some things.

Then there is all the motherfucking shit I took off of Steve's ass throughout our marriage. I know people have sex and it should be more of it when married but I just kept feeling like I wasn't a Lady with my ass in the air. I felt like we were fuckin' instead of making love and I didn't want to fuck. Steve harassing me saying things like "Loosen up Bee, I'm your husband now," "What's the matter, do I not turn you on," "Why can't I hit it from the back," "Leave the light on, let me see you," "We can't have children with me always fighting to get some ass from my WIFE," and the one I hated the most, "Don't wait up, I'm not coming home tonight because I will be getting my dick wet from a mouth and pussy, and I should be getting it wet from YOU" ... SLAM ... goes the front door. Disrespectful ass motherfucka!!

BeLynda realizes readjusting of her mind needs to be done. It is said that Satan comes in all shapes, forms, and sizes. Not that she is thinking her grandmother was but she knows even though she meant well, she used her mother's actions as a means that inhibited her in her relationships with men. The slam of the door in BeLynda's mind jolts her from her thoughts and back to class. She looks around the room to see what everyone is doing and they are very much into what Kelly is saying. BeLynda returns to listening to the instructor.

"Now, the term 'physically powerful feelings of peaks of bliss' deals with the sudden moments and feelings that leave you in awe, excitement, full of happiness, loads of euphoria and great ecstasy, just full of life and love. All of us have these moments but many of us may not be able to recognize them or understand what is going on. So it might be hard to embrace what you are feeling. Improved relaxation is self-explanatory, right?" The Ladies nod their heads in agreement.

"If you have listened to everything I have said about the phrase 'the entrance to primordial intimate feelings and more physically powerful feelings of peaks of bliss along with the improved relaxation' you will begin to understand how it is connected to our sexual worlds as well. It is also connected to our world of love and acceptance.

Learning to breathe properly to get the right feeling within your body is what we are going to do here. It will help you feel and become free. Free of all the things you have bottled up in your mind and assists with how you react and behave. Deep breathing is really the start of getting rid of those sexual hang-ups. I can tell by some of the expressions in this room, there are many hang-ups that may not have been yours to begin with.

While you are listening to me, I want you to close your eyes and work on some slow deep breathing techniques. Get into the habit Ladies of making what you do in the performance of sex benefit you at all times throughout your day. It has been an act, a performance for many of you as a means to get, keep, please, recreate with a man and it needs to start being more than that. It needs to be about what you want. Stop just being about an act but a part of your nature and well-being.

Now, breathe in with a slow eight count … release in a slow four count. Let's do that again. Continue this count sequence while I am talking to you. It is going to take some practice in order to be able to breathe this way without thinking about it or without looking like you are practicing your breathing."

The instructor is walking around the class observing everyone. "How are you starting to feel? Do you feel a little different? Not that you have to so soon but some of you just might be feeling different. It all depends on how deep you really are breathing and if you are concentrating on what you're doing. Please do not hyperventilate," Kelly laughs. "The appropriate breathing brings an existence and vivacity to your body. The deeper you breathe, the more lively your body should feel."

Mmm, "vivacity" … I like the sound of that word, BeLynda says to herself, thinking she says it in her mind but actually out loud to herself. Regina turns her head in the direction of BeLynda's voice, peaking out of her left eye with a smirk on her face, and turns her head back to the middle. *Mmm-hmm, I hear you Bee. Inner freak is starting to coming out, but I won't tell anyone if you don't want me to. I will tease her later. She ain't slick,* Regina says to herself to what she heard BeLynda saying.

"Our breathing is very imperative to our existence so we might as well put it to great use. Trust and believe, you will thank yourself when you do. It is not to just make certain we are actually alive. It really does support us in focusing more on pleasure and puts extra oxygen into the bloodstream. This oxygen is very vital to our cells in order to have enhanced health and movement of our muscles. You must recognize that oxygen is what puts the 'O' in orgasm." Kelly is smiling when she says the last statement. She notices that everyone's eyebrows raised showing excitement and the need to listen for more information.

Sandy is sitting up with her eyes closed slowly breathing as the instructor suggested. However, she starts to feel as if she needs to be on her back. She lies down and continues with her deep slow breathing. As time goes on, she is no longer listening to Kelly. She has her legs bent at the knees with her feet planted firm on the floor. Her mind drifts off to somewhere outside of the classroom and none of the Ladies can see her for their eyes are closed too. Besides, they all are busy participating in the breathing exercise. Or at least they should be.

All of a sudden, Sandy could feel her pelvis tightening as she continues with the breathing. It is almost as if she is sleep ... or even hypnotized but her pelvis tends to have a mind of its own right now, making her tilt upwards. She feels herself getting moist through this exercise. She has forgotten that she is not at home on her queen size plush bed. The sensation is strong and is taking control.

As Kelly walks around the room talking, she notices that quite a few of the women seem to be lost in their own private worlds. However, she observes Sandy getting more involved into her private session. Sandy now has her mouth open, with both of her hands on her lower abdomen, arching her back moving her knees from side to side slowly. Sandy is actually massaging her clitoris with this motion and Kelly knows it. Kelly smiles at Sandy and shakes her head up and down, saying to herself *she is entering the world of euphoria.* She kneels down on the floor beside Sandy and whispers in her right ear, "Your endorphins have awaken inducing your euphoria." The sound of Kelly's voice and warm breath up against her ear made Sandy want to feel more than her voice. Yet it would work better if it is the deep voice of a man getting ready to stick his tongue in her ear.

Kelly stands up and continues to walk around the room observing everyone to see who is really into it, who is pretending, and who may have fallen asleep. Kelly asks everyone, "How are you feeling now? Are you enjoying the feeling? Or are you a bit confused?" No one responds. They are too busy with the pleasure they are receiving from their breathing. Or maybe some of them are trying to figure exactly what it is they should be feeling at this moment.

"I am going to assume everyone is starting to experience what I am talking about. This is excellent. I like when I am doing my job. I want you to *feel* it. Let it go. Enjoy where you are right now. Keep doing what you're doing. Your mind and body should be very quiet, warm, and relaxed now. Think about nothing but what you are feeling."

Kelly sits down and watches everyone while she is checking out her finger nails. When she was walking around a few minutes ago, she noticed Colleen's French manicure is done in black tips instead of white. That is different. She hasn't seen that before and is trying to imagine how her nails will look done that way.

After about ten more minutes of talking, Kelly hears a loud sound of ecstasy coming from one of her students. Kelly stands up smiling excitedly. "*Oh my*!! Someone sounds as if they are experiencing a wonderful joy. It feels good doesn't it?" Looking around the room, to her surprise, she sees it is Colleen wailing in unadulterated bliss. *Colleen?! Is she faking? Minutes ago, she didn't even look like she was paying attention. I felt sure it would have been Sandy that I hear.*

Kelly looks over at Sandy and sees that Sandy still looks the same way she did earlier but she is drooling. Her hands are massaging her pelvis. Unaware of her actions, Sandy starts to rotate her hips and buttocks. Kelly nods in approval saying to herself, *Aaah, you like taking in the moment, getting all you can get because it feels so good, huh? Okay, I got you. You're a woman that likes to take it slow. Ain't nothing wrong with that.*

Sandy arches her back and spreads her arms out across the floor, yet no squeals are released from her mouth. However, Kelly could tell she was having a very large "O." *How is she experiencing that so quiet*, Kelly wonders slanting her head to the right looking at Sandy. *Now that is art. She must be used to getting it in while others were close by in other rooms like roommates or siblings.*

When she observes BeLynda, the strange thing Kelly notices is that BeLynda's hands are shaking. *Why is she shaking? Is she holding back her feelings too afraid to let go in front of the other women? Come on Bee, let it go. Everyone has their eyes closed and are not paying you any attention.* She really wants BeLynda to get in touch with her body and sexuality but she really has to clear her mind in order for that to happen.

She is a very beautiful woman and something must have happened in her past that keeps her closed. I would think for her to have friends like Colleen, Sandy, and Regina that she would know how to get down with the best of them. But every Monday, every class she is very attentive, listening to me and taking notes, yet too embarrassed to fully participate. For as long as they have been attending classes, BeLynda just refuses to relax while over thinking everything. *Being free doesn't require thinking and concentrating Bee.*

"Don't be afraid of the orgasm. Experience it. Have a few of them if you will. Forget you're in the room with others. Imagine it's just you and I am a CD. I want you to embrace what it means to be sexually secure and uninhibited. We all are sexual beings. We were made that way. Acknowledge and be pleased about it. Pay attention to your breathing. Connect with your body. Right now, you are learning how to be present for your experience."

BeLynda can hear Kelly but she immediately feels as if everyone is looking at her. She doesn't want to open her eyes too afraid that she will become the guinea pig for this evening's class. *Shit! Let Kelly use someone else if she needs to. Please don't call out my name. I can hear your footsteps near my head and I know you're slowing down your pace. I will get up and walk right out this bitch if you come over to me Kelly!!*

Her mind is no longer clear and free. It is now full of apprehension. BeLynda tries very hard to get back to that wonderful place she was just a few seconds ago. It is not working. She can feel Kelly near her and her eyes are on her trying to see what she is doing. *Uh-oh, what the hell is that?*

BeLynda turns her head towards the sound, rolls over, and her eyes fly wide open. She didn't know what the hell was going on but after what she heard, she needed to actually see. Someone is crying out. Others are whimpering. The scream she heard was just too much. BeLynda needed to see. She gets real nervous and starts feeling real uncomfortable until she has a queasy feeling in her stomach. But she continues to look around the room to catch where the sounds are coming from. *Damn! This breathing exercise is doing all that for the Ladies? I don't want to be doing that in here with them. How do I know it's gonna work for me when I try this at home? This is weird.*

Kelly hears some other cries of joy and a few that sound like they were in pain or hurt. Looking around the room, she sees that BeLynda has rolled over onto her stomach with her head up looking around. She already knew what that was about. *Damn, I have lost her for the evening. I already know that she will not get back to that place. I know one day she is going to surprise us all. I'm just waiting.* Continuing to speak, ignoring BeLynda …

"Get into it Ladies, let it out. With deep breathing, you will experience a myriad of emotions and that is very important. Release them. Purge them from your soul. When you breathe deeply, that is how you will exist through many experiences in your existence. When you breathe shallow … well, I don't have to finish that statement do I? I'm sure you get the point. Free your inner being. Your sexual being."

All of a sudden, BeLynda throws up all over the floor. Kelly hurriedly retrieves antibacterial wipes and some paper towels, heading over to BeLynda. She comes prepared for the breathing exercise because it never fails. The inhibited students always seem to get sick at some point in the exercise. Maybe it is their body's way of releasing all of those pinned up emotions they had been carrying around for years. Kelly is realizing that for as long as she has been teaching this class, she has never researched why that is the reaction from her inhibited Ladies.

She throws many paper towels over the vomit but starts to wipe the sweat from BeLynda's face with the wipes. "That's right, let it out Bee. Be free of the psychological bondage. This sometimes happens when we try to fight what we are feeling. Don't hold on to it. Let all the negativity pass and let the positivity in. Welcome peaceful relaxation. Accept complete euphoria. Appreciate the awakening of your intimacy. Don't be ashamed of what you feel. I'm here to help you. You will feel so much better once you do. Be who you want to be sexually. It doesn't mean you are a freak. It means you are a woman."

Kelly finishes wiping BeLynda's face and notices that BeLynda is now pale and drained. She stops talking to her thinking that will make BeLynda calm down. She kisses her on the cheek. Kelly is pleased with what BeLynda is experiencing but she isn't sure if she is receptive to what is happening to her.

She thought that she had lost BeLynda's attentiveness for the evening but she somehow found her way back to that place. All of that holding back she has been doing of such wonderful feelings, that apparently she could no longer hold captive inside her body. BeLynda is coming into her own sexuality. Kelly isn't sure how open BeLynda is going to be to it but she is happy that BeLynda now knows what it feels like to let go of all that repressed emotion.

BeLynda is totally embarrassed. She couldn't believe she had just thrown up all over the damn floor in front of everyone in class. She couldn't even look at anyone. Why did I have to be the one to throw up? *Why couldn't it have been someone else? Was this supposed to happen? I know they heard me but did anyone see it was me? Hell, I know Regina knows it was me. She's lying right beside me.* Looking around the room, she notices that everyone is still into the exercise paying her no mind. Regina appears to still be into the exercise too.

It didn't make matters any better for the instructor to be wiping her face with the damn antibacterial wipes. BeLynda wanted to slap her hand away but she really couldn't move. She was exhausted as if she has gone through a purification session. As if a huge weight has been released from her body, mind, and soul. However, she knows her face is going to be broke out when she looks at it tomorrow morning. But one thing she can't stop thinking about is:

What are my friends saying about me right now? Are they gonna have conversations about me during the week? I know they are going to have plenty of uncomfortable questions for me when we meet up at the spa Thursday. I am not looking forward to that. Maybe I'll play sick.

Chapter Six

6

Back to current day, Thursday …

"BeLynda, how are you today? What have you been doing? Your skin is glowing today."

"I'm fine Lorna, thank you. I'm not sure why my skin is glowing today. I've not done anything different. At least I don't think I have. How are you doing? Has it been busy in here today?" BeLynda runs her hand over her face.

"Oh, I am just fine as well. Well, your skin is looking more beautiful than before. Yes, it has been quite busy in here today. It is Thursday. Are you here by yourself today? Or will your friends be joining you?"

"Ha, ha, ha they will be here as always, I'm sure. No one said they weren't coming. Then again, I've only spoken with Colleen and she said she would be here. Is Marcus working today?"

"He most certainly is. And I'm sure the other three will be with you too. They've not missed a Thursday yet." They both laugh.

"Good because you know I don't like trying anyone new. I did once and that didn't work out too well."

"Oh, I'm sorry to hear that."

"Ha, ha, ha don't be ... I'm not. I stick with what works."

"BeLynda, I know I ask you the same questions every week but one never knows."

"That's all right Lorna. It doesn't bother me. You're just doing what you are supposed to. I can't fault you for that."

BeLynda always gets to the spa before everyone else. For one, she lives closer to Waldorf than the other three. She likes getting to the spa first anyway. For two, this way if Marcus isn't working that day, the rest of the crew wouldn't see her disappointment. The others aren't aware of her hidden attraction to Marcus. She doesn't know why they aren't aware of it. She thinks it is quite obvious.

Maybe they just think I like the way he uses his hands on me. Well, that is part of it. Yet his body ... his looks ... and his voice are definitely at the top of the list for me. If only I can get his dick to be number one. Then I wouldn't think once about my main squeeze or ex-husband, BeLynda thinks to herself, flipping pages in a *Self* magazine, not even paying attention to what is on the pages.

She is thinking about what the receptionist said about her skin. *Glowing, huh? It probably was those antibacterial wipes Kelly was lathering on my damn face. Maybe that should be my new facial cleanse. Or it could be that damn purge I had in class Monday night. I have been feeling a little different and freer. Been breathing right and I have been experiencing more horniness than before.*

Putting the magazine down, picking up a *Prevention* magazine, thumbing through it to help past the time away, BeLynda hears two females laughing loudly walking into the Spa waiting area. They sound like two high school girls. BeLynda looks up to see who is being so loud and to her surprise, it is Sandy and Regina. She thought the laughs sound familiar. They are arm in arm, giggling uncontrollably as if no one else is around.

Look at them. Having another private conversation that neither Colleen nor I will ever hear about to laugh along with them. Well, they have been friends longer. Colleen and I didn't come along until twelfth grade. That's five years after they had already been friends. So I guess they're bound to have more secrets anyway.

Sometimes I try not to notice. Other times, it is hard not to. Especially, when Colleen makes a scene about how they seem to have secrets. They probably been shopping today and perhaps Sandy is happy Regina has spent money on her, as usual. That's something that she hasn't done for the rest of us. Granted, we are pretty comfortable financially but it just has never been offered. Not that I would accept anyway ... I'm just saying. When those two get together I know Regina is the only one spending. Almost acting like she's Sandy's man, showering her with gifts and shit. It doesn't matter who or what it is being spent on or for, Regina is the one spending, period. Thank goodness she only shops when she needs to. I guess that's why Stan never says anything. Hmmm, I wonder if they have actually slept together before. That would explain some things. Inquiring minds would like to know.

BeLynda just sits there still flipping the pages of the magazine but looking at them instead of the pages, thinking to herself and observing another scene of the strong bond between her friends. After a few more minutes, she has had enough and decides to interrupt their stingy conversation.

"Hey Ladies. What devilish things have the two of you been up to? Coming in here all giggly ... let me share in the laughter." BeLynda stands up and walks over to greet Sandy and Regina with big hugs and kisses.

"Hey girlie. You're the only one here," Regina asks after giving her a big hug and a kiss on the cheek in return.

"Well, I was. Now we're only missing Colleen. When she came over my house this morning she said she had meetings with two of her clients. Hopefully they went well. Not that she would miss Spa day anyway. Sooo again, what have the two of you been up to? Coming in here sounding like high school girls."

Sandy starts giggling again waving her hand at BeLynda. "Oh, chile please. There isn't anything private about our giggling. We were talking about what the instructor was talking about in class Monday night. Those looks she was giving trying to demonstrate breathing. Don't you think it was hilarious? All that deep heavy breathing mixed with those faces and sounds throughout the room. I eventually stopped peeping at her and everybody and got into it. It was just comical to me." BeLynda's smile disappears from her face. She is wondering if Sandy is laughing at her and the vomiting experience. She starts rubbing her fingers across her eyebrows, something she does when she is beginning to feel uncomfortable. Regina's voice breaks her thoughts with laughter and leaning on her shoulder.

"*Please*, don't have Sandy show you what she was doing or what she was seeing. You will be laughing like a high school girl too. We were already too loud when we came in here. To add another voice to it, they would put us out of here. You know how they are about quietness in the tranquil area." Regina leans over and whispers to BeLynda the latter part sarcastically.

BeLynda isn't laughing because she knows they had to be laughing about her too. She is sure that one of them heard, smelled, and saw her vomit all over that damn floor in class. It wasn't as if she could hold it in. Once her mouth started building up with saliva, she knew she was done. It still didn't make it right that they are making fun of class.

Damn, I knew I should have not come to the Spa today. But no matter when I was ready to face my friends, they would have been asking me about the episode and I am not ready to discuss what I was feeling. Especially dealing with Colleen and her damn bluntness that comes with her the majority of the time. I love her to death but I would have no problems smacking her ass today. Then again, Colleen didn't say anything about it when we got to Regina's house that night, so maybe I am being uncomfortable and irritated for nothing. Hell, had I not been embarrassed by the dark shadow at the classroom door actually watching us, I would have just gathered my things and left the class. It must've been one of the Ladies' husband watching and he didn't want to be noticed. Whoever it was though didn't budge. I wished I could've seen the face.

Just then, Colleen walks in the Spa. She greets everyone with the usual kisses on each check and a slight peck on the lips as to not mess up her MAC lip glass. She starts taking off her Ruana, revealing her outfit as if she knows she is looking real nice and expensive. So she wants her friends to take in her appearance. Sandy rolls her eyes up in the air. Regina looks at Colleen, smiles and shakes her head with her hands on her hips. BeLynda sits back down, picking up a *Women's Day* magazine, resuming flipping through the pages and pays Colleen no attention since she did see her earlier and the outfit has not changed.

"Hey, Ladies. How is everyone? Whew … are they ready for us yet? Whew, after the last four hours, I am ready now to choose what blended salts and butters I want for my body polish. Who's here today?" Looking around the room trying to see who is working today, Colleen continues, "Can a sista get a glass of wine? Hell, I need something a little stronger but I know they don't offer that here." Colleen sits down to change her footwear. Her feet are tired and hot. She removes her boots that she had been walking around in all day, trying to be cute and puts on her flip flops. Her flip flops with the tiny beads on them massaging the balls of her feet, feels so much better right now.

She walks over to Lorna and inquires about how long it will be before they go upstairs to the locker room to change into their robes. She needs to get all the way comfortable. Lorna assures her that it would be shortly. The Ladies just look at Colleen coming in, making her presence known to everyone. *She is definitely consistent with her behavior, like it or not*, Regina chuckles to herself.

Five minutes later, Jan approaches the Ladies very business-like as usual and escorts them upstairs as if it is their first time at the Spa. Once in the locker room, Jan leaves without explaining to them what they should do next. Luckily Jan knew better or else she would have gotten an ear full from Colleen. They meet here every Thursday for a five-thirty group appointment. So they already know what to do and where to go. Not that they get a discount by going in a group. This is just a way for the Ladies to get together to share in some girl talk and girl time catching up on each other's lives.

"All right girls. What have you been up to? I haven't really spoken to any of you since Monday night when we left Regina's house. What's been happening? Or shall I ask what has happened? Got caught a little off guard in class Monday," Colleen asks the Ladies looking at each of them straight in the eye, especially BeLynda. She may have not been next to her but she knows how far away from her those gurgling sounds came.

Colleen knows she had been caught off guard with all that weird breathing and what it made her do in class but the Ladies would never know it. Well, Sandy might know since they weren't too far from each other. But she made sure she wasn't too close once Kelly started talking about the experience.

However, she also knows that BeLynda has to be more embarrassed than she is. To throw up all over the floor, in class, in front of everyone, regardless of people supposedly being in tuned with the class and having their eyes closed through the exercise, Colleen knows with who BeLynda is, this is going to be an awkward evening. She knows she is going to think that they might ask her about it.

Colleen doesn't know what the vomiting meant but she won't address it in front of the others. Still looking at BeLynda, who is avoiding eye contact, Colleen just says to herself, *Oh, you and I will be having a conversation that apparently is needed. Avoid looking at me all you want. We are like sisters and I need to know how you are hurting.* Regina and Sandy notice the look on Colleen's face and try to figure out what she is thinking.

Regina responds to Colleen first. "Well, I really haven't been up to much. You know Stan was on travel and he just got back home this morning. He surprised me and came home early. He gave Maria the day off and cooked me breakfast too. So you know how that went."

"*Whaaaat*?! Gave Maria the day off? Since when did he start doing stuff that like for the maid? *AND* he cooked you breakfast? I didn't even know Stan could cook. Sounds like ol boy was missing somebody, huh? Hell, ol boy getting his weekend started early ain't he? What y'all think," BeLynda asks Sandy and Colleen. She is trying so hard to make sure her episode at class stays back in Monday night's class and not here at the Spa. *Colleen just had to bring that shit up here and not at my house,* BeLynda says to herself rolling her eyes with a smile.

"Yeah, I guess so. I was thinking the same thing Bee," Regina laughs at what was said. "Plus, as all of you know, we're leaving for the Poconos tomorrow afternoon … right after my hair appointment. So, he probably is getting amped up for this weekend. Today, Sandy and I went shopping for my little rendezvous. We had a ball too."

Hmmp, I bet y'all did, Colleen says to herself slightly rolling her eyes at Regina's last two statements. "When are y'all coming back? And why are you getting your hair done? It's gonna be tore up come Saturday morning anyway, so why are you wasting the money? You know damn well Stan has your ass standing on your head sometimes. That's why your ass talked us into taking these damn classes," Colleen says poking Regina in her ticklish spots. Sandy and BeLynda are laughing hard now.

"What's so funny? What's wrong with me looking nice for my man even if it is for one night? You know I have to represent when we first walk up in that place. Those other couples are gonna be hatin' on us. So they need to see me before the hairdo gets messed up." They all are laughing at this point, each nodding their head as if they are agreeing and saying, "I know that's right."

"Besides, I'm getting a loose pin-up which is easy to handle. I don't see that getting messed-up too bad. And … for your information, my man doesn't have me standing on my head. *I* have me standing on my head." Now Sandy, BeLynda, and Colleen are laughing so hard holding their stomachs, they have to sit down on the benches. Once they get most of the laughter out, they stand and proceed to exit the locker room.

All four of the ladies walk into the Tranquil Area. It is very relaxing. There are amber lights in the ceiling. Vanilla bean and white tea scented candles are sitting on electric warmers, filling the room with a relaxing aroma. There is Spa music playing nice and soft. There are two steam fountains with changing lights of pale pinks, greens, and lavenders. The room has two glass dinette sets for four with floral arrangements centerpieces on each table, three fabric covered benches, two fabric covered chairs, and plants throughout the room. Assorted crackers, cheeses, vanilla wafers, and trail mix adorn one of the tables near the entrance. The other table is filled with drinks of plain water, lemon water, water infused with lemon, limes, and cucumbers, and an assortment of detox teas for the guests to help themselves to.

Sandy sits on a bench with her feet propped up. Regina and BeLynda sit at a table while Colleen sits in a chair with her legs hanging over one of the arms, swinging her feet making a snapping sound with her flip flops.

Continuing with answering Colleen's question to get back on track with the conversation, Sandy says, "Well, for me, I've been working as usual. Nothing too exciting here either. Still wanting to win the lottery and looking for that special someone. The family is coming over Thanksgiving and I am having a hard time getting my menu together. Larry is supposed to stop by but I prefer that he does not." Sandy has had enough of Larry. They all lean their heads to the side knowing something is coming after that "Larry" statement.

"Why, what's the matter Dee Dee? It's not working out for you? What happened? It's over before it really gets started? Hell, pass him on over to me if it is," BeLynda says, kidding with that comment.

"Hmmp, be my guest Girl. Let his fragile ass throw tantrums for you instead. The motherfucka cums before I can get a rhythm going and looks at me as if he just did something. Talkin' about 'Baby, it be feeling so gooood. I be trying to wait for you.' Get the fuck outta here with that bullshit. I ain't trying to hear all that when I have to go in the bathroom and pay my friend in the box a visit." The Ladies are listening very attentively now. They know there is nothing more frustrating during a moment of sex than when a woman is left hanging.

"Oooh, it's getting juicy now!! Fragile, did you say? Say what now? I ain't heard that adjective in the same sentence about a man. Sooo, not tantric but *tantrums*?! How old is he? That surely isn't his idea of foreplay is it? Let me get comfortable. Explain yourself girl," Colleen said swinging her legs around to the other arm of the chair to face Sandy letting her know she has her undivided attention. She needs to see Sandy's lips moving while she is listening, along with seeing her facial expressions as she is describing Mr. Larry to them.

"There's nothing more to explain. I mean, that's it. He ain't lasting, I ain't into selfish sex, and I ain't into having to resort to fake shit when I just had the real shit in me, you know? What woman would? Oh yeah, and he told me I was too rough. Ugh!! He is sickening right about now and I need him to get it together. What kind of shit is that?"

"What kind of *bitch* is that is what you should be asking," Colleen corrects her while giving Regina a high five. BeLynda just shrugs her shoulders, shaking her head in disbelief at what Sandy has just told them. "I mean, sometimes we want it a little rough. There is a time and a place to be gentle and I guess he got his timing off, huh? Maybe it's too early for him to read your body signals. Aww, you have to teach him. Well …"

"You got that right. What is he talking about … rough? All of that six feet two inches 'Mr. Man of Steel' Larry, and he is talking about you are too rough. I didn't know he was such a softy. Maybe he thinks all women want it the same way. But I mean, give us some details. What you be doing to this man girl," Regina joins in with her comment and gets up to get a handful of sunflower seeds and pour a glass of lemon water.

"Damn Dee Dee … thank goodness I was just kidding about handing him over. I'm soft enough. Two softies together in bed trying to get down … hell, nothing would get done," BeLynda says rolling her eyes and waving her hand at the situation. Everyone looks at BeLynda surprised at what she just said. BeLynda doesn't notice and keeps right on talking. "Girl, I guess your toys really have been getting some work in, huh? Tell you what, Colleen and I are going out Saturday night to the *Zanzibar*. Come go with us and have some other kind of fun girl. It sounds like you need it. We will make sure you enjoy yourself."

Oh no this heifer didn't, Colleen says to herself and looks at BeLynda with her mouth open. "Dag Bee, how you gonna ask her about Saturday night? You knew I was going to ask her when I got here. Hell, I am the one that asked *you* to go." Colleen smacks her lips together and rolls her eyes at BeLynda for beating her to the invite.

Ignoring what Colleen just said, Sandy responds to BeLynda's invite. *Hell, it doesn't matter who asked me but I know Colleen is feeling as if I would think it was Bee's idea and not hers.* "Hey, that's not a bad idea. As a matter of fact, that is a great idea. I mean, I might as well go with y'all. No need for me to just sit at home while Regina is in the Poconos getting her hair pulled and back blown out and you two will be out dancing, drinking, and mingling with some testosterone having fun. Maybe I might find someone to relieve me of my duties of working on my erogenous zones." Colleen gives her a high five.

"I know that's right girl. That's what I'm talkin' 'bout. You shouldn't have to do it all by yourself. Pass that duty on over to a *man*. But speaking of zones," Colleen sits up ready to tell all. "I woke up at Devin's house this morning." The ladies' mouths fly open. It's as if time has stopped and they all stare at Colleen as if she told them she is leaving the country.

"Yes, Girls I did. And y'all know what ..." As soon as Colleen says that, she is interrupted by a hand on her shoulder. She turns around looking up to see Darla. She gives them their Body Polishes. Everyone quiets down and smiles at Darla, hoping she didn't hear any of their conversation but pissed off that she decides to enter the room right now.

Colleen smiles and points to Sandy to go first. Regina went first last week and she goes first next week. BeLynda goes whenever Marcus comes to get her, which is normally when Darla is on her second person.

Sandy gets up and is all smiles but completely anxious and irritated. "Ooh goody! It's my turn to go first. But damn!! It was just getting good. All right ladies, I'm out. Hold all conversations until we meet up in the shower. I ain't playing either."

"Yeah, yeah, yeah. Just go already, please," Colleen is waiving Sandy on laughing at her.

"I'm serious y'all. I better not miss anything Colleen has to say. I refuse to get this conversation second handed or paraphrased through someone else's words. I want to hear it from the hoe's mouth herself." Colleen bursts out laughing, looking wide-eyed and shocked at Sandy.

"Girl, we aren't going to say anything else. Do we ever? No, now go get your dry ass polished." Colleen turns around to walk towards the double doors laughing hard. "Shit, my stomach is growling anyway. I want my BLT now. I don't want to have to wait until after my eye treatment. Y'all not ready to eat?"

Regina gets up from her chair stretching and straightening out her robe. "Naw, I can wait. I am not that hungry at the moment. I'll probably get a salad anyway. I don't need anything too heavy. We ate at Ruth Chris for lunch."

"Oh, '*we*' did? Who is '*we*'? Because I was busy getting pissed off at one of my clients. She was already given a discount and she was *still* trying to get me to lower the price. She may be another client that ends up having 'grand-ma' whipping up that famous potato salad and kissing my ass. But yeah, back to my question. Who is '*we*'?"

"Sandy and I ate there after we stopped in Victoria's Secret and Bloomies." Sandy stops walking with Darla, turns around and gives Regina a look wondering why she even told Colleen about their day. She knows something snide is coming out of her mouth after that.

"I should've known you would be going into Vicky's but Bloomingdale's, huh? Both of those stores with Sandy-Dandy tagging along? Did she talk you into getting her those winter white Via Spiga boots? I know how her yellow ass can work a sista," Colleen asks Regina giving Sandy the side-eye. Sandy is pissed and stops fiddling with her cookies.

"Nooo, she didn't work me, thank you very much. A pair was already in the trunk of her car. So apparently she worked somebody else." Colleen and Regina laugh. BeLynda just shakes her head not trying to get involved. Sandy doesn't see the amusement in their laughter at her expense.

"Ump ... oh yeah? Well, we better watch out. Those boots are damn near three hundred dollars with tax. She'll be crying broke about something in a few days. Watch and see. Then again, she does get paid in four days. So maybe we're in the clear." Sandy throws a vanilla wafer at Colleen. Colleen catches it, sticks her tongue out at Sandy, gives her a wink, and puts the cookie in her mouth.

"Oh no you didn't heifer. Why you always got something slick to say out of your mouth? The *Queen* at working somebody for what she wants. If I am working people over to get what I want, then I learned from your scheming ass. But let the record show that I don't scheme and especially on my friends. You better be careful," Sandy says looking at Colleen as if she has two heads.

"Oh girl, you know I'm just playing with you. Don't get all touchy over words. Now pull your bikinis out your ass. You know I love you, so don't be getting no attitude because I tell the truth through my playing. Now, Darla is waiting patiently for you, so will you leave this room please?" Colleen is smiling but she knows Sandy is in her feelings.

"Girl, will you go ask about your food, please? You went from talking about food to talking about Sandy. Telling the truth through so-called playing doesn't prevent her from cursing your ass out. Stop being so messy. That's not a good look Colleen," BeLynda says and rolls her eyes. She hates when Colleen does that.

Colleen notices Sandy is now walking out the room with Darla right behind her. Sandy has her "attitude" walk on. She looks at BeLynda, then at Regina, then back to BeLynda being caught totally off guard at what she just said to her. She gets up and sashays across the room fuming. *She is so lucky she is my girl, because I would have bust her ass out in here too. Ms. Throw Up Giles,* Colleen says to herself.

"Yea, let me go ask about my food. I need to eat to calm my nerves and my mouth. I see Mother Giles has just popped in on us. I wouldn't want to be in time out."

Chapter Seven

7

Sigh I have looked through my closet and drawers four times in twenty-eight hours and still come up with nothing. With an exception of a few pieces, everything is very conservative. Now, I know I have gone out with the girls and a few men in the last year. What did I wear? Where did my clothes go? I don't remember when the attire of Gabrielle Union's character in 'Deliver Us from Eva' was delivered to my house. This is too depressing. I must watch too much television or movies. Colleen was right. Let me get over to Pentagon City now. However, whore-ish is what I still refuse to look like.

Chime!! Chime!!

BeLynda goes to the door to see who it is. Never a dull or peaceful moment at her house.

"Hello precious. You're looking quite ravishing today."

"Ravishing? Thank you, Khalil. What brings you by here? I was just on my way out the door."

"Oh, nothing," Khalil has his hands in his pockets looking at her like he is lost for words.

"Nothing? Then what's up," BeLynda is ready to go and he is taking too long to answer. She hates when he does this.

Speak up! What do you want? Why are you here if "nothing" brings you by? "Nothing" doesn't live here. BeLynda is thinking this with a slight grin on her face, still appearing to give him her undivided attention. He is looking rather handsome in a young sexy way. He is wearing his dark indigo True Religion jeans slightly loose on his ass but not too far down. He has on a bright orange Ralph Lauren tee and banana color high-top Timberland boots with a brown lambskin leather jacket. Khalil has a fresh shape up too looking just like he could be Ginuwine's twin brother ... he's just dark chocolate. *Mmmm, and he smells like Gucci too.*

BeLynda tries to be patient with Khalil because of his age. He is eight years younger than she is. He is fresh out of college and very book smart as well as street smart. At times, he can be bashful but sweet and can surely do some nonstop rounds in the bed. Something is missing though. Maybe it is the maturity level or the age difference that makes him a little uncomfortable. Or maybe it is the fact that Khalil's family and friends don't know about her and it makes her feel as if he is embarrassed about her age. That is a turn-off but the good thing is, she doesn't have to worry about wondering what kind of sarcastic statements or "old" snide remarks his family might be saying about her to him either.

Most men would give him a pat on the back for having a seasoned woman. Yet, for some reason BeLynda feels like Khalil comes around when no one would notice. Such as, when the majority is at work, or on Friday nights when people are out doing their own thing and too busy to notice, or after he gets finish playing around with the main chick.

"Do you want to ride with me? Or we can take your car, that's if you want to go with me. I don't want to hold you up."

Khalil smiles as if BeLynda just made his day. "Okay, cool. I would love to spend the day with you. We can take my car. Let me drive you around today. What Mall are we going to?"

Uh-huh. He ain't slick. He came over here to get his back scratched up. So he wants to be all nice and shit thinking that will earn him some points. He's right. I can scratch it up when we get back.

"I want to go to Pentagon City..."

"Aight. Any particular store? Or are we just browsing?"

"The girls and I are going out tomorrow night. I need something to wear."

"Do you need my help?"

Thinking of his age, BeLynda quickly responds, "No, no thank you. You'll have me looking like Colleen."

"Which one is Colleen again?"

"Never mind, Khalil. It's not that important. Let's go."

Khalil opens the door and steps out onto the porch still watching BeLynda's petite hands hold the door. BeLynda looks around checking the place once over, turns on the alarm and heads out the door.

"Your nails are pretty. You got them done today?"

"Thank you Khalil. I got them done yesterday. I wouldn't have had time to get them done today."

"Hey, I showed your picture to my boy the other day and he said that he sees you on Monday nights over by the gym coming out of the building across the street from it. What you be doing over there?"

BeLynda looks at Khalil as if he might be a stalker. "Oh really? You aren't trying to keep tabs on me through your friend are you?"

"What?! C'mon Bee!! Hell naw! Why would I do that?"

"Hey, I'm just checking. You're the one that asked the question. And I am sure if your 'boy' sees me, he also sees my friends are with me too."

"We didn't get all into that. It just sparked my curiosity when he said he sees you every Monday evening. And I know you don't have time for me on Mondays."

Mmmp, you damn sure right about that. My mind and body go through some serious changes that evening and I need to be alone, she says opening the car door to get in.

Khalil just stands there for a few minutes as if he can't believe BeLynda never answered his question.

Here I go again. Sitting here at work looking out the window. I wonder what the people down there are doing. Where are they going? Anywhere but to work, I hope. I have to be here today though. I was on slick leave yesterday afternoon. Can't do that two days in a row. Probably should have called in today and took the whole day. Who would I have called in to? Plenty of people are off today Mrs. Winston. Well, I'll be off a few days next week cooking for Thanksgiving anyway. So yeah, I'll save my leave and just make the best of today. My day should go smoothly and peaceful. Anything in my In Box can wait until Tuesday since I'll be off Monday. Good!! Don't have to deal with these folks two days in a row.

Ring! Ring!

"Ms. Robertson speaking. How may I help you?"

"You can help me by blowing me a big kiss through the phone."

"Mama! Hey! How are you doing today Lady?" Sandy gives her mother a big kiss through the phone. "Where are you? It sounds like you are outside." Sandy tries to listen hard to what she hears going on in the background of her mother's phone.

Sandy's mother blows her a kiss back through the phone. "Thanks Dee Dee." Dee Dee is a nickname for her nickname. That's Sandy's mother's doing. "I'm well, thanks. I am outside on my way to the grocery store. Have you decided on your menu for next week yet? I need to know if I am cooking something. If I am, I want to know what I am cooking. I would need to make sure I have all of the ingredients"

"I'm still not sure. We all know turkey, dressing, cranberry sauce, and candied yams are on the menu. I haven't decided on collards or green beans."

"Why not have both? You make all those starches and you can stand to add another vegetable to the menu. There will be a house full so you know you're gonna need another vegetable."

"Who's going to be cleaning and cooking ten bunches of greens and five pounds of green beans? Mickie normally brings fried cabbage so that's two vegetables."

"What happened to Sister? She's not coming over to help you? I thought she said she is helping. You can do the collards and she can do the green beans. I didn't say have two vegetables. I said you could stand to add another one."

"Like she does every year Mama? She'll be helping all right. In between talking on the phone, primping in the mirror every five minutes, and going through my closet, she may snap a green bean or two. Once I say something to her, she gets an attitude and is ready to go home. I'm really not in the mood for all of that this year. It only slows me down and since I'm the main cook, I don't need distractions."

"Here we go." Her mother lets out a big sigh.

"*Here we go?* What are you talking about? That's what happens. Is there a reason why I am the only one that observes that? I guess I am because everyone else is at home."

"Okay, Sandy. I will do the greens and two cheesecakes. I have to go, getting ready to get out the car." *click*.

Sandy looks at the receiver frowning, then hangs it up.

"How is she going to be mad with me? What did I say? Wait a minute ... cheesecake? Then who's making the apple pie?"

Ring! Ring!

"Ms. Robertson speaking."

"Sandy? How ya doing?"

"Larry," Sandy asks looking at the receiving twirling her pencil, closing her eyes tight because she didn't want to talk to him.

"Yea, it's me. I called you yesterday but the secretary said you went home sick. Then I called you at home later and I got your answering machine. Are you feeling all right?"

"Larry ... uh ... hi. Yes, yes ... I'm feeling much better, thank you."

"Good. I was a little worried when I couldn't reach you. Is there anything I can do for you?"

"Um, uh ... no thank you Larry. I will be just fine." *Dammit, he would be calling me today, right now.*

"I wanted to come by and see you last night but since I couldn't reach you, how does tonight sound? Are you up for some company?"

Fuck!! "Uh, nah ... no, that's okay Larry. I'm going straight home and going straight to bed. I actually should have called in today. You know me, loyal to my job" Sandy says with a sarcastic smile on her face.

"Are you sure? I can't bring you something? I just wanted to be there for you."

"Oh, no seriously, I feel much better and I will be okay. I am a big girl, really. Thank you though."

"Okay, well you take care Sandy. Hope you feel better. Do call if you need me to do anything. I'll give you a call tomorrow to see how you're doing. Okay?"

"Okay, all right Larry, thank you. I'll talk to you later."
click

Five minutes later, Sandy had to think about what she was actually doing. *Why am I acting like this? Larry is a softy and does have tantrums when things don't go his way, which gets on my damn nerves. However, he is sweet and kind, he is still a man and he has what I need. Let me call him back.*

"Hello??"

"Hey Larry, it's me, Sandy."

"Sandy? Hey. What's wrong baby? Is everything all right?"

But maybe he is too nice. "Nothing is wrong. I was being rude earlier and my rudeness was misdirected. What time did you want to come over? I could really use your company. I mean, I could really use some company."

"Oh! Oh, okay. Are you sure? I don't want to interrupt your rest." Larry was sounding too anxious. "How does seven o'clock work for you? Did you want me to bring anything?"

"Seven is fine. No need to bring anything extra. Just bring you." Sandy has to laugh to herself at how he is sounding.

"You got it babe. I have some making up to do with you." **click**

Sandy frowns at the phone wondering what Larry is talking about.

Whew. I am soaking wet with sweat. Luckily, I wrapped my hair and put on a sweatband before we got started. Oooh ... my thighs are trembling, my abs are aching and my biceps are tender. Fifty-five minutes of Cardio is hell on the body in one sense and heaven in another. All this jumping around, ab work, using the step, and four different size weights is hard. Why do we have to workout? Why can't the body just stay tight, firm and shapely? Why things gotta start shifting ... and so damn early? I haven't even had children yet.

"Hey girl. You look whipped. You all right? Should I or should I not ask if you liked class today," the instructor asks Colleen.

All these damn women in here and she has to be talking to me. I looked that damn whipped? She needs to get out of my face with the quickness!!

Colleen is huffing and puffing bending over holding on to her knees trying to regroup. She walks over to a stack of mats, sits down, and starts wiping her face, neck, and chest with her towel, ignoring the instructor. *She is sickening. She is only slightly huffing and puffing. There is only a small horizontal line of sweat under her breast line as if she sprinkled water on her top. How cute. That can't be possible.* Colleen rolls her eyes at her.

"How come I'm panting so hard and you're hardly panting? I am sweating profusely and you got a cute little perspiration line. Like the ones they have in the exercise videos. You look like you just walked off the dance floor instead of an exercise floor."

"Ha, ha, ha, I was just like you when I first started exercising. You'll get used to it in no time." Colleen is watching the instructor dab at the beads of perspiration on her forehead.

"What are you talking about? I didn't just start exercising *Honey.* I'm sure this body doesn't look like I just started," Colleen says with her hands on her hips.

"Well, you aren't diligent with your exercise plan. You probably do more toning and strengthening when you should do more cardio. I teach this class Mondays and Wednesdays too. I only see you on Fridays. You can't squeeze in a Monday or a Wednesday? How about both? My Monday classes are ending soon. Well, actually, the class will still be held but I won't be the instructor. The routine will be totally different too."

"More cardio? What are you implying? Girl, please. This is tiresome as it is. Don't you instruct something else," Colleen asks while taking a swallow of her water.

The instructor smiles, knowing she has hit a nerve. "Actually, I do but it's not Cardio. I will be teaching a Sexercise class in a few weeks."

That caught Colleen's attention. *Could she be talking about the same class me and the girls are scheduled to take in a few weeks?*

"Sexercise? You're teaching a sexercise class?" The instructor moves her head in fast up and down 'yes' motions. "Where? Not across the street, right." Colleen is looking at the instructor closely now, trying to feel her out.

"Yes, that is the one. Oh, so you already know about the class, huh? Are you registered?"

"Oh, my goodness!! Yes, I am registered for the class. My crew and I have been taking the classes over there for the past three months. How did you get into teaching?"

"My mother is a gynecologist and she has taught her daughters very well about their bodies and sexuality. The two instructors that you have had so far are my sisters."

Colleen is shocked. "Ain't this a bitch? Your sisters? You look nothing alike, not that you have to, but this surely is a small world. And y'all made a group decision to go into the world of sex enhancement for women, huh?"

"Yes, they are my sisters and we hear all the time we don't look alike. I look like our mother. Tina looks like our father and Kelly looks like our grandmother, our father's mother. Yeah, this is a small world. Well, again, our mother is a gynecologist. We weren't sure this business was going to be successful but we love what we do. Sooo, I'll see you in three classes then."

"Three? Hell naw, just two classes. I can't add another Cardio. Sorry. Maybe when the third session starts."

"No, it's three. Here on Fridays for Cardio and across the street on Mondays for Sexercise and Pole Dancing."

Colleen looks at her as if she has lost her mind. These are their private classes. Now, she is having a conversation about them with someone other than her crew. Colleen looks the instructor up and down saying to herself *I don't even know this bitch from anywhere but here.*

"Are you telling me you instruct the Pole Dancing class too? Damn girl, you have talent. Now, how did you get into that?"

"Well, I used to dance ... professionally and as a stripper."

Colleen's mouth is hanging open. Somebody needs to help her close it. She starts laughing and leaning over with her leg in the air. She has to take another look at this chick. As frail as she is Colleen wonders what kind of money did she used to make taking her clothes off. Maybe that's why she's teaching.

"Oh wow. My, my, my. I've surely been on a roll lately learning something new every day about the people I interact with. Please continue. I'm all ears."

"You see Sexercise and Pole Dancing are sort of a joint class. They are back-to-back, as you know. I mean you can't just jump on the pole without proper strengthening in certain areas. Pole dancing is an art and if you want to entice your man or men ... or woman, you surely don't want to embarrass yourself. You'd be surprised how many strippers have sprang or broken something, or threw their backs out."

Colleen bursts out laughing. She remembers the remarks she made towards BeLynda yesterday at the Spa.

"Woo, chiile. I know that's right. But I really didn't look at it that way. That surely is not a time to be embarrassed."

"Yeah so, anyway, think about adding another Cardio class to your week. That helps in many areas. You can drop the second Cardio class when the classes across the street starts. Besides, I am going to work you in those Monday classes until you're going to need the three day break."

"Whatever Cardio instructor. I won't do anymore than I want to. Everybody that knows will agree." *Is this broad getting cocky? She doesn't really want to meet the real Colleen Jeffries does she?*

Let's see, do we have everything we're gonna need this weekend? Hell, I guess I should be asking if I have everything I'm gonna need for this weekend. I know Stan is gonna look at me like I'm crazy with all these bags. Hell, men feel as long as they have clean underwear and their dick work, they have packed all that they need. But they should know by now how it is when a woman is going out of town. Can't ever have too much stuff. Let me go check to see if Maria saw my list of things I need her to round up for me.

Regina walks down the hall to the other end of the house to the Maid Quarters to see if she would find Maria there. Knocking on the door and peeping her head inside she calls out, "Maria, are you in here?" There is no answer. She calls out again, "Maria, its Regina … are you busy? Are you in here?"

Regina decides to walk into the room. She hasn't been in this area or room of the house in a very long time. She likes to make Maria feel welcome and give her privacy. *Hmmm, she keeps it quite neat and clean in here. Thank goodness. Where did she get this comforter from? I don't recall this being the one I purchased for this room. Hmmp, maybe she brought this with her to give the place her own feel*, she says to herself.

As Regina was about to turn around and walk out the room to look for Maria in another part of the house, she notices the top drawer of one of the nightstands is slightly opened with an 8.5 x 11 envelope visible. Stepping back to take a closer look at the envelope, she looks around to see if she is really alone. *I know damn well, I shouldn't be snooping.* Picking up the envelope, she sees it is sealed. *Damn!!* Turning the envelope over, there is a label on the front with the words *"For Your Eyes Only"* typed in Calibri 24 font. *Hmmm, whose eyes? What's in this envelope? It's probably nothing I care to know about. Let me put her shit back before she catches me and decides to quit from me snooping.* Regina puts the envelope back the way she found it and heads towards the door to continue looking for Maria.

On the way out of the room, she bumps right into Maria almost knocking her down. They both are startled. Maria is shocked to see Regina coming out of the Maid Quarters. Regina almost jumps out of her skin, looking guilty.

"Senora Wooten? What you doing down this way?"

"Oh Maria!! You scared the shit out of me!! Where did you come from," says Regina holding her chest trying to calm down her heartbeat and looking around to see which direction had Maria actually come from.

"I'm so sorry. I didn't mean to scare you. I have never seen you over here. Is there something wrong? Are you all right," Maria asks while leaning her head into the Maid Quarters to look around. She notices the nightstand drawer is open. *Did I leave that open like that*, she asks herself. She pulls her head out of the room and looks back at Regina, wondering if she had seen the envelope.

"Oh, no Maria, everything is okay. I was in my room making sure I had everything set for this weekend. Then I decided to come see you about the list I left for you. I wanted to make sure you saw it and that everything is just right. Did you get it?" Regina nervously rubbing her hand across her hair, moving her hair to hang behind her right ear.

"Yes, yes, the list! Si Senora!! I got things from store. I will fix and place in frig by Sauna Room so Senor Wooten won't see, okay? Everything will be all ready for you trip." Maria notices that Regina is acting a little uncomfortable. *Were you really looking for me or were you snooping in my things? What did you see? What do you know?* Maria looks at Regina wondering.

Regina notices Maria's stares and decides to end their strange meeting working very hard to not appear guilty of anything. "Okay, great!! I knew you would have it all together for me. I was just checking. I know this is not a store day for you. Thanks Maria." Before Maria can respond, Regina walks down the stairs to the movie room instead of turning around to walk back down the hall towards the Master Suite. This way, she would avoid feeling Maria's eyes burning a hole in her back from staring so hard.

Why am I feeling so guilty? All I did was knock, call out to her, look around her space, and pick up that curious envelope. Right? Nothing wrong with that, right? But what the hell is in that envelope? I've only seen shit like that in the movies. Maria you better not be into no bullshit while you spend most of your time up in my fucking house. I better be over exaggerating Maria.

Regina walks over to the bar in the movie room. Opening up the refrigerator, she pulls out the sugar-free Triple Sec, lime juice, and Patron to make a Low- Carb Margarita. Her hand is shaking so she sits the drink down on the bar. Walking over to the window, Regina looks out and notices a Black Charger with black tinted windows sitting across the street. The window is slightly down and she sees flashes going off.

Is someone taking pictures of my shit?! What the fuck is going on?! Is there going to be a full moon tonight or something? All this weird ass shit going on today!! And I am always by myself when it happens!!

Chapter Eight

8

"Ooo-wee. Look at you Ms. Giles. Let me step in and get a better look at you." Colleen sashays into BeLynda's house. She dramatically turns around so BeLynda can get a good look at her as well. BeLynda rolls her eyes at her. She isn't too happy with Colleen right now. Colleen is walking around her carefully looking her up and down at the entire ensemble making sure not to miss any details.

"You're thirty-five minutes late. Why can't you ever be on time? I know you didn't have any clients this late and it is Saturday. You work on the weekends too?"

"Mmm-mmm, knee-high stretch suede square-toe boots with a funky four inch heel. I like those, Bee. If we weren't friends, I would've gone to the store and got me a pair too. But you know, we can't meet up with the same shit on, walking around looking like bopsie twins. I have to keep my individuality."

"You know I don't like sitting here dressed and waiting either. *You* asked *me* to go out with *you*. The least you can do is be on time to pick me up when you're the one inviting. I bet you Sandy is already there wondering where we are."

Colleen pretends to not hear BeLynda and continues to check out her appearance. "Cashmere sweater ... beautiful. You chose the perfect color. It complements your complexion. *Suede* mini? Oh, I see you Bee. Designer pantyhose? And your jewelry is sparkling too. Oh you went all out for tonight Girl! My Girl was really listening to me when I was talking the other day. I'm proud."

"Don't ignore me, dammit! You heard what I said. You're late and I don't appreciate sitting here dressed waiting on you. I had to walk around to make sure the back of my blouse didn't get wrinkled. That ain't right. Fashionably late isn't for all settings, especially the club!!"

"When did you go shopping for all of this? I know you didn't have this already hanging up in your closet. I'm sure I would have seen it before. Then again, it has been a minute since we dressed up and hung out. Who went with you because you surely didn't ask me to go with you?"

"Colleen!! Stop it!! I'm serious!! Stop acting as if I'm not talking to you!! I'm not tryin' to be irritated before we go out. You need to hear because I don't want a repeat of this!!"

"Okay, okay already. Damn!! I heard you. I know I am late. That didn't have to be pointed out to me. I can't turn back the clock, shit. I was dealing with a few issues. Give me a break with the yelling. Looking at you is lifting my spirits but your mouth is killing me."

"A few issues? About what? What's going on?" BeLynda's emotions have now switch to being concerned. She gets her purse from off the couch preparing to leave.

"Well, first, my hair wasn't acting right. Then the pants I wanted to wear weren't looking right on my bloated stomach. I guess my cycle is getting ready to start. Thirdly, I lost one of my clients today. Well, I had a feeling our contract was going to be cancelled anyway."

"Aw, Colleen, I'm sorry about that. What happened? Which client is this? You were actually working today?"

"No, I didn't work today. She called me. This is the chick that wanted chicken to be served five different muthafuckin' ways at her Grandfather's ninetieth surprise birthday party. She said she found a cheaper coordinator. I'm trying to figure out how this other coordinator is going to be cheaper with all that she wanted? But I'm not gonna worry about it. At least I won't be worrying about it tonight. I will deal with that Monday when I'm going over my books."

"Are you sure that's all? Well, I know your cycle is getting ready to start so you're trying not to be emotional. But, I know how you get. So don't be going off for no reason tonight."

"Yeah, that's all. At least that's all she said. And I'm cool. I took some Midol before I got dressed. So it should've kicked in already. No emotional dealings tonight."

"Girl please, yea you will be fine. I wouldn't even worry about it. Once she starts asking for what you were giving, they'll pretend to be able to do what she wants for her price. Once she sees that hidden cost, she might be calling you back. Ump, she found a cheaper coordinator all right ... I bet you it's her Mama 'n nem." BeLynda made Colleen laugh and she is feeling a lot better than she was a few hours ago but she is still slightly annoyed. She don't need clients like that messing up her reputation.

"Girl, you can be crazy when you want to be." Colleen walks over to the powder room to look at herself in the mirror.

Ring! Ring!

"Hello." BeLynda is still laughing.

"Hey girl. What's so funny? I see you're at home and Colleen still hasn't picked you up yet. Have you heard from her?"

"Yeah, I've heard from her. She's here now and we're about to leave. I can hear you're already there." BeLynda can hear the loud music in the background. Plus Sandy is talking extremely loud.

"Girl, yes I am. I have a table for us too. Y'all better hurry up. The fellas are looking mighty scrumptious tonight. Tell Colleen she needs to work on her punctuality."

BeLynda laughs at Sandy, saying "We're on our way. See you in about twenty-five minutes."

"Aiight." *click*

"C'mon girl. Sandy is already there and has a table for us. You know how hard it is to try and hold a table for your friends. If we are any later, the only chair left at the table might just be the one she's sitting in."

Colleen takes one last look at herself in the mirror and walks out the door, not saying another word. BeLynda looks at herself in the mirror too and smiles. She knows Colleen isn't like the competition. *Yea, I'm serving them tonight. She did all that and never actually gave me a damn complement.*

By the time BeLynda and Colleen arrive at the Zanzibar, they smell like they have already been there. In twenty minutes, Colleen had smoked three cigarettes while drinking something out of her flask. It probably was Tito Vodka because she is a white liquor drinker. BeLynda only had one cigarette. Thank goodness BeLynda's new boots aren't hurting her feet. They had to walk two blocks from the car to the club.

"Good evening Ladies." A gentleman opens the door for them as they are approaching the entrance. They are so pumped up ready to have fun neither of them spoke to the man at the door. They start to look for Sandy on the first level but quickly change their minds to go upstairs and look there first.

Walking up the winding staircase, there are men going down, coming up, and just standing to the side on the stairs checking out all of the females that pass them. BeLynda is enjoying herself already. Maybe it has been a minute since she has been out. The sites are quite lovely to her. The men are handsome, dressed nice and smelling good. However, once they walk upstairs to the bar and table area, the scene and smells change. The men were all sweaty, and the air is very musty. *They dancing hard up here with all this funk floating around*, says BeLynda to herself.

"C'mon, let's go get a drink. The bar doesn't look that crowded. I'll order while you look for Sandy."

"Okay," BeLynda responds.

Walking over to the bar, several men make eye contact, speak to, or touch BeLynda on the arm. She is riding high and loving the attention but they are too damn drunk and funky for her to take any of them seriously. Colleen pretends she doesn't notice the men checking out BeLynda. She keeps walking until she finds a spot at the bar.

"Hello ladies. You're looking lovely. What may I get you both," asks the bartender, trying to show off a sexy smile.

"Hi. I'll have a cranberry and vodka, please. What are you going to get Bee?"

BeLynda is still looking around for Sandy and checking out the sights. Sandy used the right adjective to describe the men because they are making her hungry. At least the ones that haven't sweated up their shirts.

"Oh, um, give me a Singapore Sling, please."

"A Singapore Sling? Girl, get current with everything. How are you going to be dressed like that having a drink that old? Sir, make her a Blue Martini, please."

The bartender smiles at Colleen and BeLynda saying, "You got it. I'll make it real nice for her."

"Oh, well make sure you make mine real nice too," Colleen jealously responds. The bartender gives her a respectful head nod as if to say "I got you."

The club is jumping. People are talking, laughing and mingling. The dance floor is packed and people are dancing in the table area as well. Colleen lights a cigarette. She is bopping her head and looking around to see who she can see. Even though she asked BeLynda to look out for Sandy, she forgets all about looking for her when Frankie Beverly and Maze comes on. She is looking around the crowd roar when the tune started up. Those first few beats before Frankie's voice comes in always get people up out of their seats and bombard the dance floor.

♪Before I let go.

Before I let go.

Whoa whoooooooa!

You make me happy

This you can tell

You stood right beside me♪

The club is filled with screams. The floor slightly empties because this is a slower tune than what the DJ was playing at first. However, it quickly fills up with Frankie Beverly fans and everybody are still grooving to the music.

"Oooh, that's my song." BeLynda is dancing to the music. "Frankie can always get me up out of my seat."

"That will be nine dollars total ladies." The bartender hands them their drinks. Colleen pays for the first round. She takes a sip of her drink and smiles. It is made perfect with the right amount of juice and vodka. Colleen is watching BeLynda dance and shakes her head. Taking a drag of her cigarette, she says to BeLynda, "This is your song? Then why are you doing the two-step? How do you dance if it is *not* your song?"

"What's wrong with my dancing? How am I supposed to dance? This is not a butt rollin' put your booty on the floor type of song. Let me see what your hot ass does when you are dancing off of *your* song."

"Oh don't worry, you will see. Just not right now. This is *your* song, not mine."

At that point, Colleen spots Sandy. "There's Sandy over there. C'mon let's go get our seats so we can put these drinks down. I'd hate for some of these wild heifers in here to spill my four – fifty drink."

Sandy is sitting at the table guarding it with her life. She has her drink sitting in front of one chair and her clutch sitting in front of the other. She sees Colleen and BeLynda walking towards her. She stands to greet them. She is very surprised at BeLynda's ensemble. She gives both of them a hug and kiss on both cheeks, still checking out BeLynda.

"Hey. Y'all finally made it. What happened? You couldn't find a parking space?"

"We found one, just not right out front. We've been here long enough to get a drink, check out the sights, and look around for you."

Colleen is checking out Sandy's outfit. Sandy is wearing wool cuffed quarter-length pants, a cotton-stretch blouse with French cuffs, winter white boots, and a beautiful choker. She and Sandy are almost dressed alike except for Colleen's pants are floor length and her blouse is a wrap yet it has French cuffs too. Colleen likes wrap blouses. With the right bra, the blouse makes her breast look bigger and stomach appear flatter.

"Look at you!! Don't you look nice? Not that you don't any other time. This is just a switch for you but a good switch Bee. Oh hold up ... are those boots by Stuart Weitzman?!" Sandy asks looking down at her feet really shocked.

"Yes, they are. You sure do know your designers don't you? I'm impressed," BeLynda laughs. She is really surprised. She didn't realize how much time Sandy spent in the expensive shoes section of the stores. Even though she is always dressed expensive.

Colleen is puffing on her cigarette and sipping her drink as if she isn't listening. She is listening but with an attitude. No one has said anything about her mink purse or brand new diamond necklace yet. Maybe they didn't notice. So she places the purse on the table and opens her collar a little more just in case it is covering the necklace.

"Hey, Colleen, you look nice. Why are you so quiet? What's wrong," Sandy asks.

"Thank you Lady. Oh, I'm all right. Got some bloating issues going on. I'm just listening to the music and enjoying my drink. What have you been sipping on? I see one glass is already empty."

"I'm drinking Syrah. The other glass was already here. So I used it as a cover for the chairs. You know people always want to take chairs so they can sit ten deep at a table for four. I like those pants. I see we're almost dressed alike."

"Thanks Lady, do you too. Yea, we are almost dressed alike. Great minds think a lot, right," Colleen responds.

"Syrah? What is that, a wine? What happen to your Merlot?" BeLynda knows she been out of the "going out and drinking" scenes but this is new. Sandy isn't one to do much changing.

"Yes, Syrah is a wine. I wanted to try something new. Larry drinks this. It isn't too bad."

Did BeLynda and Colleen hear her right? She didn't just say Larry and a new drink all in the same response did she?

"Sooo, let's get this straight. You are trying a new wine because Larry, Mr. Softy drinks this? Where is this coming from?"

Colleen wants to know. Sandy has some juice and is being stingy with the details.

The DJ is now playing Beyoncé *"Baby Boi"*

♪ Certified quality
A dat da girl dem need

and dem not stop cry without apology
Buck dem da right way – dat my policy
Sean Paul alongside – now hear what da man say – Beyoncé
Dutty ya, dutty ya, dutty ya
Beyoncé sing it now ya

Baby boy you stay on my mind
Fulfill my fantasies
I think about you all the time
I see you in my dreams

Baby boy not a day goes by
Without my fantasies
I think about you all the time
I see you in my dreams ♪

Sandy has her eyes closed and moving her head and neck to the music. She is into it. It might be Beyoncé but with Sean Paul in it, makes it reggae and Sandy loves reggae music.

"Don't ignore me winch. You're awfully giddy tonight. You got something to tell us?"

"Yeah, what's up? Inquiring minds want to know," BeLynda takes sides with Colleen.

"Well ..." Sandy is interrupted by a deep voice.

"Excuse me, would you like to dance?" A tall handsome brother asks Sandy while tapping her on the shoulder. He has his hand out waiting for her to accept by taking his hand. Colleen is so engrossed in what Sandy is about to say, she doesn't even notice the man when he walks up. BeLynda notices him and is ready to say, "I do," if Sandy doesn't accept.

Sandy looks up at him as if he is a movie star. She puts her hand in his and replies, "I most certainly would." She looks at her girls, gives them a wink and rushes off to the dance floor.

"Oh, we'll be sitting right here when you get back. You won't get off not telling us how hard or soft Larry was whenever you saw him," Colleen yells after her.

"Colleen, give me a cigarette, please. This martini is kind of strong. I'm glad I had something to snack on before I left. On an empty stomach, I'd be underneath the table with this thing."

"Oh Chile, toughen up. It can't be that bad. You're a woman now, stop drinking like a girl. College is over."

"I need to record you sometimes." BeLynda is laughing so hard at Colleen.

"Record me for what?" Colleen starts laughing too not really understanding why BeLynda said what she said.

"So you can actually hear some of the shit you say out of your mouth. Even you probably won't believe you say half the things you say. I can't even get mad though. 'Drinking like a girl'? I'm all right with that because if that's the case, then your ass drinks like a damn nigga."

Colleen looks at BeLynda surprised at her response and laughs. "That's okay though. As long as I don't look and act like one, I'm aight with that." Colleen turns her head in the direction of Sandy on the dance floor and puffs her cigarette. "Look at Sandy. Now you see ... *that's* dancing. I don't know if that is her favorite song or not, but girlfriend is into Beyoncé right now."

"Yeah, like she's into that man. Larry must've done something different this time. Then again, that is a reggae song and you know she loves that kind of music."

"You think? She is gyrating that ass all over the place. You know Sandy dances real provocative anyway. Throw some reggae into the mix and we might not see her for the rest of the night. I love to see her get in her mood. And look at him. The damn man doesn't know what to do with her. His mouth is hanging open with his tongue damn near on the floor." They laugh.

"He isn't the only one with his tongue hanging out. Take a look at the scene. Look at the brothers standing on the sideline watching. They are probably hoping that he gets off the floor before she does so they can be next to dance with her. Look at the women." Both Colleen and BeLynda sit back and enjoy the show watching everyone watch Sandy.

"That's right Ladies. Make sure y'all take notes. I know my girl is giving every last one of you a dance lesson. Work it Sandy," Colleen yells towards the dance floor as if anyone could really hear her over the thumping beat of the music.

BeLynda and Colleen are cracking up at Sandy's audience. The men are loving what they see and the women are wanting her to leave the dance floor. All the while, Sandy is in her own little world with her eyes closed at times oblivious to what is going on. Other times, she is toying and teasing her dance partner admiring how fine he is.

"If she combines those dance moves with what she learned in the classes, she will probably have a man whimpering in bed."

Colleen laughs. "Ah, hello. Have you been listening to anything tonight? Apparently she did that already and that's why Larry is Mr. Softy."

Sandy is mechanically swaying her hips. When she makes her dips, she is making slow circular motions almost like working a hula-hoop. She makes half turns where her back is to her partner and makes perfect square and figure eight movements with her behind as if she is originally from the Caribbean instead of Washington, DC. Sandy incorporates the hip and bellying rolling in her dancing. Her risqué moves have her partner slightly hard. She smiles and continues. She is feeling good about herself and the effect she always has on a man whenever she dances.

The DJ is deep into reggae now. Sandy is lost in it music. She has been on the floor for about three songs now. Some of the ladies look like they are picking up dance moves. Her partner is behind her and has his hands by her hips but not touching her. He is beginning to sweat gyrating along with her enjoying her ass rubbing against his slight erection and vice verse. He is watching her ass while imagining it without the pants she has on. Sandy is hot. She wants him to be someone she knows. Taking a stranger home or going over a stranger's house has always been a no-no for the Girls. The rule has always been that they leave with whom they came with … no exceptions.

That thought messed up her moment. She is instantly turned off and comes back to her senses. She knows she won't be taking this fine man home welcoming him into her humble abode. Sandy turns around, bashfully smiles at the man and says, "Thank you so much for this wonderful dance. I am about to go back to my table.

My girlfriends might want to dance and I am hogging up the floor time."

As they walk off the floor, a few people start clapping as if they enjoyed the performance. Sandy walks back to the table to sit down not paying attention to the applause. She isn't aware her dance partner is following her back to the table. BeLynda and Colleen are all smiles watching their girl as his sexiness follows her.

"Damn girl. Were you trying to make him have an orgasm on the fuckin' floor? Once you started moving that ass in his face, his pants puffed out like a balloon." Colleen smiles at Sandy, leans back in her chair, crosses her legs, and lights another cigarette.

"I'm serious. You worked that poor man some kind of terrible. Had him all confused as to what he should do next. He was chasing his own ass after a while trying not to touch yours. And you let all of the other men down by walking off the floor the same time he did," BeLynda says while laughing. "But, look, he even followed you back to the table."

BeLynda is motioning with her head and eyes for Sandy to turn around. Sandy turns to see the gentleman making his way over to the table. As he approaches the table, he helps himself to the extra chair sitting down. Sandy is blushing and he is making her feel wanted. BeLynda decides to stand up to go get another drink. Colleen sits there looking at the man whispering in Sandy's ear. Sandy is blushing and responding giving him a conversation. *I wonder what he is saying to her. Hell, I want to hear too. This is a table for three, not a table for two. Don't make it a private conversation. Did Sandy forget her damn manners? A guy just doesn't come to the table without being introduced. Then his rude ass is whispering in her ear as if no one else is sitting here.*

Colleen clears her throat to get their attention and takes a sip of her drink. The gentleman and Sandy both pause to look at her. However, Colleen gives her that look Sandy knows all too well.

Chapter Nine

9

Regina and Stan pull up to the front of Caesar's Poconos' Paradise Stream. It is a pretty fall evening. The sun is starting to go down. The leaves are changing and some have fallen to the ground. There are plenty of couples here. Some are smiling and friendly speaking while holding hands. Others are caught up in the moment of just being with each other hugging and giving light pecks on the lips. Some of the women smile at Regina as they pass by, looking so in love. As she smiles back at the ladies Regina hugs Stan around the waist and smiles up at Stan. He hugs her around her shoulders, looking down at her, placing a soft peck on her forehead. She closes her eyes when receiving his warm lips.

Regina is taking in all of the different scenes before her. There are hearts everywhere, areas for putt-putt, horseshoe, archery, tennis courts, and paddle boating. There are so many things to do here and Regina can't wait to try some of them. She is excited and glad to be here with her husband. She joins the crowd by holding her man's hand as they enter the Check-In area on the ground level of the building.

"Good evening. Welcome to Paradise Stream. It is such a lovely day, isn't it? How may I assist you today?"

"Good evening," Regina and Stan respond in unison. Stan clears his throat and speaks up. "We're Mr. and Mrs. Wooten. We have reservations for this weekend."

"Okay, let's see. Is your last name spelled W-o-o-t-o-n?"

"No, it is -e-n."

"Okay. Let me check for you." The receptionist types into the computer their last name. "Ah, there you are. Mr. Stan Wooten, arriving on Friday, November twenty-first and checking out Sunday November twenty-third. You have reserved the Champagne Tower by Cleopatra. *Nice*, very nice. I see you have paid in full. That's great. Makes my job that much easier. Your room is ready for you and here are your keys," the receptionist says as she hands Stan their keys.

"During your stay, you belong to the Key Around Club. With the Key Around Club, you get to visit the other Caesars Poconos Resorts and participate in all of their activities too. The other Resorts are Pocono Palace, Cove Haven, and Brookdale. Brookdale is family oriented if you have children and want to bring them at a later date. They will have fun there. If you want to visit the other resorts, we have shuttles leaving here throughout the day. Here is a map to show you where everything is." Regina takes the map.

"This calendar and schedule tells you what is going on this weekend just in case you want to participate in any of the activities. There is a shuttle schedule in there too. It also tells you the times of meals. Or you can request room service and eat-in. If you want to see any of the other rooms, there are tours certain times of the day. Just look at your schedule. If you need anything don't hesitate to ask. Enjoy your stay here at Paradise Stream."

Regina just stands there looking at the receptionist's mouth while she hands Regina the calendar and schedule. She has a glued on smile and moves her head as if she is a robot. Regina wonders if the lady breathed any during the speech. It definitely was rehearsed. After they were given directions, they leave out to get back in their car heading to their room.

As they pull up to their room, Regina is so excited. While Stan gets the bags out of the truck, Regina runs to the door. She tries unsuccessfully three times to open the door before she notices she needs to turn the key card around. Inserting the key card correctly, the green light comes on and Regina opens the door to walk inside. She gasps, placing her left hand over her chest, smiling.

It is beautiful! The room has an Egyptian theme and is on four levels. The Champagne Glass bathtub is for two and is huge. It is the focal point of the room. The base of it is on the first floor and it extends up to the top floor of the room. She's trying to figure out how she gets in it.

Going down four steps, she sees the heart shaped pool. Regina can't swim but she can think of other ways to utilize it. No need to pay for the room and not experience all of it. The third floor only has wooden walls with a matching door. She knows this is the dry sauna and massage area. She just got her hair done so the dry sauna is out until her hair gets messed up. She opens the door to look around. It is big enough for only two people to be nice and cozy.

The last and upper level is the bedroom. It is painted midnight blue and there are stars on the ceiling. The bed is a king-size round bed. It is perfect for Regina but she isn't sure about Stan since he is tall and likes a high bed. She is not too crazy about the print on the comforter either but who needs that anyway? She already knows it's going to be too hot for that.

Turning around to look at the rest of the room, she notices the bathroom and then she sees how to get in the Champagne tub. *Ah, that is cute. Just step in it like a regular tub.*

Running back downstairs, she yells, "Hurry up, Stan! Come see the room. It is sooo nice. It looks just like the brochure! You gotta see it!!"

"I'm coming baby. After I gather *all* these damn bags you brought just for two nights. How many times you plan on changing? We're only here for a weekend."

Regina reaches the door and looks outside to answer him. Just as she thought. It isn't the bags holding him up. Stan is wiping down his wheels and twenty-two inch rims. He drives through a little water and the rims as well as the wheels have to be wiped off. She can't be mad because he treats her the same way. She gets wet and he has to wipe her dry ... with his tongue.

Shaking her head, Regina smiles and says, "I should have known what was actually taking you so long. You haven't even taken out one bag. You're gonna wipe the rubber off of those tires."

"C'mon now. You know the truck can't be clean and shiny then when someone looks down at the wheels, they look a mess."

Regina walks out the room to the truck, deciding to help with the bags. Especially the ones she needs first. She has an idea to implement while he is outside. While getting the bags, she asks, "How many wheels you have left to do?"

"I just got started. I still have the other three. It won't take me long. I promise. Just a quick wipe down is all they need. And I will be right in to check out our room. Give me a kiss." Regina turns to Stan and leans up to offer her lips.

Regina smiles and says to herself, *Good*, but replies, "Okay Wooten. I'll be in here waiting."

Back inside the room, she opens the bag with the food in it. She came prepared. Taking the tray out of the bag, she sits it on the coffee table. Next, Regina takes out the sandwich bags full of strawberries, grapes, apple slices, cheese cubes, and French bread. Regina nicely arranges the fruit in triangular shapes on the platter. After getting the bag of romaine lettuce and the plastic bowl out of the bag, she places the bowl in the center of the tray and fills it with the slices of the French bread. The romaine lettuce is used to divide the fruits and cheese on the platter. Now the tray looks like Maria has fixed it.

There! Very nice. Thank goodness Maria cleaned and packaged everything for me yesterday. Now, all I have to do is take out the goblets, wine, candles, and CDs. But, I think I can actually put the bread back. We won't eat that right now. I need my stomach to stay flat and those bad carbs will have me bloated." Regina opens the chilled bottle of Kendall Jackson Chardonnay, pours two glasses of it, and sits them on the coffee table by the platter.

After setting up the platter and drinks, Regina goes in the other bag to get the strawberry scented candles, matches, and CDs. The good thing about the room is with the curtains closed and the door shut, it is pitch black. That makes it perfect for candle lighting.

Regina places candles all over the room and stairs, mainly emphasizing the bedroom area. Peeking out the window, she sees Stan is just starting on the third wheel.

Now, it's time for the outfit of the hour. Regina knows she has to make it up to Stan since he was sleep when she got in from the Spa last night. She didn't bother to wake him. Plus, she knew he was tired and was just talking trash anyway.

The outfit chosen is a Victoria's Secret pink jacquard and lace corset set. It has underwire cups and she makes sure her breasts are pushed up as far as they can be pushed without feeling like she is about to lose consciousness. It has a lace-up back closure. When she tried it on at the store, Sandy helped her make sure the back closure was perfect so she wouldn't have to mess around with it right before she puts it on. Regina bought this set thinking it would be teasing fun for Stan. At first, she starts to not put on the matching thong but changes her mind. She wants him to see the entire outfit. Then Regina puts on her pastel pink open toe four inch heel mules. They match the set perfectly and show off her freshly cotton candy polished toes. To finish off the ensemble, she sprays on her favorite perfume ... *Pink* by Victoria's Secret.

Going through the CDs, she chooses Wil Downing and puts it in the CD player. She starts off with *A Million Ways to Treat a Woman*. There, she is done with food, decorating, and dressing.

While waiting for Stan to come in, she starts thinking about class. Regina goes into a deep breathing session to slow down her excited heartbeat. She follows with hip and belly rolling, ending with deep breathing again. She doesn't know if it is all in her mind or if it actually works. However, she is really getting aroused and quite moist. This is exciting to her. She starts doing more deep breathing. There have been times when Regina thought she was ready but too dry for Stan to enter her. That didn't feel too good especially when he wanted to just ram it in hard. So they would have to work him in, inch at a time until he was completely inside of her. This evening, he will almost fall inside her as moist as she is.

Ten minutes later, Regina is really ready. The candles are lit, wine is poured, and she is fully relaxed and moist. The door knob starts to turn. She gets off the couch, starts the CD over, and greets him at the door with a strawberry and a glass of wine.

"'Bout time you finished. I thought I was going to have to start without you." Regina seductively walks away from Stan backwards to catch his expression.

"Mmm, what's all this," Stan asks while taking the entire strawberry in his mouth and accepting the glass of wine. He surveys the room noticing the candles, the platter, wine, music, and Regina's outfit. "Damn baby, don't you look gorgeous." Stan steps completely into the room and closes the door while leaning his head to the side checking out what his wife has on. Particularly lingering longer on the breasts and butt parts of her outfit.

Regina walks across the room showing off the entire outfit. She has a very sexy walk and it gets sexier the higher the heel is. A lot of women have envied her walk. Men think it is seductive and probably have fantasies about Regina and what her walk represents or might lead to. It is almost as if she is walking in slow motion, taking her time with every step, making sure the steps are perfect to connect at the right moment with every sway of her hips. Her firm ass rises and falls like the wax in a lava lamp.

Stan is licking his lips. He is looking at her breast all pushed up in the bra of the corset. Her lean neck line that runs into her sexy shoulders. Her firm toned arms leading to her adorable hands. Her petite waist that enhances the nicely curved hips and thighs, supporting her round ass. Stan is sipping his wine while observing all of his gorgeous erotic wife. The heels are turning him on too.

Mmmp, my baby got on some "Fuck Me" pumps, he says to himself. He is taking two big gulps of the wine now, sits the glass down, and goes upstairs to the bathroom to wash his hands. He is ready for some action.

Coming back downstairs, he leans against one of the columns and just observes his wife more. He is honored and grateful for having a wife that isn't just sexy. Regina also dresses sexy and is very much into sex. There is nothing bashful about his wife when it comes to sex and he loves it. He hears other men at work complaining about their wives and fantasizing about other women. Stan doesn't have that problem. He doesn't get involved in those conversations because for one, he is the boss. For two, that would only create the opening of the wrong doors into his marriage. However, he has noticed something different about Regina sexually lately. He isn't complaining because the change is definitely a good thing. He just can't figure out what it is.

Wil Downing is still playing in the background. Regina has it programmed for repeat. Regina goes into a slow dance. It is very sensual and Stan is loving the gyrating of her hips. She is playing with every part of her body in a very tantalizing manner. She starts with her lips, using her finger then tongue to suggestively outline them. Her smiles at him are provocative. Stan walks over to the tray to pour more wine, grabs a few grapes going back over to where he was standing to enjoy the show.

Closing her eyes, Regina has one hand in the air, the other is outlining her breasts, then the nipples, and starts squeezing them simultaneously. With the candle lighting, it gives her body extra radiance in the right areas. Regina slowly moves her hands down to her stomach, wraps her arms around her waist and starts her belly dancing mixing in her hip rolling. Stan has no idea she is actually incorporating class moves into her performance. Her hands land at her thong rubbing on her hairy yet trimmed mound.

Regina further torments Stan by turning her back to him, bending over so he can see her pussy from another angle while she is rubbing on it through the thong. Stan has had enough of the standing so he sits on one of the steps which give him another viewpoint of what is before him. Regina walks over to him and steps up on the stairs where her pussy is above him and squats so it is level with Stan's face. She grabs Stan's head and rubs his face all in her stuff. He grabs her ass and she teasingly snatches away.

Stepping down the stairs backwards, she turns around, and backs up to Stan. He unties her corset. Regina turns to Stan again still hip and belly rolling, secretly getting her pelvis ready. Teasingly bending over to touch her feet, her breasts pop out in unison. Massaging them, she puts them in Stan's face. He's licking them while she is outlining his dick with her pointer finger. He is about to burst through his pants. Regina bends down and mischievously nibbles at his manhood through his pants. Stan leans back, closes his eyes and says, "Aww baby. Take it out. Let me feel your lips on it." Regina gives Stan a wet "I-want-you-to-fuck-me-real-good" kiss, and takes him by the hand to begin walking upstairs.

As Stan stands up, he starts loosening his belt to take his pants off. Regina turns around smiling, removes his hands, puts one of his fingers in her mouth, and starts opening his belt. She is teasing him the entire time in between sucking and licking his finger. Open the belt … massage his dick. Unbutton the pants … massage his dick some more. Unzip his pants … squeeze it a little. Pull his pants down … brush it against her chin. Pull his boxers down … teasingly lick the head. Stan releases his finger from Regina's mouth to take off his shoes to help his pants and boxers come completely off.

Regina is sitting on the steps with dick in her face. Every time it sways her way, she licks the head of it. Stan is hissing and sighing about to fall off the steps. She catches him by the butt cheeks and swallows him entirely. She takes it strong and is deep throating him. Stan is going crazy. Regina has never taken him completely in her mouth before. Her tongue is playing with the underside of the head, making circles and squares and flattening against his dick, then jumping like a fish. Stan is looking down at Regina go to work. Her jaw muscles are contracting in a delicious rhythm, her head is moving back and forth, around and around, her mouth is hot and wet. He is looking at his wife in amazement. Regina is giving it all she has. Men like standing for dominancy but this evening, right now ... Regina is in complete control. Stan is ready to give her whatever her heart desires.

In precisely three minutes, Stan is growling and hollering while Regina is swallowing all of his hot thick cum. Stan is weak but feeling good and shocked all at the same time. Orally, it usually takes Regina ten minutes to even make him feel like he is about to cum. Regina has reduced the time by seven minutes. She didn't even gag and swallowed without a trickle down her lips and chin. Stan is truly impressed. He is breathing heavily while feeling the last of his nut shoot in her mouth causing him to jerk forward. He is just looking down at Regina not knowing what to say or think. *Damn where she learn that at,* he says to himself.

Regina allows Stan to get control of his legs before she takes him by the hand for more fun. Stan willingly allows Regina to lead the way. He wants to see what is next because he has a feeling Regina is going to show him. She is walking in front of him so he can't see her smiling. She is tickled but ready to give and receive more. Yeah, those deep breathing, tongue exercises, games taught in class are working.

Once they reach the bedroom area, Stan starts unbuttoning his shirt. He is trying to be cool about it but he is watching Regina laying on the bed waiting for him. He can't get the buttons open fast enough. Regina is tracing the shape of her crotch and thong with her fingers. She is pretending to have her eyes closed but Stan can tell she is peeping. Stan is getting frustrated with the buttons. He decides to pull the shirt open ripping all the buttons off. Fuck it. Regina opens her eyes fully to see what is going on because one of the buttons pops her on the forehead.

She wants to laugh but she smiles real hard asking, "What you got to offer Mr. Wooten?" Stan lunges at Regina making a big thump on the floor with his knees. Regina hopes he didn't hurt himself. At the moment, he doesn't care if he is bruised or not. Stan wants some pussy. He reaches under her thighs, grabbing her hips to bring the inviting clitoris and lips to his face. His face is so buried between her legs she can only see his head moving around. Looks like he is trying to win a pie eating contest. Regina is loving the look and feel. *"That's right, eat this sweet potato pie baby,"* she is saying in her mind. Her husband is making her feel real good and her juices are definitely flowing all over his mouth.

Once Stan starts moving his tongue in and out of her, Regina envisions it is a small penis. Regina encloses Stan's head between her thighs and guides his hands to her breasts. She feels the explosion slowly building. Her orgasm is intense and her pelvis is contracting so hard, she has slight cramps. This doesn't stop Regina. She is ready to ride Stan like he has never been ridden before.

Stan climbs on the bed ready to get down too. His face is shining from all of Regina's juices. However, to Regina's surprise, he is completely limp. Smiling, she gives him a tongue bath, licking him all over from head to toe. Making sure every crease, crack, and crevice has been licked. This is turning Stan on. He definitely is enjoying it but, apparently not enough. He is still limp. Little Stan hasn't budged, raised his head, jerked ... nothing.

Regina takes him in her mouth again, gripping his butt, teasing it with a finger. She has never thought about playing around with Stan's ass before but he's loving it. *Hey, the instructor did say men like a little tongue stimulation on the anus.* Hell, Stan even turns a little so she could get closer to it. Yet, he is still limp. *What is going on?* She is ready for some good loving and Stan is spoiling the moment. It has been forty-five minutes now and she feels herself getting frustrated which is drying up her juices. Stan decides to try hand stimulation while sucking on Regina's breasts. She has lost complete interest right now but she is not signaling this to Stan.

What the fuck just happened here? Did I just suck my man into gear "Over Excitement" and now he can't do anything with his dick? I wonder has this happened to any of the girls. Damn, I put on the outfit I like most and never got to take it off. Hmmp and his ass has the nerve to get mad at times when I don't put out the way he wants me to. He likes talking, well, we will be talking about this one. I'll wait until we get back home. I might as well try to enjoy the rest of the weekend.

Regina smiles at her husband and gives him a tender kiss on the lips. No need to say anything good or bad. She can tell Stan is already feeling bad and frustrated. She lays there beside him making little circles on his hairy chest. Kicking her mules off, she gets up to go downstairs to get the platter, thinking that maybe he wants some of the fruit. Regina wants a glass of wine so she goes back down to get her full glass and his one-fourth full glass. While taking a couple of sips of hers, she hands Stan his glass. He doesn't want the drink or the fruit. He is fucking pissed. Regina can tell he is messed up over this. She was angry at first but now to see it happen to Stan makes her feel a little better. *He's human after all.*

"Hey, baby, you want to dance," she asks her man trying to cheer him up. "I have Vivian Green and Kendrick in the bag. Which one you wanna hear?"

Stan looks at her and rolls his eyes. He gets up off the bed annoyingly slinging his dick as if trying to wake it up. Regina turns her head so he doesn't see her laughing. The moment isn't funny but the way he is slinging himself it is hilarious to her. However, the current events are truly messing with his superego. No one could ever tell Stan he doesn't lay pipe. Normally he does yet, here … today … right now … he has NOT!!

"Dance?! Do I look like I wanna fuckin' dance? We were just in a heated session of foreplay which was leading to me entering a nice, warm, juicy environment. Now why the fuck will I be interested in dancing right now? I need you to do something with this," he says shaking his phallus at her.

Oooh, Stan Wooten is pissed. Is he angry at me or at himself? Is he going to blame me somehow for this?

"Well, dancing can be a part of foreplay too baby. C'mon, what do you say? It might help." *Oh- oh … WRONG THING TO SAY.* Stan's superego is showing through his manhood now.

"Might help? What the hell are you talkin' 'bout it might help? What is the 'it' you are referring to Gee Gee? There's nothing wrong with me. I must be tired. That drive up here was about five hours. Or it could have been that wine. Maybe we should have had white instead of the red." Stan doesn't know what is going on. He will point the finger at anything as long as he is not directing it towards himself. This has never happened to him before and he is hoping it doesn't happen to him again.

"Okay, Stan. Just calm down. It's me, your wife. Not a stranger. Why are you getting so huffy with me? Getting angry at me isn't going to help. Just relax and get your mind back into the flow. You were just overly excited, that's all. It happens. I'm going to put Maxwell in the CD player. How's that?"

Stan starts calming down. He knows he is wrong for lashing out at her. Regina is right and he knows he isn't being fair to her right now. She didn't do anything to cause this but it felt better to somehow blame her, or something. *This shit might happen to other men but I'm Stan Wooten. This shit don't happen to me!!*

The melody begins to come through the speakers and serenade throughout the room. Regina has the old Maxwell CD playing. She starts off with *'Til the Cops Come Knocking.* That used to be Stan's jam back in the day when they first started dating. Stan funks with Maxwell like that.

Stan walks over to Regina and grabs her around the waist. She wraps her arms around his neck. They are slow dancing slower than the music. Regina is being her seductive self and Stan is enjoying the feel of her skin. By the third time the song repeats, Regina feels a little twitch from "L'il Stan". They both smile and Stan says, "Now, that's what I'm talkin' 'bout. I'm ready for round four."

"Round four? How did we skip over round three? Sounds like a day of Tantric sex to me," says Regina.

Stan frowns at her. *What is she talkin' 'bout?* He has never heard of that. "What is Tantric sex? How did you hear about that? What does it involve? It sounds kind of voodoo-ish."

"We can talk about that later." Regina notices Stan is hard enough to enter her. She guides him over to the bed and motions for him to lie down. Stan follows her directions without reluctance. He is completely ready now. Neither is trying to waste time dancing and talking just in case.

"Yes, Ma'am. I said the same thing," Stan responds.

He is watching as Regina moves the thong to the side and climbs on top of him. He clenches his teeth making hissing sounds, saying, "Mmm," as he feels Regina's inner walls clamp onto him strong. Regina is about to go for it. She grins at Stan sneakingly as if she is up to something and she says to herself, *I'm in full jokey mode and I am ready for this rodeo, are you?*

Chapter Ten

10

"Excuse me. I'm sorry. Colleen, this is ..." Sandy hesitates and looks at the man she is getting ready to introduce to her friend realizing she doesn't know his name. He notices the look of "assistance is needed" on her face.

"Ray. My name is Ray Daniels." Sandy smiles and continues her introduction. "Colleen, this is Ray Daniels. Ray, this is my girlfriend Colleen Jeffries."

"How do you do pretty lady," the handsome man gives Colleen the sexiest smile she has seen in a long time.

"I'm doing just fine Ray Daniels. How are you?"

Ray extends a big masculine hand to Colleen. She extends her hand for the handshake but he kisses it instead. She is blushing. His hand is soft and that is a sign of no hard work. He has well manicured nails. Ray has a goatee, a perfect shape-up, green eyes, and clear skin. Colleen is attracted and knows Sandy is too. That means the boundary has been set so she's letting his hand go, reluctantly.

Sandy is noticing Colleen's look. She can't get an attitude with her because she has only danced with the man. Besides, she just learned his name and knows nothing else about him. He is fine and appears to be a gentleman. That can be a cover-up for the *real* Ray Daniels. So she politely introduces herself.

"Hi Ray. And I am Sandy. Sandy Robertson. It is nice to meet you. It was also nice to dance with you." She holds out her hand for the same treatment Colleen just received. Ray kisses her on the cheek instead. *Mmm, soft lips and fresh breath* she says to herself.

BeLynda is on her way back to the table. She observes a conversation happening between two of the three occupants. She sees Sandy is all smiles and the man is too while they are absorbed with each other. Colleen appears to be watching the conversation instead of participating. BeLynda isn't sure what this scene means. She really didn't want to know either. Arriving at the table, she places her drink on the table and pulls out her chair to sit and decides to speak.

"Hello, how are you" says BeLynda smiling at Ray.

Ray and Sandy look up at BeLynda smiling. "Ray, this is my other girlfriend BeLynda. BeLynda, this is Ray Daniels. Ray, this is my friend BeLynda Giles."

"How do you do BeLynda?" Ray takes her hand and gives her what he gave Colleen. She closes her eyes appreciating the moment. Colleen observes BeLynda's reaction to the kiss on the hand. She smiles to herself and takes a sip of her drink. *We must be some horny ass Sistas. Getting lost in the moment of a kiss on the hand.*

"I'm doing just wonderful Ray Daniels. And you?" BeLynda's hand is slightly shaking and she is feeling extra warm between her thighs. She releases her hand from his firm yet soft grip trying to recuperate.

"Oh, I couldn't be better. I just met a beautiful young lady and her two beautiful young girlfriends. I must've done some things right today to be this fortunate. And to think I was going to go straight home this evening."

"Why, thank you Ray. You must've been over here dishing out all kinds of compliments before I got back." BeLynda notices the familiar look on Colleen's face now. *Ah-ha, Ray must be a real charmer and Colleen wants him to talk to her but she won't make a move because Sandy is interested.*

"I wouldn't say all that," he says beginning to stand up. "But look, I know you ladies are out together so I won't hang around too much longer. Sandy, I actually would like to see you again in another setting. Will that be possible?"

"Another setting? I'm sure that can be arranged. How are we going to keep in touch Ray?"

Ray gives a smile of thanks. "Here's my business card. All my contact information is on the card. I will appreciate if you don't take too long to use it." He winks at her, plants another kiss on her cheek, stands, tilts his head towards BeLynda and Colleen, and walks off into the crowd.

Sandy isn't too happy about the contact information. He didn't ask for hers nor did he give his home number. She knows he knows he doesn't have that on the card.

"What does his card say," Colleen asks leaning over trying to read it.

"Yeah, what kind of business is handsome in," asks BeLynda.

"Umm, he is a video game designer," she says after reading the card.

"Video Games? That's different. A handsome nerd," BeLynda responds with a smile.

"Yea, it's different all right but he is far from being a nerd. The man is smart. That's the way to go nowadays. That bank account is just what Sandy has been looking for," says Colleen.

"Can I get to know him first before we start talking about bank accounts, please? All he gave me is a card that didn't even have a home number on it. He may be married or living with someone. Hell, he didn't even ask for my contacts."

"Oh please!! Who has their damn home number on their business cards? Besides, you can get to know him all you want to later on. When you call him he will then have at least one way to reach you. I'm sure he has caller ID, being a game designer. He's all into electronics. But right now, let's get back to this new drink that was inspired by Larry."

"Okay. Let me get another drink first. Does anyone want something while I'm going?"

"I'm fine with my daiquiri," responds BeLynda.

"Bring me two cranberry and vodkas back," says Colleen.

"Two," Sandy and BeLynda asks at the same time looking at Colleen as if she is crazy.

"Did I stutter? I said and meant two. You're about to tell me what you started to tell me thirty-five minutes ago. I don't want any interruptions. I'll have my drinks, cigarettes, and I'm about to go to the bathroom. When we both get back to the table, I'll be all ears." Colleen gets up and heads towards the bathroom. BeLynda looks at Sandy, with raised eyebrows.

"You got enough money," asks BeLynda. She knows Sandy has the smaller income of all the Girls.

"Yeah, I'm all right. Oh, don't worry. She'll be reminded that she pays for the next round."

"Actually, it'll be me. She paid for the first one. But again, she paid for ours. She still owes you one."

"Well then you should've come back with three or four drinks instead of one. Oh, trust me. I will remind both of you," Sandy responds giving BeLynda the side-eye as she goes to the bar.

The DJ switches up the music again. The beat is a lot faster now. BeLynda wants to dance but there's no one left to hold the table and the handbags. Five minutes later Sandy comes back to the table.

"Where are the drinks," asks BeLynda seeing that Sandy comes back with empty hands.

"A waitress is going to bring them to the table. I only have two hands, you know. I wasn't about to try to carry three drinks in glasses. All my shit is dry clean only." They both laugh.

"Oh, ok. Well, since you are back, I am going to the dance floor. The DJ is playing some of my old tunes." BeLynda gets up from the table and begins to walk to the dance floor.

"I thought I was about to talk about me and Larry."

"Girl, you know there's a line in that bathroom. I'll be back before Colleen is washing her hands. Watch."

"Okaaay. I'll be right here on pocketbook duty."

BeLynda steps onto the dance floor. The DJ is playing Chubb Rock Treat 'Em Right. This was one of her songs back in the day when she was hanging out at Hogate's.

♪ *Nineteen ninety, Chub Roc jumps on the scene*

With a lean and a pocket full of green

The green doesn't symbolize I made it on the top

But Robo Cop last year was a shock

The tone of the Popeye cut shook your butt

Kids are screaming; the media says, "What

Kind of music is this for you to dance to

The man with the plan and the man demands you

Leave the smack and crack for the wack

Or the vile and nine; keep a smile like that

Leave the knife and gun in the store

And ignore temptation sent by the nation ♪

BeLynda is doing her two-step but faster to keep up with the beat of the music. She is dancing by herself and watching the other dancers. Everyone is doing their own thing yet the moves are similar. However, no one is dancing similar to BeLynda though. Right now, she doesn't care because she is enjoying herself. She can practice later.

A man walks up to BeLynda and starts dancing with her. He smiles at her and she smiles back because she is at least dancing well enough for a man to join her on the dance floor. The man keeps a respectful distance. He can tell BeLynda is the "you-can't-touch-me" type of woman. They dance for two songs and go their separate ways. BeLynda gets to the table and just as she figured, Colleen is not back yet.

"All right, I'm satisfied at the moment. I've had drinks, I've danced, been entertained, and now I am about to hear a story. Before you get started, just tell me whether or not you and Larry did something," inquires BeLynda.

"I'm not saying anything until my entire audience is here. So you'll just have to wait."

"I just thought I'd ask."

Not another word is spoken. Sandy and BeLynda sit enjoying the music and sipping on their drinks looking around at the sights as if they don't know each other. BeLynda gets one of Colleen's cigarettes, lights it and makes a few smoke circles. Just that fast, she starts to wind down and is ready to go. Her daiquiri is almost gone. She and Sandy are on drinks number two. Colleen is on drinks two and three yet they are getting watered down because she isn't at the table to drink them.

Colleen comes back to the table. "I thought I was gonna have to pee in the damn sink. The line in there is ridiculous and there are only two stalls working. Then the funk ... GIRL!! I was about to past out in there. I guess it is not a requirement anymore to wash your damn ass before you come out to shake it."

"Damn, I'm glad I don't have to go, yet," says Sandy.

"Yea, me too, girl," BeLynda agrees.

"Moving on. Start talking Ms. Robertson. Oh, yeah, thanks for the drinks," yells Colleen over the music.

"You're welcome. Okay, let's see. Where do I begin?"

"How about starting with where the penis and booty connects," Colleen sasses Sandy. BeLynda shakes her head 'yes' while taking a sip of her drink.

Ignoring Colleen, Sandy begins. "Well yesterday, Larry called me at work. At first I brushed him off but then I called him back to say he could come over. He got to my house around seven – fifteen. I told him he didn't have to bring anything but him. He was sounding real anxious. He even said he had some making up to do with me."

"Mmmp, nothing but him, huh? You were straight forward with your intentions, girlfriend. Or was he too soft and slow to understand. Then again, he did say he had some making up to do with you. He felt you were getting ready to kick him to the curb," says BeLynda.

"Shhhh, don't interrupt her. Be quiet Bee, let her talk. Go 'head Dee Dee," Colleen rolls her eyes at BeLynda and scoots closer to Sandy so she can hear her better.

"Let me continue. So Larry comes in with a bottle of Merlot, a bottle of Syrah, and steamed shrimp. He gives me a peck on the cheek. The wines were already cold but I still put them on ice to keep them that way. I fixed pasta to go with the shrimp."

"Okay, I know you're leading up to the good stuff. However, since we're talking about what he brought with him, you weren't supposed to put the wine on ice Lady. That is red wine. And the food, why did you fix pasta? Why didn't you fix something quick like a salad," BeLynda asks.

Colleen rolls her eyes at BeLynda, bangs her fist on her thigh, and yells, "I don't care if she actually put ice cubes in the wine and fixed tomato soup. Let her finish Bee, damn!! Please go *ahead* Sandy. Ignore her ass."

"As I was saying, I fixed pasta seasoned with real butter, garlic, and fresh Italian seasonings. He was being very romantic. He asked if I had an old blanket and I did. I gave it to him and he spreads it out on the floor in the living-room in front of the fireplace. I was just standing there looking at him. He reached in the bag and took out plates, forks, and napkins and decorated the blanket. Larry gave me a kiss on the lips and got a vase out of the kitchen cabinet to fill it with water and placed one rose in it. I was speechless."

"Ha, ha, ha okay. Forgive me for laughing but, plastic forks and foam plates? And he gets a big ass vase out of *your* kitchen cabinet for one rose to swim around in it? How does he know where you keep your vases? So Larry knows his way around your house? Not to mention, couldn't you have skipped all of this," Colleen rudely interjects.

"Now, you wanted me to be quiet. You shut up and stop being so critical. I think what he did was romantic. Sandy don't pay her any attention." BeLynda feels like saying, "*Maybe some of your men should try it sometimes,*" but she knows that would make

Colleen forget all about what Sandy is saying and turn her focus on her comments.

"Just forget it," Sandy responds waving them off. She is tired of the interruptions. "Y'all want me to tell the story but you keep asking silly questions."

"No! I'm sorry. I didn't mean to say that. Go on, please,' Colleen says apologetically.

"For one, I didn't mind the plates and forks. It kept me from washing fucking dishes so that was considerate of him to bring them. Secondly, the vase was only big enough for the one rose. Everything doesn't have to be to the extreme Colleen. And to you Bee, I didn't want a damn salad to go with my shrimp. Now, if I am interrupted again, I won't finish and will go home. I'm screaming over the music as it is." Sandy is pissed.

"We're sorry. We won't interrupt anymore, honestly. We can converse afterwards, okay," BeLynda says and Colleen agrees.

"Okay. Now, after decorating the eating area, he turned on the fireplace. I prepared the plates and he poured the wines. We sat on the floor, ate, talked and laughed a lot. I was really enjoying his company, I will admit that. Larry has always been great with the romantic part of our relationship.

So, after awhile he started massaging my feet. Ooh, he was applying the right amount of pressure on my heels, arches, and the balls of my feet. He was using the finger, thumb, pinch, and knead techniques. If I didn't know any better, I would've thought he was giving me a therapeutic foot massage instead of a normal one. Larry had to have worked on each foot for about ten minutes before he moved on to my toes and ankles. It was so relaxing.

I thought he was finished until I felt my foot being raised and he puts my big toe in his mouth." *Okay now, it's getting juicy,* Colleen says to herself. "Hopefully my feet weren't too sweaty. I didn't have time to freshen up before he got there. So, he was sucking my toes and still massaging my feet and ankles.

I hadn't realized I was no longer sitting up. My nipples were hard and I was overly moist. After a while, Larry was actually taking too long with my feet. I was ready for the next move."

Mmm, a foot fetish, huh? Maybe that's why he's so soft. He likes delicacies, Colleen is saying in her mind.

"He started working his way up my leg then to my thigh. He was so close to my coochie, Girl, I had a slight orgasm from anticipation. Well, when Larry realized what was happening, he removes my panties and pulls his pants down. He lifts my butt off the floor a little and enters me deep. I mean *deep*. I couldn't believe it. I opened my eyes to look at him to make sure it was still Larry. The next thing I know, he was on his feet in a squatting position with my butt up off the floor. He pulled me up until I was sitting on his lap with my feet on the floor."

Colleen tilts her head while trying to imagine the position. BeLynda is sipping from a dry glass, not realizing her glass is empty. Sandy continues. She's looking like she's actually reliving the events.

"Once he got his balance, he begins rocking me. I was very still at first not knowing what he was going to do. I started moving and he said, 'uh-uh, don't move.' With my fresh waxing, I was receiving some serious stimulation. He kept rocking, and rocking, and rocking until I reached a second orgasm. That was unbelievable!! I had never experienced a second one and it was powerful." Colleen and BeLynda are all into Sandy's mouth making sure if they didn't hear her right, they could at least read her lips since they were still surrounded by club levels of music.

"I thought we were done but I was wrong. He laid me back on the floor still inside me and gets off his feet. I know his thighs had to be aching by now but he didn't show it. Anyway, he lifted my leg and brought it over to meet my other leg."

"So you're on your side now, right," asks BeLynda. Colleen didn't bother to say anything to BeLynda because she wanted Sandy to answer that question for her too.

"*Exaaactly.* He must have a curved penis because it felt like it was hitting my left tube. Oh, he starts going for it then. Larry was out of control at this point. I couldn't believe it. I was ready for his ass this time though. I rose up on my elbow, clamped my inner muscles and let the pelvis go to work. He grabbed my butt and started cursing, his eyes rolled up and he grabbed my leg and pushed it towards my breast. I was hanging with him though but it seems like he wasn't hanging with me. He got me with that first position. I wasn't going to let him have this one too.

I titled my pelvis back and forth and all he kept saying was, 'Sandy baby, what are you doing? I can't hold out. Wait … stay still. It's too damn good.' Sandy starts laughing at herself for imitating how Larry sounding. "Girl, he flipped me over onto my stomach, grabbed my hips, and I went to work with the Kegel exercises and belly rolling on his ass. He moaned like a wounded animal … and then girl, it was all over." Colleen and BeLynda are looking like they wanted more. They didn't want the story to end just yet. There has to be more. It sounds like she is leaving something out.

"So, you never took your clothes off," inquired BeLynda.

"Nope, we sure didn't. That was the exciting part about it. I enjoyed myself and him, I can you tell you that much," Sandy was sitting there proud. It's has been awhile since she has had anything exciting to talk about.

"Now, what the hell happened in one day. Did I miss something," asks Colleen.

"What do you mean," Sandy replies. BeLynda looks on because she wants to know what Colleen is talking about too.

"Okaaay, what I mean is just two days ago, you weren't happy with his ass. You didn't want to be bothered with Larry. It sounded like you were the dominant one between the two. Now all of a sudden, he's performing Kama Sutra stunts on your ass? How did he flip that shit? Then you tried to be so clean with telling us the story. What is this 'coochie' stuff? I wanted to hear the raw details. Give us the porn version. You know, dick …ass … pussy … words like that."

"Maybe that's what he needed to do. There is a time and a place for everything and the unadventurous technique isn't getting me there. And Ho, you tell your exaggerated stories your way and I'll tell my stories the way I want to. Everything doesn't have to be raunchy. Tellin' it vulgarly doesn't make you more explanatory than me. Remember that." Sandy is looking straight into Colleen eyes in a matter of fact way.

"So you didn't do anything with the wine," Colleen smiles devilishly ignoring Sandy's last statement. She wants to hear some real grit. Something that sounds like it comes out of a smutty novel.

"Ha, ha, ha that's another day, Ms. Horny. I am not here to help you privately get off. The wine was red, I guess you forgot that tidbit of information. Must've skipped over that when you were trying to get to the raunchiness. However, the wine was really good.

I won't give up my Merlot but I won't mind a glass of Syrah every now and then either."

"Mmm-hmm, I bet you won't mind … with a side order of Larry to go with it too, of course. Sooo, what about Mr. Ray? What's his last name again?"

"Daniels. Ray Daniels. What about him? I just met him and no one said that this is going to be a blossoming friendship." Sandy looks over at BeLynda wondering why she is so quiet. "What's the matter Bee? Why you so quiet?"

"Nothing, I'm just sitting here remembering some of the things you said. A waxed coochie? Kama sutra? Strong thighs? Shiiiit, I better have something other than my checkbook to smile about come Thursday at five-thirty." They all laugh out loud.

"Well, the night is still early and I think we're about done here anyway. Did y'all wanna go get some breakfast? I can enjoy a steak and eggs. Are we gonna go," Sandy asks her friends.

"Umm, that sounds good to me. Bee is riding with me so she has no other choice than to go. But, I don't think we're quite finish just yet. At least you're not," replies Colleen and points behind Sandy.

They see that Ray is on his way back to the table. Sandy can't figure out why he is coming back to the table. She doesn't see where he might have left anything on it. *Hopefully he is coming back to make me blush some more but I'm sure that isn't it.*

Ray approaches the table. "I'm sorry Sandy. I rushed off earlier and forgot to give you my home number. Forgive my manners. Normally, when I give out a card it is for business purposes only and there is no need for them to call me at home. This is an exception because I gave you a card for personal purposes."

Damn, he is goood Colleen smiles to herself. Sandy is blushing. BeLynda has her face propped up on her hand leaning on the table all into Ray's words.

"Oh, okay," Sandy smiles excitedly inside and hands him the card. Sandy watches as Ray writes the number on the back of the card. He hands the card back to her, winks his eye at her, and says, "Again, don't take too long to use any of the numbers." He turns to face all three of them and say, "You ladies enjoy the rest of your night."

Sandy, Colleen, and BeLynda watch him walk away, each smiling with separate mischievous thoughts written all over their faces.

Chapter Eleven

11

It is four o'clock and Sandy is getting off work. Class starts at six o'clock. It is her turn to drive so she has to pick up Regina. BeLynda and Colleen normally come together because they live on the same side of town. Sandy will change into her class attire when she gets to Regina's house.

Sandy pulls into Regina's driveway. Sitting there she observes the house for a minute. She really likes Regina's and Stan's house. Sometimes Sandy likes it too much. A family of six can live comfortably in the house without invading each other's space and privacy. No wonder Stan hired Maria after they were in the house only seven months.

Sandy turns off the ignition, gets her bag and purse from the backseat, gets out the car and walks to the front door. Ringing the doorbell, she thinks out loud, *I could really get use to this kind of living. And Regina has the nerve to complain about not having enough to do everyday. I can sure think of quite a few things to do in EVERY damn room in here. Please, she's living the life ... and always has."*

The massive wooden front door opens ending Sandy's thoughts. "Good evening Senorita Robertson," greets Maria.

"Hello Maria. How are you today?" Sandy enters the foyer, looking around as if this is her first time in Regina's home.

"I'm just fine, thank you Senora. Go ahead inside. You know where the Guests' bathroom is by now." Sandy and Maria both laugh. "Do you need anything?

"Ah, yeah, are there any apples and cheese here? Is that doable?"

"Ha, ha, ha you know there is plenty of fruit and cheese here. What kind of cheese would you like? We have Cheddar, Swiss, Gouda, and Gruyere. We are all out of Port wine. The apples we have are Red Delicious, Gala, and Honey Crisp. You can't have any of the Macintosh, they are for my pies."

Sandy laughs at Maria. She adores her. "I know that's right. I'll take Red Delicious with cheddar, please. Thank you Maria."

"Okay. I'll go tell Senora Wooten you are here. Your snack will be waiting for you in the usual place."

"Thanks Maria. You are so sweet." Maria smiles, waves her hand at Sandy and walks down through the foyer towards the kitchen. Sandy goes in the Guest bathroom to change her clothes.

She smiles remembering Saturday night out with BeLynda and Colleen. She hasn't called Ray yet. Actually, she hasn't thought about it. *He didn't even ask for any of my numbers. That can be a plus or a negative. If he's crazy, then it's a plus that he didn't ask. If he thinks I'm gonna be stroking his ego by calling and leaving messages appearing to be desperate that is a negative. I will never be desperate regardless of how much I long to be in a relationship.*

Walking out the bathroom towards the meeting room, Sandy literally bumps right into Regina. "Hey, hey. What's going on Mama," asks Sandy, giving Regina a hug and kiss on the cheek.

"Hey you!! Not too much going on with me girl. I'm just ready to get to class. I've been in the house all day," replies Regina while giving Sandy a kiss as well. They both walk into Regina's meeting room. Sandy sees her snack and begins to eat while they continue their conversation.

"All day? You didn't have any errands to run?"

"Nope. Not today. I just have lain around. I literally just got up one and a half hours ago to take a bath and get dressed. I had been upstairs watching all the court and talk shows all day. Oprah was really good today too."

"Ooh, stop. Don't tell me anymore. I love those kinds of days."

"Hmmp, I don't. At least not all the time."

"Girl, please. You wanna trade? And it isn't all the time so be quiet. How was the Poconos girlie? No, wait until later to tell me. We need to get going. Class is waiting."

"Yeah, let's go." Regina grabs her jacket, house keys and purse. On her way out the door, she yells, "Maria I'm leaving! Don't forget to lock the door!"

"Yes ma'am!" Maria yells coming around the corner from the kitchen, wiping her hands on a towel.

Sandy puts on her jacket, grabs her back pack and purse. She stuffs the last slice of apple and slither of cheese in her mouth and waves good-bye at Maria.

"Hey ladies. The rest of the crew is here," Regina prances over to BeLynda and Colleen with opens arms.

"She's baaack! Hey girl. We weren't sure what day you were returning. How was it? Was it everything you thought it would be and more," asks BeLynda.

"Girl, we had a ball. We had a good time. There were so many things for lovers and groups to do there. I mean, except for one little mishap, we really enjoyed ourselves. I definitely would go back."

"What little mishap," inquires Colleen, zooming right into the drama but really concerned.

"Saturday, when we got back to the room from dinner to change our clothes into something comfortable for the Newlywed Game, someone had been in our room Girl. The entire room had been ransacked. It caught me off guard."

"Say what," screams Sandy.

"How do you know someone had been in your room," asks BeLynda. Sandy and Colleen look at her as if she has stolen something. "Bee!! She just said that the room was ransacked.

Duh?! That wouldn't have been obvious to you?" Colleen wants to smack BeLynda for sounding so slow. BeLynda just stares at Colleen and then look at Regina and Sandy to see if they felt the same way as Colleen. Their looks tell it all.

Regina is looking at BeLynda as if maybe she didn't hear exactly what she had said. So she starts talking slow to assure the clearness of her message. "Well, because when we entered the room, our clothes were thrown all over the place, the CDs were broken, and the wine had been poured on the sheets. One of the lingerie outfits I had just bought for the trip was slashed to pieces and smashed down in the toilet."

"Who in the world would do some shit like that? Did Stan piss somebody off earlier that day," asks Colleen.

"Regina ... are you serious?! That sounds real creepy as a motherfucka. Who in the world would be doing that type of shit out of town," Sandy asks.

"I don't know but it surely had me on edge. We played couples basketball earlier that day and won. A lady from one of the other couples teams was mad at her husband or boyfriend ... or whoever he was to her. She was bragging earlier about going to win but they lost and she started saying we cheated. Hell, the referee was the one keeping score, not us. I didn't want to blame her for the damages because we didn't see her coming out of our room. I don't even know if she knew where we were staying. We did complain to management. So they gave us a new room ... an upgrade at that. They gave us a free weekend that we have to use in a year too. It was just crazy."

"Crazy is an understatement. Sounds like someone needed a straight jacket and an ass whipping," comments Sandy.

"Luckily for her, *IF* it was her, you didn't catch her in the act. She would have gotten a serious beat down had that been my shit," Colleen says.

"Okay, y'all hush. We can finish this later. Here comes the instructor. What is her name again," BeLynda asks.

"For the tenth time, her name is Kelly and the other instructor's name is Tina. What's the matter Bee? You all right? You're so into the classes you can't remember?" Regina shakes her head at BeLynda and starts laughing. Colleen and Sandy joins in with the laughter.

BeLynda ignores the comment and puts her attention solely on the instructor. The rest of the class does the same. Some are sitting on the floor and others are sitting in chairs. They already know what the topic is but they aren't sure how Kelly is going to approach it. The class considers her the mild instructor.

"Good evening ladies. How's everyone doing today?" Kelly greets everyone as she walks around the class observing who is present and who is not. She notices her faithful four are there and as always, ready.

"Today, we will start talking about the genitals and follow up with a review from another class. Now, let's talk about us first. Us, meaning women. Some women say their vagina is too small. Others say theirs is too big. However, the vagina stretches to allow a baby to pass through. So surely a penis can't compete with the size of a baby, right? So is it safe to say the vagina can accommodate different sizes of the penis?"

The class nods their heads in agreement with Kelly. They are quiet and listening except for Colleen.

"Whew, that's good to hear," Colleen mumbles, thinking about Devin. *If I ever get a chance to go down that road with him again, I'm not gonna stop at the first corner. I'm gonna go to the end of the block and around to the next corner.*

"Now, the vagina is more than just a hole for child birth, penises, pleasure, tampons, diaphragms, dildos, cucumbers, and anything else one might want to insert. It is a delicious, self-preserving, interesting, mouth-watering, high-potency, and alluring member of the female body."

"Mmm, I love the way she describes it," says BeLynda.

"As I said earlier, the vagina has stretching capability. However, if you have a small vagina and link up with a mate that has a very large penis, there might be some discomfort. There are some things you can do to help ease the discomfort and really enjoy yourself. Does anyone know of some tips?"

Sandy raises her hand and responds unsure of her answer, "One can use K-Y Jelly?"

"Yes, that is correct. But in this situation, you will have to use a lot of lubrication. Even if your secretions are flowing, you will still need lots of lube because your secretions alone will not be enough. Anyone else?" Colleen says to herself, *Did she just say "lube" to us?*

"What about those breathing exercises we've been practicing," asks another lady in the class.

"Well ... breathing is correct if it is being used to get relaxed. Because if you aren't completely relaxed, the vagina isn't going to stretch or lubricate enough for you when you want it to. Other things you and your mate can do are, extend your foreplay and try different positions. Now, I am not a doctor so make sure you ask plenty of questions at your GYN appointments. They can tell you some other methods to try as well. They are there to help. Does anyone have any questions before I move on? Make sure you're taking notes. You will have a written test in a few weeks." *Hmmp, I know I won't be showing the paper or grade to this test to Stan,* Regina says to herself.

"I have a question," BeLynda raises her hand.

"Go on. Ask away," responds the instructor. She knew no matter, BeLynda was going to ask her something.

"I'm not sure whether I have a small or large vagina. However, let's say I do have a small one and my mate is large like you are talking about right now. What kinds of positions work for this situation?"

Oh, okay Bee, I see you, the instructor says to herself. "A good and popular position is always with you on top. This way, you control the movement and how deep the penetration is. The penetration is in fact quite shallow. That's why at times you probably will find that your mate grabs your hips and brings you down further while he is thrusting upwards. There are different variations that make this position shallower. You can face him, or you can have your back turn to him which is what they call the Reverse Cowgirl. You can even be side-ways on top. Try them all and see what works for you. That's the fun part, but once you find the position that works use it to your advantage. Hell, they do." The class erupts into laughter.

Colleen is very quiet and taking notes. She also has her mini tape recorder on just in case she isn't writing fast enough. Then she can write everything completely when she gets home. She will laugh later when she plays the recorder back.

"Now, when a woman's vagina is large and her mate's penis is small, some of the same techniques we just talked about can be used. You definitely can try new positions. I will repeat, trying new positions is always fun no matter what size vagina you have. Women like talking about the size of the penis and how it matters. Yea, we have all heard the little saying. You know, "It's about the motion in the ocean." Well guess what Ladies, unless you're laying there like a lump on a log, you are apart of that ocean. That means you need to be moving too, not just him. So with both of you working in that boat with those positions and movements together, some of you might rethink your penis size opinion." The Ladies are looking at Kelly as if after all this time they just realized they had been missing a part.

"Remember what I said in the breathing class. Let go of other people's hang-ups that have been instilled upon you. Learn what you need to for you and your body as well as for your mate and his body. Now, does anyone know of any other methods that can help out with a large vagina/small penis encounter?"

No one raises their hand. They seem to be too stuck on her last few sentences. Some probably know the answer but afraid to say it just in case it is wrong. Sandy, Colleen, BeLynda, and Regina look at each other and the other women.

"C'mon ladies. We've already discussed one of these methods before." The instructor looks around the room. No one budges. "Are we awake this evening? Am I boring the class today?" Some of the ladies snicker. "Okay ladies. Haven't we discussed and perform Kegel exercises and pelvic movements?"

"Yes, we sure have," responds a lady moving her head up and down in a "yes" motion.

"That's right. I forgot all about those," another lady responds.

"I started to say that but wasn't sure," says Colleen.

"How do these two help a woman with a large vagina," whispers BeLynda to Sandy.

"Girl, I'm not the instructor. Ask her so both of us will then know," Sandy replies. BeLynda is embarrassed to ask. Even though she realizes the classes are for women to be in tuned with their bodies, sensuality, and sexuality. She just doesn't want anyone laughing at her. Maybe she should already know how they help but she really doesn't. They did have those classes already but she can't remember the importance of the techniques. That must've been the part she didn't hear in order to write in her notes. Then again, no one answered that last question. So she's not alone with being lost. She'll ask anyway. If they laugh, let them laugh. Everybody's just sitting back and not saying anything but probably want to know the answer. BeLynda raises her hand.

"Yes, you have a question," the instructor points to BeLynda.

"Yes, I do. I am not clear on how or what the Kegel exercises or pelvic movements help in this situation."

"Can anyone help BeLynda out?"

"Well, different pelvic movements help the penis have more contact with the walls of the vagina," says Regina.

"Excellent answer Regina!"

"Can you help her to understand the importance of the Kegel exercise? Or does someone else need to do that?"

"The Kegel exercises make the vagina muscles stronger and tighter so you can grip the penis during sex." Regina is feeling good that she knows her stuff. She should know, especially after the rodeo she had this past weekend.

"Great! Let's give Regina a hand." Everyone claps and roots Regina on. She smiles and bows her head in acceptance.

"Ump, been practicing Regina," Sandy asks barely opening her mouth so no one could really hear her. They both snicker.

"Does that help you BeLynda," asks the instructor.

"Yes it does, thank you. Thank you Sandy."

"You're welcome. Are we ready to move on class?"

"Yes," everyone says, sounding like they are in a choir.

"Okay, well let's move on to the men. We all know that, for the most part, intercourse involves the penis entering the vagina. So as women, we need to be knowledgeable of the male anatomy as well. Having more knowledge may increase your sexual desire and pleasure. For some women, they might stop feeling uncomfortable during intimate encounters. They will want to be more open with their partner. Ha, ha, ha some women are just free with their sexuality without knowing anything about their male partner's anatomy."

"Get with it and stop the speech," mumbles Colleen.

"Our organs are actually the same. The only difference is ours are internal and theirs are external as well as they look different. The ovaries are the same as the male testicles, the shaft of the clitoris is the same as the shaft of the penis. The scrotum is the same as the labia majora. The penis is the same as the clitoris. Are we getting the picture here ladies?" They all nod their heads.

"Yes. I never thought about it that way," says one of the ladies in the class.

"A lot of women don't know that. However, if they did, it may help them to understand that we all like a lot of the same stimulation. Later on, you can teach your man about his stimulation for you." Kelly winks her eyes at the women and continues with her speech. "For our more advanced women, what is the corona and frenulum," she says walking around the class.

Sandy raises her hand. The instructor motions for her to speak.

"The frenulum is the skin underneath the penis and the corona is the brim of the head.

"Almost Sandy, that was good. You got corona right. Try frenulum one more time." Sandy is trying to figure it out. What didn't she say? She thought that was the answer.

"Where the head meets the shaft," whispers Colleen leaning over slightly towards Sandy yet still watching the instructor. Sandy hears the answer.

"I got it! The frenulum is the skin underneath the penis where the head and shaft meets."

"Yes! There you go. That's what I wanted to hear. Did everyone get that?" The class nods. "Okay. Now as I said, the penis is the same as the clitoris. So both are extremely sensitive. Treat the penis like you treat your clitoris or how you want your clitoris to be treated. You can have your man climbing the walls if you use those tongue techniques or give him a massage on his frenulum."

The class is very quiet. Maybe everyone is thinking about their man's frenulum. Some are staring off into space. Others are tapping their pens. A few are running their fingers through their hair or propping their chins on their hands. All of them are in deep thoughts about something.

"That's all we're going to cover today about the genitals. Next week, we will discuss things we can do with the different sizes of the penis and when it is soft and hard. Okaaay, let's review what we have learned on oral stimulation. There are five steps and there are ten of you. I want you to pair up with someone. One person will tell the step and their partner will demonstrate for the class."

Everyone laughs. No one wants to demonstrate the step. Everyone wants to tell the step. Colleen has an idea. "Kelly, no one seems to want to demonstrate. So, why not have everyone do both with their partner," suggests Colleen.

"That's a good idea Colleen. We will do it that way. Now, who wants to go first?" Kelly gets the review started. The rest of the class isn't too happy with Colleen's suggestion.

"I'll go first. C'mon Sandy," Colleen says. She and Sandy stand in front of the class. Sandy has her tongue hanging out making silly faces. The class laughs at her.

"Okay. We're going to show touching the nose with the tongue." Sandy tries real hard to do that. She folds her top lip over her teeth to help stretch the tongue more. Her tongue almost reaches the bottom of her nose. The class claps for her.

"Wow, that makes my inner jaws ache," Sandy says moving her jaws around massaging them with her hands.

"That's right Sandy. The more you practice, the stronger you jaws will get. Right now, you're forcing your tongue. Your tongue will become stronger and more limber after awhile also. This helps with oral sex. All right Colleen, your turn."

Colleen is feeling awkward doing this in front of the class. She closes her eyes so she doesn't have to face anyone or see anyone giggling. Apparently she didn't watch Sandy at all. Colleen's tongue doesn't past the top line of her upper lip. The class is silent watching her. It is obvious she is very uncomfortable with the demonstration.

"Okay, that's good Colleen. Just keep practicing. You will get the hang of it. They did a great job didn't they class? Now, who's next?"

Two ladies walk to the front of the class. They are secretly discussing who is going to do what first. Once they get ready, they face the class and start right away.

They state what they will be demonstrating. "Move the tongue up and down in fluttering motions," lady No. 1 says. Lady No. 2 demonstrates for the class. However her flutters were going all over the place instead of up and down. The class tries not to laugh. Colleen isn't laughing because she knows how she felt when she was standing in front of everyone. They switch and lady No. 1 is now demonstrating. Hers is too perfect. That is some serious practice and concentration. The class is amazed and too stunned to clap.

"Very good ladies," instructor says moving on, "Next?" No one volunteers. "Am I going to have to choose? Where's Dina and Teresa? Don't try to hide. Get on up here."

The women reluctantly walk to the front of the class. Dina immediately speaks, letting Teresa know she will be demonstrating first.

They state what they are about to demonstrate. "Move your tongue in circles to the left and then to the right," says Dina. Teresa smiles because this is easy. She moves her tongue real fast and then slow. Dina does her version with lots and lots of enthusiasm. Almost as if she has a penis in her mouth already.

"Oh my goodness. Calm down Dina," Kelly responds to Dina's explicit demonstration. "You'll be home soon enough." There were a few snickers from the class. "Okay ... Regina, who is your partner?"

"BeLynda is my partner."

"Well, get on up here. What are you going to do for us?"

Regina and BeLynda look at each other and bust out laughing. The class joins in on the laugh. Regina can't stop. She has a sudden case of the giggles. It went on for a few minutes.

"Okay, okay, okay. I apologize. I'm serious now. For some reason, I got the giggles," Regina straightens her face and composure. "We are going to demonstrate sticking out the tongue, move it left to right, and pull it back in." BeLynda gives her version. She's moving so fast like a lizard. Her eyes are going in the same direction as her tongue looking like she is watching a tennis match. Some of the women snicker. Regina quickly does hers and sits down. BeLynda follows her back to their seats. The other women look around at each other wondering what just happened.

"Wow that was fast. Regina, you didn't want us to see it huh?" Neither Regina nor BeLynda responds.

"It looks like someone is missing from the last group. So I will do it myself. She must've snuck out to the bathroom. Tell her when she gets back, I have something special for her next week. Now, our last step for now is reaching your chin with your tongue. Here it goes." Kelly bends her bottom lip in and over her bottom teeth to allow her tongue to reach further. Kelly has a long tongue anyway so she actually reaches her chin.

"Goodness gracious," says BeLynda.

"I'm serious. Her man must love her," responds Colleen.

"That's from these exercises," Sandy joins in.

"You think so," asks Regina.

"Hell no. Sandy is just talking. Her tongue didn't get to that length from rolling, reaching, and stretching," Colleen says.

"Whatever. We'll see," Sandy responds with an attitude.

"All right ladies. That's it for this evening. Remember practice makes perfect. Next week bring cucumbers and bananas. If you can find a large potato, that can work too. Enjoy the rest of your week."

"Did she say bring cucumbers and bananas," BeLynda asks shockingly, "and what's with the large potato?"

"You heard her Missy," Regina replies.

"What's next class about? Why do we need fucking food? Especially shaped like those?" BeLynda is looking real confused.

"To practice. What do you think?"

"Okaaay ... practice what?!"

Sandy smiles, leans on BeLynda's shoulder while twirling her hair and says, "Come on sweetie. Relax and let the imagination *flow*. What would we need them for? *Think*!!"

Regina and Colleen laugh at Sandy's response and behavior. Sandy finds it funny also and participates in the laughter.

"You can laugh all you want but my imagination is having a hard time *flowing* with the involvement of them damn fruits and vegetables." BeLynda isn't finding anything funny about the conversation.

Still laughing, Colleen says, "Girl, just bring them to class next week and stop being so inhibited. The next class is about to start. Let's go see what Tina has planned for us this evening. Maybe she'll have us experimenting with chocolate and honey. Tina be off the chain!! You can handle that can't you?"

BeLynda rolls her eyes at Colleen. When it comes to her sexuality, the last thing she needs is for a know-it-all to try and make her feel inadequate or dumb. Hmmp, she peeped Colleen's card earlier. She thinks BeLynda isn't aware she was feeling uncomfortable with those oral exercises. *Colleen may be telling on herself after all.*

Chapter Twelve

12

"Hey Ladies. How you been? Did you eat too much turkey last week? Some of you are looking mighty stuffed. I can't believe I didn't see any of you last week for class or the Spa." BeLynda stands to greet the Ladies as they all walked into the Spa one by one but at the same time.

"Hey yourself Lady. I've been just fine. I ate what I was suppose to eat. Nothing more and nothing less. You know I don't do all of that bad carb mess. I may fix all that but it doesn't go in my plate. Plus, after all that cooking, I didn't feel like doing too much eating anyway." Colleen says while giving BeLynda the normal kisses on the cheek and peck on the lips and removing her gloves.

"I know that's right Girl. I did a lot of cooking myself and to be the Aunt Jemima at the table while everyone else comes over all dressed up and taking pictures for memories, that doesn't work for me. I need to find a new solution to that. I don't want memories of me looking like that," Regina says coming into the conversation while giving BeLynda the same greeting as everyone else.

"I know what you mean Girl. Thank goodness we went over Sandy's house Thursday. But I did bring my famous pecan pies. And you know Sandy's mom had her lips poked out because everybody was falling all over themselves trying to make sure they got a piece of my pie to take home." BeLynda says with a smirk to Regina and Colleen but making sure she doesn't look at Sandy's expression.

"Oooh, now that was a sight to see, I am sure. I bet you if you get to go over Sandy's house next year, you will NOT be on dessert duty. Mama Robertson might leave you outside with your pie on the porch," says Regina making Colleen and BeLynda laugh. Sandy rolls her eyes but she has to laugh at what Colleen says. They know her Mama all too well.

"Or if she is told to bring dessert, it better be anything other than pecan pie. Or we might be visiting Bee's ass in the hospital. We might walk in the room to see her in a neck brace, arm up in the air in a sling and a leg in a cast elevated." The Ladies all laugh at what Colleen says. Sandy just shakes her head while laughing. "Y'all stop talking about my Mama. You know she don't play when it comes to her baking."

"Right and that is why I am surprised that Bee even waltzed up in your house with any type of damn pie. She must was trying to make the Shit List" says Colleen.

"Well, you know Bee can throw down too. I don't even know why she hasn't gotten her other business started. But we all have talents in the cooking and baking department. We should have been started a joint venture. As a matter of a fact, we will call it Cakes 'n Bakes," says Sandy forgetting that the topic was BeLynda vs. Mrs. Robertson.

"Girl, stop. You are forever talking about starting a business. Anything to get out of that damn government nine – to – five job of yours, huh? I mean, I feel you because that's why I left years ago. But knowing damn well, the minute you run that food business by your Mama, she is going to have her lips poked out because YOU will be showing her up at all the family events." Colleen says looking at the other Ladies for approval in what she was saying to Sandy.

"Exactly!! And there won't be a section on the menu titled "Mama R's Old Fashion Sweets. They will be old fashion but they will be mine. I love Mama Robertson and the last thing I want is to end up in the ring with her over whose pound cake taste better and is moister. Oh no, this sista will have to throw in the towel to not hurt your Mama's feelings." Regina and Colleen are laughing hysterically now.

"Hardee-Har-Har, Ms. Not So Funny Giles. What, you ate my Mama's pie to make her feel good? Or to see what was the difference and to learn something about the ingredients? Please, my Mama has a husband and had seven children for him to use as test dummies to figure out what should and shouldn't be used as an ingredient. So don't try it. Who did you test yours out on? Steve's ass? And what you laughing at Regina? Sitting over there every year cooking all that food and for who? Who comes over to eat all that food you take two days to prepare? Colleen … I'm not even about to start on you because that would take the next ten minutes." Sandy gives them the "talk to the hand" gesture, rolls her eyes and walks over to the reception desk to check on when they will be escorted upstairs to the locker rooms.

Regina observes whispering to the Ladies, "Y'all, chill out. She is in her feelings right now. I mean that is her Mama. Colleen, you always jokin' around with someone's feelings. You know she is sensitive." Regina smiles because she is kidding with Colleen.

Colleen leans back looking at Regina, with her hand on her chest, whispering, "Me?! Why is your finger pointed at ME?! I don't recall my mouth being the only one releasing words on this matter. And I thought we were just having fun, right?" She sees Regina laughing and smiles. "Girl go 'head. I thought you were serious for a minute. I was about to say!! Sandy knows I love her ass. Hell, I forgot Mama Robertson had all those damn kids. And still with the same man too? Hell, we wasting money taking these classes. We should've been going over Sandy's Mama's house all this damn time."

They all get quiet when Sandy returns to the group. "They said someone is coming down shortly. I'm ready to get into my robe," says Sandy trying to lift her spirits from where they just went a few minutes ago.

Ina comes downstairs with her smile plastered on her face as if she has Vaseline on her teeth saying to the Ladies, "Good evening Ladies. Follow me …

"You know what, the last time we were here, we were in the middle of a juicy conversation and we got interrupted by Darla coming to get me. Now I clearly remember Colleen saying that she spent the night over Devin's house."

"That's right Slick Ass. Thanks for reminding me Sandy," Regina then turns to Colleen saying, "Devin? Devin who?! Devin

Maddock?! Hold up, what a minute, let me take a seat and get comfortable. You've been sitting here all this time knowing you haven't finished the story, holding onto some juicy four-one-one like that?! You tried that the last time, trying to slide that in the conversation all smooth and shit. How did you end up over there? You were there all night," Regina asks.

"*O ... M ... G*!! Wow!! I mean when she said that the last time we were here, I surely didn't see that coming at all. You always act like you all are only and will forever be friends. Well, at least tell us if he has a nice place," Sandy eagerly asks. She has always been attracted to Devin. His chocolate complexion, strong shoulders, built-up chest, nice size ass and thick thighs all being held up by a set of sexy bow-legs has always created heat between her legs whenever she would see him. However, she always thought he was kind of quiet though.

"Well, first let me just say that Bee thought I didn't hear her ass say "we" went over Sandy's house. Who is "we" Bee? Who have you been seeing on a regular? And why BeLynda gets to meet him first and not all of us at the same time? *Now*, who's slipping stuff into conversations," says Colleen. Regina surprised and smiling, looks over at BeLynda waiting for a response. BeLynda blushes. But before she can answer, Colleen makes sure she keeps the floor and continues.

"We will get back to you later. So hold that thought. But, Girl, YES!!! His house is like that. For as long as we have been friends, I have never been over to his house. It is huge!! His place is laid out but I can tell a female helped him decorate. Three guests bedrooms on the upper floor. His bedroom is huge and is on another level all by itself. His bathroom ... girl! I can't even describe it but the bathroom I used was something I've seen in a movie before. He has a game room and a bedroom for his little brother whenever he comes to stay too.

The kitchen is to die for. Regina y'all running neck and neck with the kitchen but Sandy, you would be in heaven with all that cooking you like to do. All the regular rooms are on the main level and his basement is finished with a complete exercise room in it. We need to have a party there just one time. Chile, I could go on and on but, the house is nothing compared to what we did."

"Mmm – hmmm just like I said. There you go again trying to slide the real juice in, making us sit here listening to you go on and on about his damn house. Spill it winch!! And don't leave out any details," Regina says standing with her hands on her hips tapping her foot on the Berber carpet.

"What," Colleens asks looking around at all the Ladies. "Didn't Sandy just ask me to tell y'all all about house? Hell that was the short version. I didn't go into any details to what the rooms really looked like. But, okay excuse me."

Sandy is still stuck on Colleen saying "what we did." Her mouth is hanging open and eyes are blinking. "Huh? What did you say? You ... and *Devin*? The 'Devin' I've been trying to get you to introduce me to? The 'Devin' that you pretended to not be interested in? You did more than just sleep at his house? Is that what I'm hearing? Well, how was it heifer? I knew you were liking him from the beginning," Sandy responds totally surprised. Colleen and Devin have been friends for three years and their interaction always appeared to be strictly platonic. Maybe Colleen was waiting for the right moment. *I guess I will step off from wanting him,* she says to herself.

"Why I gotta be a heifer? First it was Bee calling me one the other morning when I was at her house and now it is you. What, you mad that I didn't call you to come join us? It wasn't even like that." Colleen laughs at Sandy. *Damn, Sandy is really serious about this, huh? I had no idea how she actually felt about Devin.*

"I ended up at his house because I had too many martinis and he didn't let me drive home. So he took me to his house and I slept in one of his guest bedrooms. I didn't even remember going to his house, that's how drunk I was. All I know is I woke up that morning in an unfamiliar room with some arms holding me. I turn around and it was Devin." Colleen explains to make sure they all understood that it was not a planned date of sex.

"Awww, that was nice of him. I've always liked Devin. He is such a sweetheart. Always polite and courteous but in a manly way, you know," BeLynda says getting up to get her a few crackers and spread Port Wine cheese on them. "So, is there more you would like to share with us?"

"Well, first before I finish," Colleen turns to Regina. "Regina, you wanna call me a heifer too? I mean, you know … I didn't want to leave you out." Colleen roles her eyes, smiles, and then winks because she was only playing. BeLynda and Sandy start laughing. Regina shakes her head saying, "Nah, I'm good. Please continue … Slick Ass." Colleen's eyes get big and the Ladies are laughing.

"Okay!! Now, as I was saying before I was rudely interrupted, and then called a 'Slick Ass' … it was a surprise to me too. Yes, he was very gentlemanly. He had taken my clothes off *and* gave me a facial without trying anything with me. That was very respectful of him and I really appreciated that, you know? He was going to cook me breakfast but all I wanted was ginger-ale and crackers. So when he said he was going downstairs to eat breakfast, I thought I was alone. Well, he walks in on me satisfying myself and decides to help a sista out. I couldn't believe it! I think I may have jumped a little bit from embarrassment."

A pin could be heard dropping in the Tranquil Area from the quietness. Mouths are open, eyes are open wide, and no one is moving just in case they may miss the next detail in Colleen story.

"Satisfying yourself, how? He helped you, how? What were you doing?" Regina now moves to the empty seat at the table tripping over her fluffy slipper to keep from having to turn around to look at Colleen.

"Hell, Girl, I had a perfume bottle up in my pussy. When he walked in on me, and saw what I was doing, he got turned on and started working it for me. Then his fingers were getting a piece of the action too."

Regina's mouth is hanging open in astonishment at the story she is hearing. Sandy is blinking and choking on her water assuming that Colleen is inflating the story somewhere. BeLynda covers her face trying to hide her laughter. She doesn't want to visualize Colleen being so horny that she resulted in using something out of her purse.

"Say what?! A perfume bottle?! Oh my God!! Colleen?!" Regina screams with shock and excitement in her voice and written all over her face. Sandy and BeLynda are laughing too hard and running around the room. They couldn't believe it. They are giving each other high fives and clapping their hands. Regina just sits there smiling, fanning herself and sipping on her lemon water.

Trying to regroup, Sandy asks, "Okay. Now tell us where the dick comes into this story. I'm sure if y'all went that far, the bottle had to be replaced with his dick, right?"

Regina is ready for the next juicy detail too. So she leans in closer, placing her elbows on the table. "Yeah girl, where did it come into the scene?"

Colleen waves them off, smacking her lips together. "Chile, he is very well-endowed and I do mean VERY. I wouldn't have been able to even put it in my mouth. That would have been some serious lock jaw in a maximum of ten seconds. So it went no further than my hand because he wasn't putting that in my pussy."

"What?! Girrrrrl, c'mon … slow it down for me. I'm getting too excited," Sandy is ready to see for herself. However, she knows that isn't going to happen. So she wants to slowly imagine this brother with a dick like that in her mind as Colleen talks about him.

"Okay, well as in the words of Isaiah Washington's character Savon from my favorite movie *Love Jones*, 'let me break it down for you so that it will forever be broke.' I'm telling you, it really is that big. Hell it's enormous as a matter of a fact. So I worked it with my hand. I had no other choice, seriously. That is the closest he has gotten to some pussy in a long time and I do understand why. Bitches probably start putting their clothes back on before he is all the way hard after taking a look at his package. To say that he is packing is an understatement, for real. And if you could have seen all that cum shooting all over the place …"

"Damn … shoot it all over *ME*," Sandy says with a daydreaming look on her face. "Well, all I have to say is, he may be big like you said but this right here," she massages in between her legs and continues, "stretches to release babies. You do remember that our instructor told us, right? And it has been known to release some very large babies at that. So if his thickness is wider than or just as wide as a baby, then he needs to sign up for the *Guinness Book of World Records*. Other than that, he would have been inserting that in my second set of lips. It would not have been wasted on no damn hand job."

Let me find out Sandy is more of a freak than me, Colleen thought to herself while soaking in what Sandy just said, looking at her like she is crazy.

"Mmm - hmmm, or enter the Side Show as 'The Man Who Is Hung Like A Horse.' Hell, no offense Colleen but I'm with Sandy on that one," BeLynda responds to Sandy and stands up to stretch looking at the clock on the wall. "Y'all know I am about to go in and see Marcus, right" BeLynda is loving every detail of Colleen's story. It sounds like something straight out of a novel. *I always enjoy a hot steaming novel full of smut.*

"But what makes you think he was backed up, though," Sandy asks, still wanting to hear more.

"You didn't see what I saw. If you did, you may have ran. The combination of dick and cum was something straight out of a movie girl. Cum was all over the place. The walls, night stand, headboard … my arm. Hell, if that had gone in my pussy, y'all would have been telling me congratulations on the 'having a baby' announcement." All eyes are on Colleen really wondering if she is exaggerating.

"Why would I have ran? You didn't. This would have been a perfect time for you to be practicing some of what we've learned in class. Yet, you choked under pressure." Sandy smiles. She is getting to Colleen and she is enjoying it.

"Actually, it does sound like she *was* practicing from several classes," Regina interjects and that sends them all on the floor. If anyone walks in right now, they wouldn't believe grown women would be acting like this. Then again, they are talking about sex, so maybe it would be believable.

"Maybe, maybe not Ms. Robertson. Besides, I was concentrating on the three fingers and thumb that were working me over. Speaking of class, what do all of you think about Monday's lesson?"

"Don't try to skip the subject, winch. Anyway, I think it was very interesting. She started off talking about the vagina and penis but then went on to review about the mouth and the importance of breathing but she was looking more like she was having an orgasm standing up. When she fell back into the chairs, I thought I was going to lose it. But, ladies ... who'd thought when we started these classes, we would be doing half of the stuff they have us doing? I mean, belly rolling, hip rolling, mouth exercises, feeling on ourselves. The session that dealt with pleasuring with the hands ... now I can see that. I was learning some things. I mean, I know y'all are all right with it but I wonder how many women in the class are uncomfortable," BeLynda replies, no longer laughing but looking serious.

"Oh I'm sure you weren't the only one uncomfortable. But you should have understood the purpose of the belly and hip rolling. No man wants you just lying like a stiff board looking like you're just waiting for him to finish so he can get off of you." They all laugh agreeing with each other.

"Hell, that's like Whoopie Goldberg in *The Color Purple* when she said that 'Mister' would climb on her to do his 'business.' Just think about when you are riding that head of your mystery man. The rolls are perfect to work those abdominal muscles to get that pelvis going Girl. You have to know how to move right so you can get buck wild and have his ass screaming and curling his toes. Ump, I surely will be trying it out starting tonight. Stan has been waiting all day. He got a quickie this morning but he better watch out!"

"The instructor was talking about breathing right too in that class. Something about increasing our arousal levels, prolonging our orgasms, and having more of them big O's. Chile please, I don't need to work on no damn breathing. I'd be going for it all night if that's what it does for you. A man may think I am a nympho." Colleen swings again her legs over one of the arms of the chair.

"Hey, maybe we need to start classes for men so they can keep up with us. What you think? You never know how many of them may start taking the classes. Regardless, I have been taking notes, notes, and more notes. I'm ready to see if these classes do what the instructors are claiming they do." Sandy is thinking this is a good idea. Maybe this will be her way out of the nauseous nine-to-five workforce.

"Calm down Sandy," Regina shakes her head at Sandy.

"You're talking about starting classes for men? Heck, who'd thought there would've ever been classes like the ones we are taking? Hell, if you are serious, I will be responsible for registering them for the class. I will not be teaching," says BeLynda.

"And for four friends to be taking them together? The other women in the class come alone. And Stan still has no idea what kind of classes they are. Ha, ha, ha, you know I'm the first one in class every week getting new pointers on how to make my man skip to work and not ever think about having me get a job. Shiiit, I'm in as an instructor." They all start laughing.

"Ha, ha, ha, I know that's right!! My supervisor keeps asking me, 'So what kind of classes are you taking again Sandra?' Hmmp, maybe she'll give me a promotion once I tell her what I got my degree in. I can teach her a few things." They are laughing even harder now. They think it is exciting to attend the classes as well as it being a secret what kind of classes they are.

"That's all right. They'll be called our *Private Classes*. No one knows what we are being taught. They just know we are somewhere learning something. If I ever get another chance with

Devin, these classes are definitely going to be needed. Next week's class is about the genitals and different things we can do with them, right?"

"I think so. Maybe you'll get some pointers on how to work that well-endowed friend of yours." Sandy is smiling playing around with her vanilla wafers. "Who knows, he might be your Christmas dinner." They are really laughing now.

"Yeah, girlie. Eat that ham and turkey. Giblets and gravy too," Regina comments and winks her eye at Sandy and BeLynda.

Regina, Sandy, and BeLynda are laughing. They really are having a good time while they wait to be seen. They truly forgot they were in the Spa. Yet, that's how they are every week. They go to their private classes on Mondays and at the spa on Thursdays they catch up on each other's lives, anticipating hearing something really hot and juicy.

Colleen stands up, straightens out her robe, and gets a glass of water. "What time is it," she asks looking over at the clock on the wall. "I'm ready for my Spa cuisine now. All that laughing and talking about sex got me hungry. Whose turn is it to go first this week anyway?"

BeLynda gets up to check the time. She's relieved that they never asked her any questions about that Monday night she vomited all over the floor but she knows it is coming. "Yea, I'm a little hungry myself. However, you know Marcus comes out for me, so I'm not included in that rotation. Hey, when do the pole dancing classes start? I'm about to get a pole and stage put in my basement," BeLynda jokes around with the ladies trying to loosen up a little. They all stop what they are doing and look at her like she is crazy.

"For what? So you can sprain a wrist, break a leg, or throw your back out trying to swing around the damn thing? Can y'all see

Bee dancing on a pole? Not a good look. Not a good look at all Bee baby. And who will be it be for? Oh yea, the other half of 'we' that went over Sandy's house Thanksgiving. What's his name?"

Regina snickers at the two of them. They can be too comical at times. Just like two friends in a kindergarten sandbox. One minute they are inseparable, the next they are enemies, but in between they compete a little bit.

"Well, the class starts in about four weeks, right after this one," Sandy answers BeLynda's question, ignoring Colleen's question. She is still playing with her vanilla wafers. She doesn't even know why she got them. She and Regina hung out again today. So after having lamb chops, creamed spinach and cheese cake for lunch, she didn't need the cookies anyway.

Colleen catches on to what Sandy is doing and tries to keep down the friction so she directs the change of conversation at BeLynda to prevent her from getting upset with her.

"Bee, you're interested in more than just Marcus' hands, aren't you? You think I didn't notice? Always requesting him and when he is not here, you snap our heads off. Well, I guess he must be here today. All this time and you never said anything to him? Girl, go for it. I ain't mad at you. I think he is single but there may be a woman .... maybe two. Hell, as fine as he is, I am *sure* there is definitely a woman. Shit, he may even have a few stalkers Girl." Colleen almost chokes on her water after saying that.

"Ooh, stalkers. Please, don't go there and spoil my mood. I don't need any reminders of that damn trainer I had. I wonder what ever happened to him anyway. Hopefully he left the area," Regina says.

"Or left the fuckin' earth. Who gives a rat's ass what happened to Mr. Psychotic? Hopefully we don't have to see his ass again … ever!! That fool was past crazy. And he had the nerve to have a fucking girlfriend? How?" Sandy is frowned up crunching hard on the cookies thinking about some of the things he had done. She had been with Regina on a few occasions when he showed up from out of nowhere. "He was straight from the Looney bin and I hope he somehow found his way back there."

"As they say, there's someone for everyone." BeLynda says and they all get quiet shaking their heads in agreement.

Chapter Thirteen

13

They arrive at the next class which is on the same floor as the first class but two doors down. The good thing about this class is, they are the only students which really makes it a *private class*. They almost think class is cancelled. Or at least that Tina hasn't arrived yet. The door has a glass pane and they can see nothing is going on inside. Well at least, they think nothing is going on.

"Tina isn't here yet. Well, I guess we will just go in and wait a few minutes and see what happens,' Sandy says. Before she opens the door, they see Kelly walking down the hall.

"Excuse me Kelly. Is Tina coming to class today," inquires Regina.

Kelly softly laughs saying, "Oh yes! She is coming. As a matter of fact, she is already here. She was setting up in class earlier. If she isn't in there, just have a seat. She'll be right with you." Kelly continues walking down the hall towards the exit smiling.

"Thanks." They watch Kelly walk off down the hall.

"That girl got some hips and thighs on her," Sandy observes.

"You got that right. And look how she commands the hallway with that glide in her walk," says BeLynda.

"I'd hate to go out with her ass. She would get all the attention while I'm jumping up and down on the sideline trying to let the men to see I'm there too," says Colleen looking on too.

"Oh, so what you sayin'? That you don't have that problem with you're out with us," asks Regina.

Colleen waves her hand and Regina saying, "Girl, please. I was exaggerating. It is all in the heels baby. All in the heels. With the right size heel, our hips and ass would be moving like that too." They all laugh at Colleen's remark.

Regina opens the door. Colleen, Sandy, and BeLynda follow here into the room. They are walking slow and quiet as if they are afraid something is going to jump out at them. However, they are relatively surprise at what they see. The lights are off but the entire room is lit by candles of all different sizes in a pear and vanilla scent. There are tea lights and votives in pretty holders, and pillars in five sizes. Some are on tables. Others are on the floor or large candle stands.

There are big pretty pillows all over the floor in shades of orange, red, green, fuchsia, gold, and blue. Slow music is playing and a little ball is making different color circles appear on the walls.

The Ladies are in awe at the decorated room. They continue walking around looking at the set up. It is lovely and quixotic. *I need to set up one of the rooms in the house like this*, Regina says to herself.

There is one question about the room as they continue walking around witnessing it. The shocking thing is, a naked muscular male mannequin with a short afro is lying on a massage table. There are some oils, powders, jars, and other things on a cart by the table. What stands out as strange is the main part of the mannequin is missing.

"What in the hell are we about to do in here?" Regina is curious as she stops at the table looking at the mannequin. Taking in the entire scenery, she realizes the room is actually set up for a night of romantic intimacy.

"I don't know but I think I am going to enjoy myself. Candles, pillows, soft music. Looks like we have come to an adult toy party Ladies," says Sandy.

"Yeah, you would say that but it will be a tease for me. And what you know about adult toy parties? Oh, is that where you get your little *friends* from. Who you know sell toys? I might want to get a few," Colleen laughs.

"Oh, I bet you do. So the next time you end up at Devin's you won't have to use a damn perfume bottle. I guess that will be added to the essentials in your big ass HCL handbag," Sandy says and all the Ladies laugh.

"Well, where is the mannequin's penis? How come there is a hole instead," inquires BeLynda. "The room looks nice but how much does she really expect for us to do in front of other people?" They look at her strange because they are the only ones in the class.

Surely she isn't uncomfortable in front of her friends, wonders Regina

"Hey, maybe we need those cucumbers and bananas in this evening's class," Sandy laugh.

The women are laughing so hard they don't hear Tina enter the room. Tina is standing with her arms folded across her chest smiling. She has an idea what the laughter is all about. Tina starts walking slowly around the room but hard enough so that the women could hear her heels clicking across the floor.

Still laughing, the women turn around to see who entered the room. They are shocked at what they see. Tina has on a red sheer off-the-shoulder poet style sleep shirt that falls to the middle of her thighs. She has on the matching v-string and a pair of six inch clear color stilettos. She has a bag in one hand and a dildo in the other licking it like an ice cream cone that is melting fast and she's trying to catch all the ice cream before it falls.

BeLynda's mouth is hanging open and her eyes are open wide. Regina turns away from Tina and covers her mouth still laughing but now laughing at the scene that just entered the room. Sandy and Colleen look at one another, smile, and turn back to look at Tina.

"Oh, this is going to be *gooood*," mumbles Sandy still smiling and watching Tina.

"You think so? Well, it better be. With all this decoration and ass she gives us and a seductive entrance, I will be pissed if it isn't," responds Colleen checking out Tina's outfit. *She's wearing the HELL out of that outfit. I wonder if that's how I look in mine.*

"Well, unlike her sister Kelly, she is known to be creative with these classes. So let's hope she is not too creative. Comin' in here lickin' and shit," says BeLynda a little worried.

"Hey, ain't nothing wrong with her giving us our monies worth. We get educated, taught, and a show all at once. That is what I want," Regina says sitting down on a pillow still watching the instructor's performance.

"Hmmp, either she bought those breasts or she is younger than she looks," Colleen mumbles again still watching Tina checking out her assets. She is starting to see the resemblance between Tina and the Cardio instructor.

"Hello ladies," Tina provocatively greets the women still licking her dildo but slowly now.

"Good evening," responds Sandy. Colleen, BeLynda and Regina wait for the rest of Tina's introduction.

"How is everyone this evening?"

"We're fine," BeLynda responds this time. She doesn't want to appear to be rude. She is watching Tina sashay across the floor licking the dildo. She then turns away, not wanting to appear too interested in watching a female perform fellatio.

"Did you enjoy class with Kelly this evening?" No one responds because they're too busy watching. "C'mon, you can tell me. I won't say a word. We don't live together or compare notes. Her class is hers and mine is mine. We teach the way we see fit. So, how was it?"

"It was aiight. Nothing to jump up and down about," Colleen says very nonchalantly. Sandy looks at her thinking she must've been really uncomfortable doing those tongue exercises.

"Just all right? They will help you in quite a few classes, starting with this one. Well, relax and get ready for some fun. You may be here a little longer than an hour."

"Huh? Longer than an hour? What in the world are we about to do," asks BeLynda. She is starting to get uncomfortable.

"First, I hope no one is offended by the way I am dressed. I like to get into the mood and moment as much as possible. So if that means I get dressed, that is what I do. Is that all right Ladies? Dressing for the occasion always makes it easier to participate. Would any of you agree?"

"Don't mind us girlfriend. Go right ahead and get into it. I think you look rather sexy in your poet shirt," comments Sandy.

"Mmm-hmmm," Regina agrees with Sandy.

"Yes, you do. I walk around my house like that on my feeling sexy days all the time," adds Colleen. BeLynda rolls her eyes. She is over Colleen's foolery.

"Yeah, playing with yourself," Sandy's says with a devilish smile to Colleen.

"Don't hate because I don't mind loving me. Maybe you should try it. You just might learn something about yourself. That goes for you too BeLynda."

"Oh, don't drag me into that mess. I was just fine standing right here listening to Tina. I already know about me without having to love me *that* way," BeLynda says with an attitude.

"Awww, did I hit a nerve? I'm sorry poop-poop."

"Colleen! Cut it out. Stop aggravating people. BeLynda's aren't the only nerves you are hitting right now," Regina says.

"Oh, no disagreements in my class *friends*. You're all in this together. In between classes, have conversations with each other and see how you might can help a little more. Colleen is actually right. You will not know exactly what a man needs to do for you if you've not explored your body. It is not his job completely to satisfy. Sometimes there will be times when he won't meet his mission. But if you know how to take yourself there with him, you both will be satisfied all the time."

Colleen smiles at Tina but rolls her eyes at Regina and walks over to stand by Sandy. She hates when Regina gets forceful with her. It isn't often because Regina is a very patient person. It takes a lot to get on her nerves. So whenever she gets forceful with one of them, that means the person really needs to stop. Colleen doesn't think she is really saying anything wrong. That is a big problem because Colleen never thinks she is doing or saying anything wrong.

The instructor notices the slight tension and decides to speak up before the class ends early or be less one student. Not that the number of students matter because they have already paid. She knows they are friends and it bothers her to see friends upset with each other over small things.

"Good, I'm glad no one wants me to change my clothes. At least I have on more than what I originally had planned to wear this evening." Regina's eyebrows rise at the statement. "Now let's get started. BeLynda, will you get my bag please and hand everyone one of the items inside?" Tina knows BeLynda is the more bashful and conservative one of the group. She wants BeLynda to loosen up.

BeLynda gets the bag and walks over to her friends. She is quite nervous yet anxious to know what is in the bag. Once BeLynda approaches Sandy, she reaches inside to retrieve one of the boxes. She hands the box to Sandy noticing that it has a picture of a dildo on it. The label on the box read "Woman's Best Friend."

BeLynda knows that is not the original label. *Tina must have put this label on here,* she says to herself. Sandy smiles as she takes the box from BeLynda and begins to open it. Regina sees what it is and starts imitating Tina licking the dildo. Colleen smiles at Regina because she had the same idea. Sandy is giggling and shaking her head at Regina's antics.

BeLynda is concentrating on passing out the items that she doesn't notice what Regina is doing. After she hands Colleen and Sandy their dildo, she reaches in for hers. She is looking at it and feeling very uncomfortable. To have a fake penis in her hands is rather embarrassing and she is starting to feel like a desperate woman. BeLynda knows her friends have and use toys and objects but she just never thought to do so when she can make a phone call and enjoy a real one.

"Okay ladies. I see everyone has their gift from me. It is yours to keep. You will use it in class and at home for practice. So make sure you bring it with you because you never know when you'll need it," says Tina.

"Does using this require us to get naked at some point," asks BeLynda. Colleen's smile disappears as she looks at BeLynda with irritation on her face. Sandy just holds her head down shaking it in disbelief as to what BeLynda just asked.

"It's up to you Bee. However, I get the feeling that you aren't too comfortable with class this evening. If so, please do not hesitate to speak up. As I said a few minutes ago, I do not want to offend anyone."

"Girl please. Don't worry about BeLynda," responds Sandy.

"Yeah, she'll warm up in about fifteen minutes," says Regina.

"Ump, she tries to be conservative but I know it is all an act. To have friends like us, she must be undercover and don't want us to know yet," Colleen joins the comments. Everyone except BeLynda laughs. Then BeLynda smiles a little at the comment. It made her feel good to know that Colleen doesn't think she is a prude. She can get buck wild like the rest of them but there are just some things she want to keep private. As well as there are some things she just won't do.

"Okay, now that everyone has their new friend. Let's get started. Open up the package. I want everyone to get acquainted with their friend. You know, introduce yourself, look it over, and become *very* personal with it. Tell it some deep secrets about yourself. Don't hold back, it's yours. So get familiar because you and your friend are going to be real close."

Everyone is looking at the instructor like she is crazy right now. The mere thought of talking to a dildo is ridiculous. What are they suppose to say? How personal can you get without looking and feeling like you need to be in a padded room wearing a straight jacket?

Sandy is the first to take hers out of the package and looks it over. *Hmmm, this is a nice size. I wished Bee had pulled out another shade of dick for me though.* She walks over to one of the big floor pillows and sits down ready to get started on her lesson.

Regina is watching Sandy, waiting to see what she is about to do. This is weird yet interesting. *I'd rather watch someone else first before I look like Nancy Downs in the movie The Craft.*

Colleen is pretending to be reading the packaging. She has never talked to a real penis before and isn't too sure about talking to an imitation. BeLynda just hasn't given any thought to what Tina has just instructed them to do.

"C'mon ladies. What's the matter? Feeling a little strange? Pretend it is the real thing." Tina looks at the women to see their expressions. The room is full of silence and concentration. "Oh, none of you have ever sat in front of your man with his 'good' dick in your face and talk to it? You've never thanked it for the pleasure that it has given you?" Still there is no response.

Regina is rubbing her hair. Sandy has her back turned to the instructor. Colleen has her mouth open in pure shock. BeLynda ... no response or expression, just listening. "You put it in your mouth don't you? Don't you? You lick and suck all on it yet you feel uncomfortable talking to it? Really? So, you only let your pussy talk to it, huh?" She gives a sheepish grin to the Ladies. A pin can be heard if it is dropped on the floor. No one is admitting to anything. "Are you tellin' me that as friends, you don't talk about giving head? You do know that your man talks about getting head, right? So no matter what you try to hide from your girls, his boys know. So whatever looks you are trying to avoid, you are already getting them. Loosen up Ladies."

BeLynda raises her hand, asking, "How loud are we supposed to be talking? I mean, is everyone supposed to hear what we are saying to it? If I am telling deep secrets, then I don't want anyone to hear what I saying." Everyone, including the instructor look at BeLynda. She has totally thrown everyone for a loop.

"What did I tell y'all? I told you she is undercover. That's why she doesn't want us to listen to whatever she has to say. Let it out, Bee. We may be able to learn some of your tricks. The only person here you don't really know like that is Tina. But she is our teacher. Who is she gonna go tell? Hell, she may like it," Colleen says as she saunters to the opposite side of the room, winking at Sandy and Regina.

"BeLynda, you can be as loud or as quiet as you want to be with your conversation. Would you like for me to demonstrate?"

"Yeah, yeah, yeah let the pro show us how it is done," Colleen speaks up fast. "I've got to see this."

Tina glides to the center of the room and sits on a pillow Indian style. She looks at her dildo and smiles at it. She is turning it around, upside down, examining it thoroughly, and admiring how it looks. Then she lays it on the pillow, gets on her knees, and leans over it. Tina begins to speak. She has the attention of all four Ladies.

"If I had a camcorder, I would surely videotape this. This is a memorable moment," Sandy says in amazement at seeing the instructor perform.

"Hey, baby how ya doing? My name is Tina, what's yours? Do you remember me? I'm sure you do. How was your day today? Been cramped up in those boxers and pants all day, huh? Oh, uh-uh, no need to thank me for freeing you. I've been wanting to talk to you all day. I couldn't think of nothing else but you today. Well, what would you want me to do with you today? I love being creatively freaky with you. Do you want me to lick you? How about suck you? Would you do a few jerks for me if I deep throat you this evening? Ha, ha, ha my mouth is getting very watery ready to invite you in. I might rub my nipples on you on when I finish. I know you want me to put you inside me. I just want to do some other things to you first."

Sandy's mouth is open wide amazed at what Tina is doing. She has had a few dicks in her face but she has never ever thought to speak to any of them. And the men she has been with surely wouldn't have the patience of watching her doing something strange as this. When you're down there, they expect to immediately feel mouth, jaws, and tongue. There is no conversation involved. For some reason, she also thinks that it is not a bad idea.

Regina is smiling and imagining doing the technique on her L'il Stan when she gets home. That would surely give Stan another surprise. She knows Stan would go crazy to see her do that, feeling her warm breath on his head and shaft while talking to it and licking it like a lollipop. She knows it is hers and she wants to make sure it remains hers. Finding different things to do with her dick keeps the anticipation going.

Colleen is trying to maintain self composure but she is being turned on by the demonstration Tina is giving them on the life-like dildo. She likes what she is witnessing from Tina but this would only be done on the main special man in Colleen's life. Since she doesn't have one, she will give her dildo a name and keep this act private until the man comes along.

BeLynda is looking at Tina like she is a damn fool. She couldn't believe Tina was crawling around the pillow licking, rubbing, and talking to a dildo. BeLynda doesn't like oral sex so she knows this would be a tough class. Then she wonders if that is what Colleen does with her toys. The mere thought sends BeLynda into laughter. Her laughter breaks the silence and concentration of the other women. However, Tina kept right on with her performance.

"What is so funny," whispers Regina.

"Oh, I'm sorry. I just got another picture in my mind. I couldn't hold it back." BeLynda is trying to keep it together but can't stop laughing.

"What kind of picture are you seeing? This doesn't remind you of some porn flick does it," Sandy asks.

"Oh, you really don't want to know what I was thinking about. Stop talking to me and look at Tina. We're being rude." BeLynda is still laughing but quieter, with her shoulders moving up and down.

Colleen rolls her eyes at all of them. All the talk threw off her concentration. Plus she can't hear everything Tina is saying. One thing she knows for sure, Tina has no shame in her game. Colleen doesn't have any shame in her game either. However, after watching Tina, Colleen sees that she isn't as free and confident as she thinks she is.

"Okay, does everyone have an idea of what I mean? That is how I would do it. Every woman has her own style so whatever feels right to you is how you proceed. Does anyone need music to help get you in that mode of concentration? If so, let me know. I have a little of Keith Washington, Wil Downing, Joe, and the Chocolate Factory man himself. Now, no one has to demonstrate before the entire class. You may find a quiet place in the room and get started. I will be walking around the class to give pointers. There are plenty of props here if you want to use any. I have feathers, tasty powders and gels, massage oils, honey, whip cream, you name it and it is here."

Colleen gets up to get a few props. "Let me get some of the honey and whip cream. I'm hungry anyway so I might as well eat it off of my new friend."

"I know that's right," Sandy responds. It'll give you some practice so you'll ready when you wanna eat it off the real dick. I wouldn't use too much honey though. That will have your mouth sticking together like peanut butter and I don't think Tina has any milk in here for you." Sandy and Regina laugh uncontrollably. "Can you imagine having a mouth full of honey and nothing to wash it down? That whip cream surely won't be the answer. But do your thang Girl.

"Yea, y'all heifers can laugh all you want. Try it, you just might like it. It'll have you licking and sucking real slow with hard sucking pulls. Your jaws will get some serious work during that session, and he'll be climbing the wall, I'll tell you that." Regina looks at Colleen as if she is thinking, *I didn't think about that. That's not a bad idea at all. Hmm.*

"Well, tonight, I'll use the feather for now. Maybe she'll let us take one of these gels home. Stan and I have never used any of those."

"*What?!* I guess Stan is all man and don't need to bring other things into the bedroom, huh," comments Sandy.

"He is all man, no doubt about that. But we do use other props every now and again. But for the most part, certain things mess with his sexual ego. The last thing I need is for him to start thinking that he's not satisfying me. That would create a monster, for real."

"Oh whaaat? Really? Men, I tell you. They need to learn how to have some other kind of fun sometimes. I mean, really. What the fuck would it hurt to bring some props to the activity? No one said it has to be all the time. But what kinds of stuff have y'all used?"

"Um, well, we have played with things like fruits and drinks. He loves to use strawberries and whip cream. Mmm, I do too."

"Strawberries and cream? What does he like about that?" All attention is on Regina now.

"Now, that's for me to know and love and for none of you to find out. You know I tell some things but I don't tell all. I won't have none of you looking at my man all crazy when you're in his presence. So steer your imagination somewhere else. Like back to the class."

"Are the two of you just going to stand there and run your mouths? Get started. Heck, I want to get out of here and make a few phone calls," says Colleen, trying to act as if she wasn't listening to Regina and Sandy.

"Feeling kind of horny Colleen," Sandy asks.

"Hell yeah I am. You got a problem with that?"

"Nope, I sure don't. However, BeLynda is your ride home. So you better be talking to her. Where did she go anyway?" They all start looking around the room.

All three of them look over at BeLynda. She has the dildo stuffed down the front of her blouse and speaking into it like it is a microphone.

"Has she lost her fuckin' mind," asks Colleen.

"Let's just say she is following Tina's instructions *her* way," Sandy says. The Ladies laugh hysterically.

Chapter Fourteen

14

Yuck! These tomatoes look nasty. Makes me not want to get any of them from here. I must've come in here on the wrong day. Need to find out the day their shipments come in because it looks like I'm wasting my damn time in here. These nectarines only look good enough for compost. All these damn fruit flies over here, what is going on? Let me go over there to see what the bananas look like. Those are what I really came in here for anyway. BeLynda grabs the handle of her cart pushing it over to the bananas to take a look at them.

Okay, good. The bananas are nice and green, just the way I like them. Once they are yellow, I don't want them. They start turning black too fast and then I have to make banana bread or muffins. There's no need for me to worry about that though. These aren't for eating anyway. Bananas! I am really curious as to what Kelly is going to have us do with these damn bananas. Oh yeah, she said cucumbers and potatoes too. Hmmm, hope we are not going to be inserting these anywhere. Lockjaw!!

BeLynda laughs out loud. She is really laughing hard. Customers start looking at her like she is crazy. A few smile because it is obvious that she is enjoying herself. She can't help it. All she can think about is Colleen talking about King-of-the-Mandingo- Tribe *Devin*. She decides which cucumber she wants and puts it in the top basket of her cart. *I think I better get two of these just in case and ask Colleen to compare them to Devin,* BeLynda says to herself. She laughs even more at her own comment.

As she is walking towards the potatoes, still laughing, she takes a look at the squash and zucchini. *Hmm, that would be an interesting veggie to use,* she thinks. Not paying attention, she bumps into a cart. The cart runs into the onion stand, making a loud noise while knocking over about eight bags of onions onto a man. *How embarrassing!* BeLynda looks around the produce section to see how many people had free tickets to front row seats to embarrassing moment.

"Excuse me! Oh, I am sooo sorry! I wasn't paying attention to where I was going. Let me get these onions out of your way. I can't believe I did that." BeLynda bends down to pick up a few bags of onions. She doesn't even want to show her face.

"That's quite all right. No problem. You were in your own little world. I saw you laughing a few minutes ago. Your mind must've been deep in thought about either the squash or the cabbage. Which one was it," the deep voice of the man said to her. She can see out of her peripheral that he is wiping onion skins off of his slacks.

Quite embarrassed, BeLynda looks up at the man in front of her still stooping to pick up the bags of onions. She stands to respond and realizes they have met before. She places the bags that she has in her hands back on the pile with the rest of the onions that are still intact. She bends down to pick up a few more and she speaks.

"Hey, hello, how are you? What are you doing over on this side of town? I don't recall ever seeing you in this neighborhood or in this Safeway before." BeLynda is all smiles while placing the onions back on the table.

This is out of character for BeLynda, for a change. Normally, she would have pretended not to have noticed the man and wait for him to say something to her first. Then, if he doesn't say anything, she knew not to even bother about bringing it up. Today is different. She feels like engaging in a conversation with a stranger she has seen at least once before. She picks up the last few bags of onions.

The man smiles back at BeLynda, looking a little confused. "Hello. I'm fine, thanks. Ah, have we met before? You're talking to me as if we've been introduced. I mean, you do look familiar. Not to be insulting, please refresh my memory. Where do we know each other from?"

"Well, we weren't actually formally introduced before. But, we crossed paths at the Zanzibar. Saturday night at the Zanzibar as a matter of fact. We danced," responds BeLynda excitedly.

"*Really*?! Is that right? We danced? How did I forget *that*?" The handsome stranger is checking her out and the look on his face tells BeLynda that he is satisfied with what he sees.

"Yes, we did. We danced for several songs to be exact. But, don't worry about it. We never even said two words to each other.

You walked up to a Lady on the dance floor, danced with her, and that was that. That Lady was me but I know my dancing was nothing to remember. Plus, we were out having a good time and not trying to get picked up by anyone, right? You have a nice day, okay? Oh, again, I'm very sorry for bumping into your cart and making such a mess all over you."

BeLynda doesn't realize she has been holding the last two bags of onions all this time. She places them back on the pile and brushes off her hands and clothes trying not to make eye contact with the stranger at this point. She is really ready to walk away. He doesn't remember her and that is enough to weaken her spirit for the rest of the week. She can't hurry up out of that section fast enough.

The attractive stranger notices her sudden rush to leave the scene. BeLynda is pushing her cart extremely fast to get to the canned meat aisle. He stands there watching her for a few minutes until she disappears into the aisle. Looking around observing some of the customers who are busy shopping, he says to himself, *Well, I fucked that up*. Running his hand across his face in a frustrating manner, he decides to go after her.

He walks to the aisle he saw her enter. When he reaches it, he sees she is half-way the aisle and her cart is down at the other end. She begins to walk towards her cart with an item in her hand. He calls after her loud enough to still be subtle without causing attention to the situation.

"Hold up!! Wait a minute Miss Lady! Did I say something wrong," he asks while jogging up to BeLynda. "Why are you rushing off? One minute you were smiling engaging me with conversation, the next, you look like you don't want to be bothered. What just happened? What did I do?" He catches up to her and taps her on the shoulder. He starts to politely grab her arm but he isn't sure of the response he may receive if he touches her. He doesn't want any problems, especially in the grocery store.

"Oh, um, nothing is wrong. Really, I'm fine. I just came in here for a few items. I really need to get going. It was nice seeing you again though." BeLynda just wants to have the moment over with. This man is making the moment linger and it is pissing her off. *First I knock over about a million bags of funky ass onions on him and then he doesn't even remember me. Just turn around and go down another aisle please. Anywhere as long as it is far away from me. Forget my face. Forget I said anything to you.* BeLynda closes her eyes and pinches the bridge of her nose.

"Oh, okay. I was just checking to make sure everything is all right. You looked like something bad had happened." *Yea, it did nigga. You didn't remember me ass-hole,* BeLynda is responding in her mind. "Well, it was nice seeing you too." BeLynda faintly smiles and begins to walk away towards her cart. The man stops her one more time with a question. *Dammit!!* "By the way, what is your name? Through the entire incident, you never told me."

"It's BeLynda. My name is BeLynda but my friends call me Bee." BeLynda gives a weak smile but is really trying to get to back to her cart fast. She just wants the handsome man to disappear out of her face and out of her way. She could care less what his damn name is.

"Nice to actually meet you BeLynda. My name is Paul. I do not live on this side of town. I was on my way home from a friends' house and decided to stop in here to get a few things myself. Sooo am I allowed to call you Bee? Or is that just for old friends?" Paul smiles showing those perfect bright white teeth encased in a pair of kissable lips.

Ignoring his question, she says, "Oh, okay Paul. Now I have a name to attach to the face. I guess I'll be seeing you around since you have friends over this way. Well, I better be going. It was nice meeting you Paul, really." BeLynda wants to gag at herself. She forces a smile across her lips and takes a step to walk away. Paul steps in her way one more time. She looks up at him trying to figure out why he is pressing this chance meeting.

"Umm, do you live around here BeLynda," Paul asks while placing his hands in the pockets of his bomber jacket.

Damn, why won't he shut up already?! He is stalling for some reason and I am already past the beginning of my uncomfortable moment. Don't make me get loud on you in this fuckin' store. "Not too far from here. Normally I don't shop here. Well, see you around Paul. I really have to get going," BeLynda looks at her watch for an effect.

Paul catches the hint, tilts his head towards her saying, "Forgive me for holding you up. I just wanted to make sure we knew each other's names before we left this place. Plus, now that I know you live in this neighborhood, I look forward to running into you again. Hopefully, the next time we don't have carts," Paul gives a handsome smile that BeLynda tries not to get caught up in. She smiles as she walks off, rolling her eyes once she is away from his face. *Fine Ass Jerk*, she says to herself.

BeLynda walks back over to produce section, thinking she has lost him for the rest of her shopping. She finally gets over to the potatoes. *Now, where was I before I showed everyone in the store that I was clumsy?* Walking over to the potatoes, she decides to leave them there. They are too big and odd shaped. Whatever Kelly has in mind, BeLynda already knows they aren't going to fit. Then all of a sudden, it hits her. She starts looking around the produce section to see who is in that section and what items they are putting in their carts. Other than the man stocking the fruits and vegetables, there are only women in the section.

BeLynda starts really paying close attention to what they are putting in their baskets and carts. Some are picking up lettuce, radishes, and celery. Others are focusing on green beans and collards. A few are picking up avocados and tomatoes but she notices many are picking cucumbers, zucchinis, and bananas. She wonders if she is the only one in the store getting food for something other than to eat. She doesn't see any of the other women from the class but, the class is offered at other times and days of the week.

At that moment, BeLynda puts on her shades and rushes towards the cold drinks aisle. She gets a few of the Minute Maid Light drinks out of the refrigerators and places them in her cart. The regular drinks have too much sugar in them and all it does is go to her hips, butt, and thighs so she tries to watch the sugar.

BeLynda gets in line to pay for her items and still looking at what other customers have in their carts. It had never dawned on her before when she would come into the store if anyone was getting items for sexual fun. This is making her very uncomfortable. *Maybe I should have gotten some other items too so it wouldn't be noticeable. Hell, what am I trippin' for? No one is paying me any attention just like I normally don't.*

At that very moment, she sees Paul again but he is turning down the crackers, cookies, and chips aisle. *Hmmp, he's a junk food eater. Lazy ass,* she says to herself. She puts her items up on the belt, the cashier greets her with a smile and rings them up. BeLynda looks around to see if she sees Paul one more time while she pays the cashier. She doesn't see him while she is grabbing her bags out of the cart, exiting the store to walk to her car.

Putting the groceries in the trunk, out of her peripheral vision, BeLynda notices a car pull up beside her. She pretends she doesn't see the car. She doesn't acknowledge the car just in case it is someone she doesn't want to be bothered with. She has had enough of that in the store. *Could this be someone from the class? Did they see what I bought and want to say something about it?* BeLynda continues doing what she is doing still pretending not to notice the car. *Maybe they are just waiting for me to leave the parking space.* She doesn't know if she is being paranoid over something or nothing.

"Hey, BeLynda, I didn't catch your last name," the handsome voice of just a few minutes ago says from the car.

It is Paul. Shit, why doesn't he move on already! BeLynda stands up, takes off her shades, and turns around to face Paul in his car. Paul is sitting in the driver's seat of a new 2003 Jaguar XK8. *Mmmmp, no paper tags or dealer tags,* she observes. *No wonder there was something jerk-ish about him through that conversation. You must think you're too good for me or something, don't you? What do you do for a living Mr. Paul?*

BeLynda stands there looking at Paul. He has a big grin on his face. He has no idea what she is saying to herself. "I didn't throw it at you. No offense, uh Paul, but why are you hanging around? Are you feeling guilty because you didn't remember me from a few days ago? Don't worry yourself. It was only a few dances. Really, I'm all right. I am quite sure if you didn't have any friends in this area, we would have never seen each other again." BeLynda turns around raises her arm to close her trunk and Paul continues ...

"No, no, no you have it all wrong. I'm not feeling guilty at all. I'm not trying to bother you either. Really, I just wanted to know if I can call you sometimes. I don't want to have to keep coming up to the Safeway sitting in the parking lot hoping that it is the right day and time to see you again."

BeLynda blushes at what Paul just said. She think it's cute. If he was trying to make me smile, he was successful. But she puts her serious face back on and asks, "Call me sometimes? Why? And to be sitting up her waiting to see me sounds a little stalk-ish, don't you think?" BeLynda turns back around to face Paul, with her trunk still open. She isn't exactly sure why she is so annoyed. She is attracted to him a little. Maybe it is because she didn't make an impression on him in order to be remembered. *Colleen may have a point about me acting and dancing so grandma-ish.*

BeLynda just wishes the scene in the grocery store never happened or would start over. She won't be sharing this situation with anyone. It will forever be between her and Paul. She would rethink speaking if she had the opportunity to rewind the scene. Hell, Khalil likes her but, right now, that isn't enough. She wants to know she is appealing and attractive to more than just one man. At this very moment, she wants to know if she is attractive to the man sitting in the Jaguar that she knocked all those bags of onions on.

"Not to make it up to you BeLynda, if that's what you think. I can see you thinking. Just slow down, please. Look, I want to call you because I am attracted to you. I want to see what BeLynda is all about outside of Safeway's produce section and the Zanzibar. I'm really glad you bumped into my cart. Honest, I am. We both could have been in the store and never seen each other. Then my opportunity to get to know you would have been lost. Who would have thought I would run into you here?" BeLynda is listening to him knowing damn well he is full of shit.

He smiles, looking at her turn back around attempting to close her trunk again and continues, "However, of all the things to rush to the store for. Bananas, cucumbers … and juice? What are they for? Some type of homemade smoothie?" BeLynda is fumbling with her scarf now trying to not seem uncomfortable by his questions. "By the way, you never told me which of those items had you in that trance. The squash or the cabbage?" Paul is still showing off his beautiful teeth, slightly leaning over to look at the grocery bags BeLynda has placed in the trunk.

BeLynda doesn't want to get into that conversation. Especially with a stranger, that she has only seen twice in her life, and is just learning his name about twenty minutes ago. Lord knows if she really tells him what she is going to do with those vegetables, he might think she is a freak and speed off. She reaches in her purse for a pen and tears off a piece of brown paper grocery bag to write her cell phone number on it. *Cell phone number is perfect just in case I am dealing with a lunatic.*

"Here's my number. Enjoy the rest of your evening Paul. I really have to go. I am running late. I should have pulled off fifteen minutes ago. I stayed in the store longer than planned." She hands him the piece of paper and walks back toward her car.

He looks at the number, then back at BeLynda, watching her hips help her plump cheeks sway like melons as she walks towards her car door. He smiles and says, "I really liked those suede boots you had on the other night. They went great with your skirt. Together, they complimented your sexy legs."

BeLynda stops putting her leg in her car when she heard him say that. She looks back at him, shocked. Paul winks at her, pushes the button for his window to close up and drives off. She watches him pull off with her mouth open in a slight grin and blushes as she sits down in the car. Shutting the door, she says, "He remembers me. He actually remembers me after all. The entire time, he was playing coy." After her moment of inner excitement, she realizes he didn't give her his number.

His ass didn't give me his number. Damn!! What is with these men not exchanging numbers? What does that mean? Oh, I'm sure he doesn't think I am a stalker or some fatal type of chic. Now I am gonna have to wait for him to call me. That's IF he decides to call. Okay, Mr. Jaguar is trying to take control of the situation, huh!! I will show him how control is done.

BeLynda puts the key in the ignition starting the car and pushes radio button number two for 93.9 WKYS. They are playing Beyoncé's *Baby Boy*, again. *Damn, they are gonna wear this song into the damn ground,* she says while putting on her Isotoner leather driving gloves. BeLynda turns the volume up to thirty just enough to pump the sounds without sounding like she wore sagging pants off her ass, and pulls off.

Maybe I will be leading the conversation at our next Spa appointment. All right Paul, let's see if I get to keep you around ... or stick with Khalil.

Ring! Ring!

"Yo!"

"Yea, what's up? Where you at? What's all that noise in the background? That doesn't sound like you're home or at the gym."

"You're right. I'm not. So don't worry about where I'm at bruh. I'm out handling some business right now. Did you get that thing done that I asked you to do for me yet? Or you still procrastinating on the shit? I don't have all year for you to make a move."

"Yea, it's done. Ain't nobody procrastinating doing a damn thing. I do have a life and it doesn't revolve around you or your bullshit. But, I just finished talking to her."

"Oh you did? Aiight. How did it go? Was it easy as I thought? Or did she make it hard for you?" The deep voice chuckles softly. "Did you have any problems getting next to her? That was a smooth move you did at the club. Just gave her enough to remember you."

"Nah, it went aiight. It took a little longer than I had expected it to, you know. I thought I wasn't going to be successful today because I sort of pissed her off by pretending not to remember her. But she finally took the bait. I just left her standing on the other side of the parking lot of the grocery store. I see her pulling off right now."

"The grocery store? How'd you do that? Damn, my nigga … now *that's* what I'm talkin' 'bout. Be about your shit!! Good! I likes that. She is a back up anyway just in case it doesn't work out with the other one. She seems to be closer to that other bitch anyway. So don't call her until I tell you to. She is plan B. I just wanted to make sure I had an alternative route if needed. What kind of car is she driving?"

"Aight. Good. I hope it does work out with the other chick. You know I can't be getting all tied up with these women for you causing problems for me and my own Lady. And she drives an Avalon. Well, at least that's what she is driving today."

"An Avalon? Damn!! Oh, so she hangs with two average ass bitches and one with money? They must've been friends for a long time. Fuck, she needs to be plan C but it doesn't matter, she probably won't be used anyway."

"Hey, I'm about to stop past Hogate's to get something to eat. You wanna meet me down there so we can finish talking? You didn't give me all the information to this plan of yours. And what does the kind of car she drives have to do with anything? What … you tryin' to see who has money? I'm not trying to be blindsided by some fucked up surprise. You know you're famous for that shit and I'm not doing any jail time being a fuckin' accomplice."

"Fuck NO I'm not meeting you down there!! You just met the bitch and her friends down at The Zanzibar the other night. *Now*, you wanna be seen with me a few buildings down from there? That ain't happenin'. I wanted to know the car she drives because I wanted to know the car she drives. And you will get tied up with whoever I say you get tied up with. If I say kiss her, then your muhfuckin' ass will kiss her. If I say fuck her, then you will fuck her. If I say propose to that straight-up-and-down bitch, then you will propose ALL THE WAY TO THE FUCKING ALTAR!! You ain't in charge of this nigga. I'm running this show and this ain't over until my plan is executed. Plus, that broad you dealing with and calling your Lady … trade her in bruh, and fast. She ain't you."

"Hey, it was just a damn question. I didn't wanna sit across from you while eating and digesting my food anyway. And don't worry about who I'm dealing with. This is my business and ain't nobody asked you for your dumb ass opinion. And look here bruh, if I don't want to get tied up with any of them bitches in your mess, then I won't. Who the fuck is in your face that you feel the need to impress? Don't act all gorilla on the other end of this phone!! This is *your* shit, not mine nigga!!! I can end this conversation right now and never have to hear anything else about this shit muhfucka!! But I tell you what, *whatever* it is you got planned, I'm tellin' you … kidnapping, murder, extortion … your ass is on your own!! My name won't be connected."

"Blah, blah, blaaah, whatever nigga. Just make sure if we don't get it to work with that other bitch, that you are gonna be ready to step to this one. Did you tell her your real name? I know she's not your type. But you just might like something different," the deep voice laughs on the phone.

"Yea, yea, whateva. Naw, I didn't give her my real name. For what? When your shit gets fucked up which it probably will, and you have to go to plan C, if she comes looking for me, she won't know where to look. And what you know about my type? How many times ... *click*.

He looks at his phone saying to himself, *This motherfucka just hung up on me? Oh he has lost his damn mind. I see he keeps forgetting who is the oldest and how many times I done had to whip that ass already. I will let this bullshit blow up in his face if he keeps fuckin' with me. I got a baby on the way and his stupid mess ain't important to me. All this bullshit over a woman who ain't ever been his. Idiot!*

The man better known as Paul to BeLynda slams his cell phone shut and puts it on the charger. He sits there for a few minutes with his hands on the steering wheel watching people from the other end of the grocery store parking lot. Letting out a big sigh he begins to perspire under his arms profusely. He is pissed and exasperated with his brother. Starting up the car, he turns up the volume on his Bob James' CD trying to clear his mind by getting into the groove of *Let's Just Say Good-bye*. Driving, he continues up Indianhead Highway in the direction of Southwest Waterfront Washington DC.

When he gets to a light, he pulls the torn brown paper bag with BeLynda's number on it out of his bomber jacket pocket and looks at it. He balls it up real tight and shakes his hand in fury.

FUCK!! I don't have time for this shit!! Why do we get ourselves caught up in his bullshit all the damn time?!!

He places the paper in his glove compartment to make sure his woman doesn't find it in any of his clothes. *Yea, I'ma put this in here. She don't check my car. I don't have time for no questions and then have to explain it. It would definitely sound like a lie. Plus, she can't stand his ass anyway. He will not be the cause of me losing my woman and not being in my child's life. Hmmp, she's not my type. Nigga fuck you!!*

Bomp! Bomp!

He snaps out of his thoughts and realizes the light is green. He pulls off and continues down the street still hoping that his involvement ends with only talking to BeLynda in the store.

Chapter Fifteen

15

Colleen is laying across her bed watching the morning news on Channel 4. It is just so depressing. All they talked about were the Sniper murder trials, the new copycat sniper cases in Ohio, the serial arsonist, Michael Jackson's new charges, and the Iraq murders, just sickening. Sometimes Colleen just wants to stay in the house, not answer the phone and ignore the outside world. She would probably feel better if she could watch Oprah but she doesn't come on until four in the evening. *If I don't watch her for nothing else, I at least watch Oprah to check out her shoes. She stays classy wearing Christian Louboutins on those feet. Watching her show is where I was introduced to the "red bottom" shoes.*

"Aaaagh," Colleen screams while stretching, "I don't want to do anything today. All my appointments ... just go away! Damn, I wish I could have known two weeks ago I wasn't going to feel like doing anything today. Aaaagh!" She talks out loud as if there is someone there listening to her.

She walks into her office to take a look at today's schedule. It's Wednesday and Colleen usually has a heavier schedule on hump day. Mainly because there aren't any personal things scheduled on Wednesdays, so she books many of her clients on this day to free up the rest of the week. Today, she has five appointments.

"Who am I scheduled to see today? Let's see, Veronica is at ten this morning for decorations and her final payment. Anna is scheduled for eleven-fifteen but will probably get here at eleven-thirty. I have her final menu ready so she can sign her contracts and leave a payment. Her deposit has been paid and she had her food tasting two weeks ago. Olivia should be real quick. Hopefully she gets here early. I don't know why I scheduled her for one-thirty. Must've been thinking about lunch."

Ring! Ring!

Colleen's business phone is ringing interrupting her checking her schedule. She presses the speaker phone button and continues to look at her appointments. She didn't bother to check the Caller ID.

"This is Colleen. How may I help you?"

"Hi, Colleen. This is Martha Sumner."

"Martha Sumner?" Colleen doesn't recognize the name.

"Yes, I have a two-fifteen appointment with you today."

Checking her schedule, she sees her name. No wonder she doesn't know the name. This is her first appointment with the lady. Colleen sees she was referred by a previous client. *That's right, help to keep my business going people*, she says to herself.

"Okay, yes, Ms. Sumner. I see you are coming in for a consultation. Is there a problem?" Colleen is hoping that she doesn't need to reschedule for a later time or another day. She needs to know if she is going to actually hire her to do her event. This is how she keeps up with her budget.

"Oh, there's no problem. I just wanted to know if I needed to bring anything with me. You know, deposits, lists, pictures, things like that?"

"Oh no, not today, just bring you. We will just be going over what you want for your event, what you expect and line them up with what I offer and provide. However, to keep from forgetting anything, make sure you write down all your questions so there won't be any misunderstandings. Does that sound good?"

"Oh, okay. That answers my questions. I am so excited yet nervous. I just want everything to be right."

"Don't worry Ms. Sumner, everything will be just fine. You are in good hands. I'm sure you won't be disappointed. Are you coming by yourself? Or will you be bringing someone with you?"

"No, my mother will be with me. Is that all right?"

"That's great. Mothers can sometimes remember details that we forget. I look forward to seeing both of you at two-fifteen." Colleen has her business voice on, sounding all professional.

"All right. We'll see you then Ms. Jeffries." *click*.

Colleen still in her pajamas gets comfortable in her chair and goes back to looking at her schedule, talking out loud to herself. "She sounded intelligent and courteous. I haven't had one of those in a while."

"Now … where was I? Oh yeah, don't need to go over this one, she just called and confirmed. This last one is … oh, Dana. I can scratch her off since she cancelled her contract with me. Well, now I have four appointments. I just might get a chance to just chill a little today. I didn't want to work with her ghetto ass anyway. Let me look at her contract. Hopefully she cancelled too late to get her entire deposit back." Colleen walks over to her files and retrieves Dana Jones' folder.

Looking at this file, I should have seen the signs. This lady changed her menu four times, trying to cut some damn cost. Yeah, it looks like Mama 'n nem are going to be her coordinators all right. She was too ghetto anyway. The first time we met, she walked in with half her head in braids and the other side in a little bush. Why would she have made a braid appointment that close to her appointment with me? Another time she came with rollers in her head, eating chicken with mambo sauce and trying to rush me because she needed to go sit under the dryer. I don't rush through shit when it comes to my business. I need to keep those referrals coming in. Yeah, it was best that she cancelled. I could see me cursing her ugly ass out and then taking her to small claims court to collect the rest of my damn money.

The good thing about it though, she waited too late so she only gets one-third of her deposit back. I'll write "void" on this contract, make a copy through this fax machine and mail it to her. Knowing her silly ass, she may be looking for more money. Let me highlight this clause so there won't be any confusion when she gets the money order for one hundred and sixty-six dollars.

"Oh well, I guess I better look like I am running a business here. So I'll put on a suit and pin this stuff up into a ponytail. I'm hungry but don't feel like cooking anything. Sure would be nice if Maria worked for me on some days. Maybe I will ask Regina how much they pay her. I might be able to find me one. For the time being, I will call Byron to see if he will be able to bring me breakfast and lunch." Colleen closes the folder and proceeds to call Byron.

"Hello," his deep voice comes through the phone sending chills through Colleen's body. She can tell he is in his car. A dead giveaway is the loud rap blaring in the background. The beat of Ludacris' *Act a Fool* coming through his Bose system is his driving song. Byron swears he is a part of the *2 Fast 2 Furious* movie when it comes to that driving. However, his driving song before this was *Move Bitch*. He is a die-hard Ludacris fan and Colleen is glad he never tried to sport that damn bush.

"Hey Byron, this is Colleen. How are you today Mr. Jackson?"

"Hey sexy, I'm doing just great now that you called. Wait a minute, hold on." He puts her on hold and she could hear him turn down the music. "Now, what can I do for you Ms. Candy? You need more supplies?" Byron had given her the nickname Candy because he says she reminds him of the Cameo song.

"As a matter of fact I do but I am calling about something else," Colleen is twirling one of her curls on her finger, blushing. She loves when he calls her Candy.

"Something else, huh? Is that right? Something else like what? What does my Candy need from me? You know I am your all-purpose man."

They both laugh at his last statement. There have been plenty of times that Byron had supplied all of Colleen's needs. From paper, pens, and toner to car maintenance and sex. When she first met him, he was coming to her house to drop off her new car. When she peeped through the blinds and saw a fine ass brother pull up into her driveway with a muscular arm controlling the steering wheel, she had to pick her mouth up off the floor. She ran up to her bedroom and quickly put on the tightest pair of jeans she could find that would accentuate her thick thighs and basketball butt.

"Byron you are so crazy."

"Hey, I'm only telling the truth. You know I am."

"Well, I am calling because I am going to be pretty tied up here with my clients. I haven't had a chance to cook and I am sort of hungry. So if you are going to be out and about, would you please bring me something to eat?"

"Oh, that's all? I thought you were going to offer me a few hours of some fun. But I'm sure I can handle that. What would you like?"

"Whatever you feel like buying. I won't be choosy today."

"Oh, you won't, huh? So what if I make myself your dessert? Will you be choosy then?" Colleen can't see his face but she can tell by his tone that he has a devilish smirk on his face.

"You know I am never picky when it comes to you," Colleen laughs. "However, I will have to have my dessert later. I told you I am going to be pretty tied up here today. I don't want no quickie."

"Mmmp, I hear you baby. I will hold you to that. I don't want to disappoint you. I will make sure you are full and satisfied until you won't want anymore dessert. Okay, Candy baby. I will be there in the hour with your food."

"Thank you so much Byron. I really appreciate it." *click*

Colleen walks out of her office and into her clothes room to decide which suit she is going to wear. Pushing the button on her motor clothes rack, she starts laughing to herself as she reminisces about the nights she spent with Byron. They were off the chain. They always started off with either dinner at a nice restaurant or a get together at his house. He is such the entertainer in all areas. He knows how to treat a woman the way she wants to be treated. Byron makes sure he isn't satisfying her based on what another woman may have told him in the past. Colleen would be extremely stuffed from food and orgasms when it was all said and done. She will have to admit though. Byron is the man and has taught her quite a few things.

She remembers one night especially. She attended one of his fight parties. Shane Mosley was fighting Oscar De La Hoya for the second time. She knew she was looking teasingly sexy that night. She purposely dressed to have the women jealous, for the men to be envious of Bryon, and to have Byron wishing everyone would go home early. She wasn't even there to watch the fight. She just wanted to see Byron's sexy ass in his element of being home, having a good time with friends, good food, and drinks. Then she had hoped that he would ask her to go home the next day.

Byron eyed her all night, smiling, winking, and licking his lips, while sipping on his drinks. A few times she had to laugh when he started tilting a bottle of beer before it was up to his lips, spilling it on his Black Label cashmere turtleneck. She knew she was in for a fun and ecstasy-filled night after witnessing that. He was in a deep trance. That's exactly the effect she was going for. Colleen was ready too because he was looking just as sexy as she was.

Some of the women that were there by themselves must have been some of his old dealings. Especially since he didn't bother to introduce her to any of them, and that was cool with her. She never asked who they were because she sure as hell didn't care. She just strutted around being cordial and keeping small talk, pretending to be sociable but really only letting them get a good look at all of the playground Byron was going to be playing in when they took their asses home, pissed.

Plenty of his male friends were hoping she was a relative. Most of them would just stare at her as if they could eat her up. A few did try to strike up a conversation, and she was polite but they got the vibe that she wasn't there for any of them. So they would walk away all cool to the visible eye but actually with their egos stuck between their legs.

While everyone was eating, engrossed into either the fight or a conversation, Byron grabbed Colleen by the hand and they disappeared outside into the gazebo and had a very memorable experience. Some of the guests noticed the move.

He sat down on the bench rubbing his hardness looking so serious and nervous she thought he was getting ready to do something like propose. Colleen asked, "Byron, what's wrong? What's going on? Why you bring me out here?" She was thinking, *I know damn well this neegro ain't about to tell me some chick he dealing with just pulled up to the house and I have to leave. Oh, I'm about to give him an earful and when I walk out this damn door, it will be good night and good riddance.*

However, Bryon instead smiled and said, "I thought I was gonna be able to wait until after everyone left and do some playing with you. I've been trying to hold out for the past two hours. I need you now baby. I know you want me right now too. All those sexual signals you've been giving me." Byron walked over to Colleen and ran his finger tips against her nipples that were already erect. Colleen shivered a little at the feel of his touch.

"I been watching your firm nipples through your sweater all night and I need to put them in my mouth. Let me please you right now to the point that *I* am calling *your* name. Tell me what you want me to do." His dick was about to break the zipper on his jeans. *Damn, it looked so good.* Colleen's mouth started to drool for just a taste of him while they were outside on his gazebo.

Colleen remembers how that night, when he said those words to her, she thought she was dreaming. No man had ever said something like that to her before. Byron was about satisfying her through his wants and that put him at the top of her list of Options. That was a true turn on and her clitoris was getting swollen by the minute from pure horniness. Luckily for Colleen, the Donna Karan denim skirt she had on may have hugged her thighs but was an A-Line cut, offering easy maneuvering. All she had to do was lift it.

There was nothing she could really say to him but, "Just please me the way you want to for now. After everyone is gone, I will put in my special request."

Byron smiled at her, stood and went to work. His tongue, hands, and warm dick had her forgetting they were outside and he had a house full of people. Every strong intense thrust and position had her body trembling on a verge of convulsion. He was reaching areas she didn't know would make her feel the way she was feeling. It was so good that she was calling his name in soft whimpers. He had her pussy singing a lovely tune to him. From time to time, he would respond to her pussy saying, "Yeah, I hear you talking to me. That's right, get sloppy wet for me baby. My dick loves that," without missing a thrust or movement. Byron was truly long stroking her.

She knew the neighbors had to hear everything but she didn't even care. Juices were everywhere and Colleen didn't want it to end. The air smelt of wonderful sex and Byron was totally turned on by it. After he had made her have four orgasms, he really went to work. He had held out as long as he could. He started moaning and growling saying, "Aww, baby. Damn your pussy is so wet and hot. Shit!" Three more hard thrusts and he exploded with so much force. Colleen squeezed her inner muscles and he grabbed her hips moaning like an injured animal. He just stood there inside of her a few minutes until he was drained.

They regrouped, fixed their clothes and finally decided to go back inside and join everyone else. Colleen was ready to throw them all out so Byron could move on to the next phase of their private night, which was to do to her what she wanted him to do. She thought some of the women were looking at her funny. It could have just been her conscious. Nope, she knew they were looking at her funny. She went straight to the bathroom to check out how she looked. She didn't want to be walking around looking all crazy making it obvious that she had just been in some delectable positions with the Host outside in the gazebo.

Colleen freshened up so she could mingle with the other guests for two long hours. She had no other choice but to exhibit patience. That was not her house however, after the fight was over, Byron was going to be all hers. Colleen had told Byron previously that she likes plenty of foreplay and every time they hooked up, he was more than happy to play for her. So she couldn't wait until the last guest was out the door so he could put his skills in motion. Of course when you are in a hurry, time seems to stand still … and the damn fight went twelve fucking rounds. Then some of the guys acted like they wanted to hang around a little longer since Shane won the fight. Or maybe they were trying to cock block.

Once Byron finally saw the last guest out the door, made sure they had gotten into their car, and pulled off, he turned around to look for Colleen and saw her walking upstairs. "Unh – unh, where you going," he says smiling at the sway of her hips looking like a wave in the ocean. She turned around, looked at him and said, "I thought I would meet you in the bedroom, unless you have somewhere else in mind for me to meet you."

Colleen stood there with her hand on her thick right hip pushed out, which made the skirt struggle against it. Byron gave her that sexy devilish grin of his and started walking towards her. Colleen could see the front of his jeans had started to puff out. He started snapping his fingers, doing a smooth two-step, and sang like Larry Blackman:

♪ It's like Candy

I can feel it when you walk

Even when you talk, it takes over me

You're so dandy

I wanna know

Can you feel it too just like I do

Woo ♪

Colleen had to laugh and shook her head at him because he was making her blush. He was so silly but in a sexy way. When he reached the steps she was standing on, he wrapped his arms around her waist and gave her a sensuous, serious, stimulating, sexual kiss full of so much tongue and meaning. They stood there for a few minutes kissing, exploring each other's mouths. She was so into the kiss, she didn't realize that when he pulled back from her, all of their clothes were at the bottom of the stairs. She didn't even remember taking anything off. That night, she named it the "4S Trick."

Byron gave her the most euphoric round of foreplay right there on the stairs. She was gone after four more orgasms just on mere foreplay. She truly stroked his superego that night. Her screams, moans, and grabs let him know he had gotten the job done. Byron had licked, massaged, sucked, and stroked every nook and cranny she had until she couldn't take it anymore.

Byron finally entered her for the second time that night and to her surprise, she was still tight. They went at it for what seemed like hours had gone by before he finally exploded powerfully. That explosion seemed more forceful than the one he had earlier that night. Byron sounded like he was in pain. His Akita started howling right along with him. Byron scared Colleen a little but she felt proud to know she had that affect on him as well.

Once Byron got himself together he grabbed her hand and led her to the bedroom. He was completely drained by this time. They laid down, spooned, and went to sleep. Colleen was in heaven and more than likely Byron was too. Two hours later, he was up, ready for round three. He had put a beating on her box some kind of delicious.

Colleen snaps out of her trance focusing back on today. She has been standing in her clothes room with the motor clothes rack going around and around. She completely forgot about choosing a suit and getting dressed for her clients. Byron is supposed to come by before her first client. After all that reminiscing, she can actually take her dessert now. Their many nights together have been delicious but none of them have been better or the same as the night she was just thinking about.

Ding-dong!! Ding-dong!

Colleen blinks out of her thoughts when she hears her doorbell ring. She cuts off the motor rack and heads downstairs to answer the door. She knows it shouldn't be anyone but Byron with her food. Colleen opens the door, still in her Victoria's Secret pajamas and UGGS flip flops. Her hair is loose hanging to the middle of her back. He loves for her to have her hair down for him. It was just a coincidence that it was already down today.

Looking at him starting from the bottom working her way up to his handsome face, she is liking what she is standing in front of her. Byron has on navy blue suede Farragamo loafers, charcoal grey Alexander McQueen Glen Plaid slacks, and a white raw silk French cuffed Stefano Ricci shirt with gold Tiffany cuff links. The first two buttons on his shirt were open, giving Colleen a peek at the very top of his wife beater and the smooth hair on his chest. A thick 24KT gold herringbone necklace lies around his neck, stopping at the top of his wife beater. All of this was slightly hidden underneath his Alexander McQueen navy blue suede jacket.

Damn, he looks fine as a motherfucka! His high trimmed beard and deep waves is looking perfect like he is one of those men on the hair product box, Colleen thought to herself. She just keeps staring at him, speechless. *I know it has been a minute since we last have seen each other because we both have been swamped with other things, but DAMN!! And where is he going looking and smelling all good? Hell, I know he is saying things about me and my outfit too. Oh damn, damn, damn ... I am still in my fuckin' pajamas ain't I?*

Byron breaks the awkward silence in the air, first clearing his throat. "Well, um, hello Ms. Jeffries. Are you going to just stand there with your mouth open looking at me? You've seen me before in casual, work, evening ... and naked attire. What's the matter?" He smiles and so does Colleen. "Are you going to invite me in?

Your food is starting to get cold," he says holding up the bag so Colleen can see that he did have a reason to be standing at her door.

Colleen snaps out of her reverie, and moves to the side to let him in, "Oh, I'm sorry Byron. I was just surprised to see you dressed like this when you were only bringing me something to eat. And then here I am still in my pajamas. Had I known, I would have made sure I was already dressed for the day."

As he is walking by her to enter the house, his bicep brushes against her left breast. They instantly feel something go through their bodies. Colleen tries to ignore it as she shuts the door. Her heart starts racing a little. She grabs the bag of food from him and takes it in the kitchen. She knows he is still standing in the same spot, watching her ass move around like bowling balls in a bag. She smiles to herself.

However, Byron doesn't want to ignore what he just felt brushing up against her. *I've always wanted her to be my woman. But our relationship never really advanced into anything more than us attending some type of event or activity and then ending in sex. Don't get me wrong, I didn't mind at all but I still wanted more. The strange thing about it is, I feel like the shoe is on the other foot with her. She is giving me a dose of my own medicine. I am feeling like she really doesn't want more from me than what we already have.*

In the midst of his thoughts, he hears her say, "What you standing there for? You can follow me in here. You've been all through my house many times. I'm just going to carry this into the kitchen. What did you bring me this time sir? It smells so good."

"Guess, I am sure you will enjoy," he says with a smile.

Colleen opens the bag … and pause. She just stands there staring in the bag. Byron's smile disappears because he does not know what is going on. He is standing behind her in the doorway of the kitchen so he can't see her face. Colleen turns around with tears in her eyes yet laughing and sniffing. She walks over to him and gave him a huge hug. Byron brought her a meal from Georgia Brown's that is symbolic to their first time going out two years ago. It was so good but they never went back there to eat. Byron had attached a note to it saying, *This is something small to show you that I never forget. Here's to our first date, June 22, 2001.*

"You remembered?"

"Was I not suppose to?"

"I mean most of the time men ..."

"Don't go there Colleen. Let me just say one thing, Byron Vhoorhies remembers what really means something to him."

Colleen just leans back on the island looking at him. *Is he trying to get me to get rid of all of my other Options?* She wants a piece of him right now but doesn't know if she should try. Or maybe she should just get dressed and talk to him while she eats, and wait on her client. There is only an hour before the client arrives and that may be pushing it. *Damn! I at least want a sample for now to hold me over until later when I can have all of him. *Sigh* Decisions, decisions.*

Chapter Sixteen

16

Should I call him? Neah. Should I ask him to come over?
Neah. Why couldn't he read my mind? Or receive signals from me?

BeLynda wants to see Khalil but she doesn't want to have to
ask. She has never been a forward woman. She has never been
much for rejection either. She asked Khalil once to come over and
he already had plans. She knew it was another woman. What else
could it had been? "Stupid" is not written on her forehead. Or,
maybe she has "boring" written on her forehead. After that, she just
never got up the nerve to ask him again. She always waited for him
to ask, even though there were plenty of times when she wanted him
to ask, and he didn't.

Ring! Ring! Ring!

"Hello."

"Hey, Bee. What you up to?"

"Hello Steve, how are you? I'm not doing much. Just chilling in my Sitting-room," BeLynda responds to her ex-husband.

"Oh, *whaaat*?! You *'just chillin''*? No orders to sort, bag, or deliver?"

"Nooo, not this evening. Are we being sarcastic today?"

BeLynda hates when Steve says things like that. They have been divorced for five years and he still blames her dedication to her business as the reason. Never mind he was always away from home be it job-related or with the boys. Or so he said he was with the boys until he got frustrated about sex. BeLynda's business is how she dealt with the loneliness, rejection, and lack of understanding from her husband. Of course, he isn't going to take the responsibility for her feeling that way.

That's cool, though. She knows Steve feels guilty. He wouldn't still be talking about it as if it happened last week. It was his decision to divorce. He wouldn't keep calling her either because there are no ties between the two of them. They never went into business together. They never had any children … and he blamed her for that too. Until it came out about his low sperm count. He doesn't know she knows that. Yet to this day, he still doesn't have any children.

"Not being sarcastic, just asking Bee. Actually, I didn't expect you to answer, but I took my chances. And you answered." Just then, the other line clicked.

"Hold on Steve. **click** "Hello."

"What's up BeLynda?"

"Hey Khalil. What are you doing? I thought you'd be out and about. Surprised to hear from you." BeLynda's face lights up.

"Huh? Why are you surprised? I call you all the time. I was trying to see you. Is that a problem?"

Yes! He wants to come over. BeLynda trying hard not to sound like she is smiling says, "No, that's not a problem at all. I would like that. What time will you be here?" She couldn't stop grinning. Khalil must've heard her silent calls out to him.

"I'm ready now, but I'll give you an hour before I leave to come over. Is that enough time?"

"Enough time for what? What is there for me to do prior to you getting here?" BeLynda is playing coy. She knows that meant, 'You better be ready for my thickness to swim in your wetness.' She will be ready all right. She might even surprise herself tonight. She knows intimacy is a part of human nature. Why it causes such a problem for her is unknown. She takes these classes with her friends and never puts to use any of what she learns. Heck, she doesn't even practice when she is alone. Just wasting time and money. "Just be here in ninety minutes. Use the deck entrance on the second level. Have you eaten?"

"I'm fine BeLynda," Khalil laughs. "No need to cook anything. I just want to be with you tonight." BeLynda is always trying to feed him.

Hmmp, Khalil wants to be with ME! Be with me TONIGHT! Why can't I say that back to him? It just rolled off his tongue with no problem. Either he's comfortable with himself or he isn't afraid to go for what he wants. Hell, he is a man and they are used to getting turned down. Then again, with Khalil, I don't know. That sexy dark chocolate youngster got it going on! Was I shy like that in my marriage? Steve never ... STEVE! Oh my goodness, he's still on the other line!

"Hello? Bee, are you listening to me?" Khalil had been talking and BeLynda was off in the world of her mind again.

"Uh, Khalil, I'm sorry. Look, let me get off this phone. I just have to straighten up a little. See you in a little bit."

"Aiight, baby." Khalil is trying to figure out what is BeLynda up to. He knows she is up to something. She keeps her house spotless, so straightening up was a cover up for something else. *I hope it is all about me. I'm really digging her,* he says to himself.

Colleen smiles looking at the phone caught off guard by what Khalil said. *Baby, huh. Even after I abruptly end the conversation. He is really wanting some penetrating activity tonight and from me. Let me apologize to Steve and get going.* *click*

"Hello ... Steve? Hello?!"

"Yeah, I'm here. I almost thought you forgot about me." BeLynda could hear the 'tude in the tone of his voice.

"I'm so sorry. I'm surprised you were still holding on." BeLynda really feels awful for having him on hold so long. Surely she is not about to tell Steve that she was on the other line making plans to see another man.

"Don't worry about it. It must've been important. I was just checking on you. Didn't want anything. Go finish what you were doing. I'll call you later."

"Good night, Steve. Talk to you later." **click**

BeLynda sits there for a minute trying to decide how she is going to set the tone and mood for the night. She wants to make it memorable for Khalil. After the breathing class, she has been feeling a little less inhibited. *Maybe it is mind over matter. Psychological. Maybe I actually did purge all the gunk from my soul in class that day.* Once she plans it out in her head, she jumps up from the chair and runs upstairs to get everything ready. She may be a little inhibited in the bedroom but she can dress and decorate her ass off for the occasion.

Khalil pulls into the driveway, parking beside BeLynda's business van that is parked behind the Avalon. He figures no one else should be coming over. There is no need to pull up beside the Avalon, making room for more company. Before he gets out the car, he checks his face and hair in the review mirror rubbing his hand across his natural waves.

He walks up the stairs leading to the second level deck, just as he was instructed to do. He opens the French doors, which puts him in the morning-room. Khalil hears Tamia's *Stranger in My House* playing in another room and sees a table full of finger foods. At one end, there is a plate of raspberries, strawberries, sliced apples, and pears with bowls of powdered sugar, melted chocolate, and melted caramel. With a finger, Khalil pokes the chocolate and then the caramel. They both are still warm. He puts his fingers in his mouth and his body immediately heats up.

Where is she? She must've run upstairs when she heard me pull up. She had this timed just right. That's BeLynda for you. All about business no matter what it is, Khalil laughs and smiles to himself, walking into the kitchen to get something to drink. He notices two stemless wine glasses sitting on the counter by the refrigerator with a notecard addressed to *Khalil Bordeaux* sitting in front of them. He frowns with a smirk on his face, picks up the card and reads it:

You are invited to a night of bliss.

Pour two glasses of the wine with a kiss.

Khalil is smiling hard now. He rubs his goatee and reads it again. "The wine with a kiss? What does that mean?" Khalil decides to look in the refrigerator to see if the wine was there. Not there. He bends down to open the wine refrigerator that is stationed next to the dishwasher to see if any of the wines are it. By the fourth bottle checked, he finds a bottle of Cabernet Sauvignon that had a mauve colored lipstick kiss planted right on the label. He fumbles through the drawers for the corkscrew. He fills both glasses half full. Khalil takes a sip of the wine. "Mmm, not bad" he says while looking at it in his glass. Khalil picks up the bottle to read the name of it again. BeLynda is teaching his young ass some things. When he does that, he realizes the "kiss" was on a posted note stuck on the bottle. As he began to take it off, there was a note underneath it. It reads:

Go up to bedroom No. 2

I have a surprise for you

Khalil gulps down his drink, pours another glass half full and leaves it on the counter beside the other glass. Going upstairs, taking two steps at a time, he searches for the second bedroom. *Heck, which one does she consider bedroom number two?* When Khalil gets to that level, he sees that she has a posted note with a "2" written on it on a door. He begins to open the door that leads to his surprise.

His manhood is already throbbing, picturing BeLynda in the room dressed in something real freaky. He knows this is wishful thinking. He opens the door wider and sees she isn't in the room. There is a beautiful queen size bed highly elevated sitting in the center of the room. The matching dressers and armoire are decorated with lighted six inch pillars giving him well-lit quarters. *Hmm, this is a strange arrangement but I like it.* He has never been in this room before. He looks around the room but can't figure out what she is talking about. As he gets closer to the bed, he sees another note card. The suspense is killing him.

Change into something extremely hot

Meet me back at the original spot

"Change into what," Khalil asks out loud to himself. "I don't have any clothes here. Was I supposed to bring something? Shit, these damn notes are blowing me now." He walks over to the closet and there's nothing in there but some boxes for her business in a corner on the floor. Walking back towards the bed, he thinks it could be in one of the dresser drawers. He opens the first set of drawers ... nothing. He skips the next two and opens the third set. There, he sees a burgundy pillow case that appears to have something in it. Khalil picks it up and opens it.

"What the fuck?! Who the fuck is gonna wear this shit? Bee trippin' right now. She is tryin to set a brotha up." Khalil pulls out of the pillowcase a pair of champagne colored silk boxers with the matching bow tie. "I gotta hand it to her, O girl got good taste in material and quality but this damn bow tie just ain't me."

Since BeLynda set up such a nice evening, he decides to put the ensemble on anyway. They are the right size. *How did she know what size to get? She must've been snooping in my clothes when I didn't have them on.* Khalil smiles, takes off his clothes and puts on the outfit. He looks at himself in the mirror and laughs but also noticing how the color appears against his chocolate skin. *Is this what women are into now?* He moves around enough to let his little man sway back and forth a few times. *I look like one of those Chip 'N Dales.* He laughs at himself again. Oh he is ready now.

Khalil walks back down to the morning-room. He notices the music has changed. Now, Musiq Soulchild *Halfcrazy* is playing. When he enters the room, he remembers he left the glasses of wine in the kitchen. He gets them from the kitchen and returns back to the room to find BeLynda sitting in one of the chairs dipping strawberries in the powdered sugar. *Does she look ever so sexy? Damn!!*

"Hello. You look nice." BeLynda is nervous as ever. She feels like she is trying too hard to be sexy. Khalil just stands there amazed at what he is seeing. BeLynda is sitting with her legs crossed, showing off a pair of orange open toe, strappy four inch heels. They go perfect with the orange multi-colored baby doll outfit she has on. Khalil is speechless. He has never seen her like this. It is always lights off. Lingerie? Who thought she owned any?

"Wow. BeLynda baby, you look ..."

"Would you like a strawberry? Powdered sugar, chocolate, or both," BeLynda asks interrupting his compliment. She is sounding sexy even though she isn't trying.

"Stand up, baby, let me see you." *Strawberry? Khalil surely is not thinking about a damn strawberry. But she looks teasingly scrumptious the way she is eating hers. I would like to eat you instead with the sugar and chocolate.*

BeLynda uncrosses her legs to stand. Khalil gets a peak of her matching panties. *Damn she has been hiding all of this in the dark from me?* He looks at her round full breast canvassing her body with his eyes all the way down to her small waist, round hips and full tight thighs. She proceeds to walk towards him, ready to offer him the strawberry.

"Mmm, turn around for me baby." BeLynda turns around, slowly walks back to the chair. She is looking confident but her heart is beating fast, praying she doesn't fall, or do something stupid. Khalil is rubbing his manhood trying to calm it down. *Damn, she doesn't have on panties, she has on a thong. Her ass is tight and has the right amount of bounce.* He knew she had a nice shape. Why the hell did it take her so long to show it to him? Maybe because he is younger than her, she was self-conscious about not being appealing to him. BeLynda turns around to face Khalil once she reaches the chair she has been sitting in.

"Damn. BeLynda, I am speechless! You surprised me girl!" He walks towards her looking as if he could tear her up. Khalil massages her left breast and with the other arm around her waist, he slides it down to her right butt cheek, and gives her a soft peck on the lips. BeLynda wonders if Khalil can feel her heart beating so hard and fast.

"Mmm, that strawberry taste good on your lips. I'll take mines with chocolate, please," Khalil says smiling. BeLynda picks up a strawberry and dips it in the chocolate. He notices her hand is shaking a little bit. The chocolate is getting ready to drip. They both watch the chocolate on the strawberry as BeLynda puts it up to Khalil's mouth. She wasn't fast enough and a drop lands on his bottom lip and his chin. BeLynda hastily sucks it off his chin. He closes his eyes and moans. Then she sucks it off his lip. "Girrrl," he says as he grabs her butt, with his semi-hardness jerking twice.

"Mmm, Bee, what are you doing to me? You gonna make me marry you Girl."

"What? You don't like it? I can stop," she says teasing and kidding.

"Hell no! You better not! We would have some serious problems if you do!" They both laugh.

"I'm glad you feel that way." She picks up her glass of wine, takes a sip, dips a raspberry in the chocolate, and pops it in her mouth. "Would you like one? These go very good with the wine."

Khalil can't wait anymore. "I tell you what, why don't we take these foods with us upstairs. I promise we will put them to good use." He winks at her and rubs his fingertips up and down the small of her back. She jerks because it tickles. This makes his dick jerk.

"You promise?"

"Do I ever. Baby, you just don't know how long I've waited for this moment. I don't know why you've been so shy around me. I've shown you all of me."

"Well, let's not have Mr. Bordeaux waiting any longer." BeLynda hands him his wine and one last card.

"Are cards going to be a part of our night ... ALL NIGHT?!" BeLynda smiles at Khalil's question as she takes the card from him and reads it to him.

Pick the room that you aspire.

And I'll show you how I inspire.

"Well, well, well, Ms. Giles. What has gotten into you? I'm liking whatever it is."

Ha, ha, ha what he should have said is what hasn't gotten into me. "Tonight is all about you. So lead the way." BeLynda steps out the way holding her hand out to signal for Khalil to take the lead towards the stairs.

"I was hoping you said that. Ooh, be gentle Bee. Please don't hurt me. Unless you hurt me real good," he says winking at her. Then he turns towards the stairs, taking her hand and proceeds towards them. Not before he plants a juicy kiss on her lips filling her mouth with as much tongue he could get in it.

"Be careful for what you ask for. I do aim to please, however, your wish may come true and you may regret it." BeLynda must've had too much drink, or drinking on an empty stomach, talking like that. She is surprising herself this evening. She must be listening to Colleen too much. None of their classes have been titled Sexual Confidence.

"Ahh, it seems like I actually heard an offer in there somewhere. I think I will accept. So, Ms. Giles, I do believe I would like to be hurt by you tonight."

"Would you now," BeLynda asks twirling her hair around her finger. She walks over to the fruit on the table and dips a slice of apple in the caramel, seductively takes a bite of it and licks the access off her fingers. Khalil wipes his mouth to make sure she doesn't see him salivating over watching her lips wrap around the apple. She takes a good look at Khalil in the outfit.

Khalil is wearing the hell out of those boxers. I knew the champagne color would look perfect against his dark smoothness. I guess he could have done without the bow tie though. I do appreciate that he wore it anyway. That is a good sign.

"Hell yeah. Show me what you *got!*" He gulps down his second glass of wine, grabs her hand and heads for the stairs.

"Where are we going? You never said which room you chose."

"Would I not be following directions if I chose more than one room? Or did you have a certain room decorated for us?" Khalil has a devilish grin right about now. BeLynda is getting nervous, wondering what he actually has in mind.

"More than one room, huh," nervously she responds. "What's going on in that nasty little mind of yours?"

"Nothing you won't be able to handle." He continues to go upstairs until he is at the very top and enters the room. Walking through the room holding his hand, BeLynda is getting uncomfortable. She passes a mirror and sees her reflection in it. She is looking rather nice and sexy but maybe it was too much all at once. Khalil is too turned on and she is not knowing what he is wanting them to do. It's too late to back out now. Her heart is beating real fast, her mouth is getting dry. Khalil is walking through the bedroom past the bed towards the outside. *The deck?! All the way up here? What in the world? We're going outside to do what?!*

Once out on the balcony, Khalil gives her a deep wet kiss, pulling her close so that she could feel how excited he was. BeLynda opens her eyes to watch him. His eyes are closed and he is lost in the kiss. She is trying to think of a way to get out of this scene. This isn't fun anymore. *Out on the deck, in lingerie, kissing, and getting ready to be explicit. Is this the kind of stuff he likes to do? Suppose someone is watching? Think, BeLynda, think!*

"Ooh, baby, it is cold out here. I don't know how long I can stay out here. You not cold?" She is hoping he decides to take their escapade back inside.

"Naw babe, I am burning up. Can't you tell?" He grabs her hand and wraps it around his throbbing thickness. "I'll keep you warm. I will take good care of you. No need to worry about being cold." He puts his hands inside the sides of her thong and begins pulling them down. He is kissing her on the neck. BeLynda is still uncomfortable being outside about to give live porn to her neighbors. But she quickly realizes that there are woods facing her deck. Looking to her left and right there could be possible eyes watching them.

By the time he has her thong around her ankles, he is on his knees. He lifts one leg to remove her undergarments and places it on the patio table. BeLynda is watching him tentatively trying to figure out what is he about to do. He notices she is freshly shaved, just the way he likes it. Without a warning, his tongue meets her clitoris. BeLynda lets out a sigh and a deep moan, grabbing his head, as her head goes back, with her eyes closed. He caught her totally off guard. She is in another world, and in that world, BeLynda is far from being cold. One thing for sure, worrying about the neighbors is farthest from her mind tonight.

Her juices start flowing down onto his mouth and chin. He is moaning and lapping up all of it. It reminds her of Tina in class licking that dildo and she gets turned on even more. She was about to climax and he stands up as if he knows she was about to. He turns her around and bends her over. Oh, she is ready to feel all of his eight inches in her. It is hard as a brick and standing straight out of the hole in the boxers. Waiting with eagerness, she feels his tongue again instead. She has never had this before and tense up a little.

Damn, his nose is all up on my ass. I know I washed up good but what does he smell? I hope it is my Bath and Body Works Mango Mandarin. Oooh, it feels so damn good. I'm so slippery. And his laps sound so damn good. She is no longer worry about who can see them. This moment is all about feeling his tongue dance with her clit. It is about the anticipation of his dick sliding in. It is about being free of all of the pinned up bullshit that has kept her caged for so long.

She feels herself getting wetter and inner walls begin to throb. BeLynda toots her ass out giving Khalil more access helping him with her lapping session. Her legs begin to tremble and he knows what is about to happen. *That's it. Enjoy it baby. Let's have fun.* He fumbles to pull the boxers down over his dick so they won't be drowned with their secretions. He knows once he stands up, he is not going to be able to hold out long enough to pull them down.

BeLynda starts sounding off whispering. "Ah … ooh … ah … Kha. Oh my God!! Don't stop baby. Right there, right there." She can really feel her orgasm building. "Baby put it in. C'mon, put it now." Khalil takes a hold of her ass and keeps right on licking and sucking. All of a sudden, BeLynda explodes and lets out a cry of pure ecstasy. She squirts all over Khalil's face. She is trembling now. Khalil is acting like he is drinking from a water fountain as he sucks her juices.

Khalil is turned on to the max. He stands up and enters her with much force but he slides in with no hesitation in the entry. He is working her over now. BeLynda is right there meeting his strokes and circling his ass. Looking down at the action, he says, "Damn, baby. You're a squirter? I've been missing out, hunh? Maybe I need to bring you out here more often." He explodes with so much force.

Damn!! That's the best piece of pussy I ever had.

Chapter Seventeen

17

"Wow, what in the world are we about to get into today? I mean, she did say to wear yoga gear, but obviously I really didn't come prepared. My upper body strength is not strong enough for this," Sandy says as she walks around the room looking at all of the gold poles that have been set up in the room for class. *I might have to pretend that Mother Nature is visiting me today so I can just sit and watch.* Sandy says to herself.

"Oooh, it looks like we are going to put more than upper body to work. We're gonna need abs for today's session too," Regina says wide eyed. "This is going to be very interesting. *Very* interesting. One thing I can say, none of these classes have been predictable yet. The title says one thing and then we get here and see they've added a twist to the lesson."

"I thought this was supposed to be the Sexercise class. Why are all of these poles up? Am I the only one here that hasn't ever been on a pole? I mean, how is this supposed to be sexy or attractive? They have these in strip clubs and I have always associated these with Ladies of the Night," BeLynda frowns and takes out her hand sanitizer, getting ready to use it. *There's no way these things can be all that clean,* she says to herself.

"Girl, what you doing? I am sure the instructor didn't set up dirty instruments for us to use. We're not in a low budget tacky class on the wrong side of town. Put that damn hand sanitizer away. What is wrong with you? I see you were just playing about getting a pole up in your basement, huh?" Regina looks at BeLynda understanding her thoughts but hurt that she keeps herself in bondage to them. *Let it go Bee, damn.*

"I don't know Bee. Why don't you ask everybody? Maybe you are the only one between the four of us, but I am sure you not the only one in this class that hasn't been introduced to the pole. And what you mean how is this sexy or attractive? Pah-leeze come out of your shell and stop acting so grandma-ish. Using phrases like 'Ladies of the Night.' Loosen up," Colleen raises her voice a notch expressing irritation. Rolling her eyes and looking up at the ceiling, she walks over to BeLynda and takes the hand sanitizer from her.

"Freak, shut the fuck up and leave Bee alone" shouted Sandy. "You always have to act as if you are so uninhibited but I can guarantee you, there is something that you haven't tried and are not willing to either. I've not been on a pole, even though I have had my curiosity with it but hell, I'm single and won't just be trying out pole stunts on random motherfuckas." Sandy walks away from the quartet to get away from Colleen and her "I'm-every-man's-bedroom-dream" attitude.

Colleen looks at Sandy with her mouth hanging open surprised at how she almost snapped her head off. Regina finds it funny and gives her a satisfying smirk, smacks Colleen on her ass and says, "Now, now, pick your mouth up off the floor before Bee stuffs a dildo in it girlie. Maybe you can lead class today and show us what you got since you're such a pro at this. Just so you'll know, I've not been on the pole either and being inhibited has absolutely nothing to do with it."

A few of the other classmates snicker at the scene the Ladies just gave them. It doesn't bother Regina but Colleen sure is beyond bothered. Regina walks past her and stands by a pole like Sandy and all the other classmates. BeLynda follows and makes sure she won't be near Colleen when she makes her way over to the poles.

BeLynda actually doesn't feel all that great about how the scene has unfolded in front of everyone. Her heart is beating a little uneasy. She whispers to Regina, "You don't think she is too mad at us do you? I was just asking a question and she starts saying all that bullshit. I mean you said some shit too but I will let that go."

"Girl, I'm not thinkin' about her ass right now. Serves her nasty ass right. Always talking shit instead of just being quiet for a change. She is not the only one that has feelings. She'll get over it and will be just fine by the time class is over. She knows we love her. Now, calm down, take about five breaths, clear your mind, and relax. Class is about to start in about 10 minutes. Oh, and I only want you to loosen up. You're young, beautiful ... live Bee. We all love you." BeLynda softly smiles, shakes her head and waits for class to start.

Regina stretches her arms to the ceiling and bends over to touch the floor, loosening up her limbs a little before class. When she stands back up, she looks towards the door of the class, and thinks she sees someone in all black watching. However, whomever or whatever it is quickly moves away from the door. She stares a little longer thinking that the image will appear again but it doesn't. A few minutes later, a lady that looks to be the instructor emerges at the door and walks in. Regina jumps, slightly startled from staring at the door too long. *Whew! Okay, get it together Regina. Stop tripping*, she says to herself.

"Regina, you aiight girl? You look like you have seen a ghost. Or were you deep in thought about tonight's class?" Sandy breaks Regina's train of thought. "Oh, nah girl, I'm fine. I just thought I saw someone at the door, but it was the teacher" Regina responds somewhat lying.

"Well, it might've been someone at the door. They probably liked the way those leggings are stretched across your ass. Once they saw you looking, they got embarrassed and ran away." Sandy and BeLynda giggle at Regina's expression to the statement.

"What?! Damn, you think my leggings are too tight? Stan told me I look good, so I thought I was appropriate." Regina is wide-eyed inadvertently rubbing around her ass, as if that would loosen the material on her round melons. She doesn't like drawing attention to herself from men. When she and Stan started dating he had plenty of fights with disrespectful men.

"Of course he said you looked good. You really do. But his body probably immediately got warm and reacted to the scene he may have been playing in his head," Sandy says laughing.

"Don't pay her no mind girl. You look nice, relax," BeLynda says to Regina. Then she turns around to Sandy with a frown on her face, trying to hide her smirk saying, "Cut it out Sandy. Don't make her feel self-conscious."

"Self-conscious?! Are you serious?! Hell, give me half of that ass then and I will show all of you how self-*CONFIDENCE* is done!! Women out here paying to get the fake version of her *REAL* ass and she's uncomfortable about my 'ass' comment? Okay, sorry to offend, geesh," Sandy raises her hands in a surrendering position. BeLynda just shakes her head.

"I'm not offended, okay. Let's just drop it. The teacher has been speaking for a few minutes and I've no idea what she is saying." Regina turns her attention to the instructor, raising her hand and says, "Excuse me, hello, my name is Regina. I didn't hear what you said your name is. However, may you repeat what you just said to the class please? I apologize for not being attentive." Colleen rolls her eyes at Regina.

The instructor smiles at Regina, Sandy, and BeLynda, noticing that the fourth member of the crew isn't standing near them. She appears to be a little distant this evening and has her back turned. The instructor has already met Colleen in her cardio class. Her sisters had already told her about the quartet, and based off of the descriptions given, she knows from looking at all of the Ladies in the class, the other three are Colleen's friends.

"Well, hello Regina. How are you this evening? My name is Candice, and I will be your instructor this evening. I have heard so much about you and your group from my sisters Kelly and Tina. They seem to enjoy all of you in their classes, and I am sure I will too. I previously met Colleen in my cardio class. Hello Colleen, is everything okay this evening?" Candice says to Colleen to let her know that they have come together once again.

Colleen turns around and sees that her cardio instructor is teaching the class this evening and politely says, "Hello Candice. I'm good. Just a little irritated but I will be ready once class begins. Just don't kill us tonight, all right?" The entire class burst into laughter at Colleen's response. Candice covers her mouth trying to hide her smile. "I promise you I won't kill anyone intentionally," she responds trying not to laugh but it's hard not to. She gets such a kick out of Colleen.

BeLynda raises her hand to ask the instructor a question.

"Yes, please state your name first," Candice says.

"Oh, okay. My name is BeLynda but everyone calls me Bee. I was just wondering why are there poles up when this is supposed to be the Sexercise class. The Sexercise class comes before the pole class, right? I mean, I'm just asking," BeLynda asks Tina, nervously rubbing her neck and scratching her nose.

"Well, hello Bee. Yes, you are correct. The Sexercise class does come before the pole dancing class. This evening, we will be incorporating the poles in this class. You will understand why as time goes on. Okay? Did I answer your question Bee?" Candice had already heard that Bee is the inhibited one of the fantastic four and she doesn't want to lose her as a student by using the wrong words before the class got started.

BeLynda sighs holding her chest with her eyes closed saying to the instructor, "Okay, I understand. Thank you for explaining." BeLynda wipes her hands on her leggings because they have become sweaty from her being so nervous. She doesn't want to always look and sound like a prude but had Candice said some crazy shit about them poles for tonight's session, she would have gladly packed up her things and gone the fuck home. She will come out of her shell when she is ready to and behind closed doors with one man is where she would start. She doesn't need an audience for something so private.

"All right ladies now that we have warmed up and everyone has found a pole, let's begin tonight's lesson. Tonight, we will start off with a workout that will benefit you in your pole dancing." Candice is walking around the class in and out of the poles to get a good look at everyone. "This workout is called strength training. It is very important to make sure to strengthen the core and upper body," she says stopping in front of Colleen pointing at to her stomach for the core, and her chest, arms, upper back, and shoulders for upper body. She continues to walk around the class. "The upper body helps with using the muscles in our arms. The muscles we will be focusing on are the biceps, triceps, deltoids, and radius," Candice explains while pointing to these muscles teaching the ladies where they are located in the arms.

Hell, I am not trying to look like I have Incredible Hulk arms when I finish this class either. Candice better chill out, Colleen says to herself.

"The first move I am going to show you will be to do a push up on the pole." Everyone grasp as if she said something in another language. "Yes, ladies … a push up on the pole. It is not as hard as you think. Just watch me. I want you to stand about one foot from the pole. If you want to be challenged a little more, then stand one and a half feet or two feet from the pole." Tina points down at the floor. "Three markings representing these places have been taped on the floor behind each pole for your convenience. Please take your position."

Everyone stands on the line they have decided to use. Most have chosen the one foot marking from their pole. Of course Colleen and few others in the class tried to show up everyone by standing on the one and a half or the two feet lines.

"Okay, now, once you plant your feet together at your marking, place both hands on the pole at shoulder level. Not at or above eye level. Make sure your arms are straight out in front of you. This should be the same level as if you were getting ready to do a push-up on the floor. Next, you're gonna lean into the pole slowly, bending your arms outward at the elbow. This involves the humerus, ulna, and radius muscles, which all form the elbow." Candice points at the elbow and bends it several times to demonstrate the movement of the elbow. Everyone is quiet and listening to everything she is saying. Or at least appear to be listening.

"Do not bend your knees. Remember you are doing a push standing up using the pole. I want you to do a three count towards the pole, then a three count back to the beginning position. This is to be done ten times. Are we ready?" Candice turns around and asks the class. Everyone nods yes as if they aren't really sure if they are ready or not but they are going to give it a try.

"Okay, we are going to do this to music to help with concentration and to make you a little more comfortable." Candice walks over to the sound system and starts the music. Evanescence *Bring Me To Life* booms through the surround sounds. Since the majority of the class is African American, along with the instructor, it sort of surprises everyone that is the instructor's song of choice. Well, everyone except Colleen since she knows the instructor has a stripper past. Based off of the slow beat of the music, she could visualize Candice dancing and swinging on a pole to the song. Colleen smiles and gets started on the move.

After the ten reps, everyone can feel a little soreness in their muscles. They shake their arms and begin another round of ten of the push-ups. By the end of the song, Tina has everyone doing reps of five slow push-ups, one of three count holds, a rep of five fast push-ups, and one of three count holds. Arms are trembling, faces are drenched, breaths are fast, and heart rates are slightly elevated. They shake out their arms, do some arm circles, and stretches to loosen the worked muscles. Everyone thinks they are finished with the arms but realize that is only one song length and there is still fifty minutes left in the class. Torture is an understatement.

After doing squats with the arms behind the back using the pole, holding the pole and lifting feet off of the floor towards the butt, holding the pole towards the side of the body lifting the legs towards the chest, and doing military push-ups on the floor with the pole between the legs, all of the ladies can't take anymore of the madness. They are whining, moaning, and complaining as if Candice is a boot camp instructor.

"All right ladies, you are done for today. You did great!! Give yourselves a pat on the back. I am very impressed with what I have seen today. I don't know if it is based off of what my sisters have been teaching you or if you have poles in your bedrooms already," Candice winks at the ladies and wipes her face and neck with her towel. "I want you to go home, get some rest and be prepared for the soreness. Your arms will be slightly sore tomorrow but the next day will tell exactly how much you worked them today. Now, don't go home and try to work the pole if you have one. Your arms are too tender right now. Good night ladies!! See you next week."

The ladies roll their eyes at Candice. She knows damn well they aren't going near a pole until the next time they come to class. Some are stretched out on the floor, some are sitting up on the floor and some are bent over holding onto their knees trying to catch their breath. However the majority are wiping off all of the sweat from their strenuous workout.

Colleen looks at the instructor ready to snap her neck. *I thought I told this bitch not to kill us tonight. Did I have to give her the damn definition of what I meant by 'don't kill us'? I don't know how many of these classes I will be attending. I'm all for working out to keep everything tight and firm at the "envious" status but this is not for me. Hell, I had a date tonight. This heifer has done put me in the exhausted ready to go to sleep mode.*

"Whew, girl, I can't even lift my gym bag to put it on my shoulder. Did y'all expect to feel like this after class just by working your arms? My arms feel like I'm carrying bricks. I won't be doing anything with these joints for the next two days," BeLynda says while she tries to get ready to leave.

"Hell no!! I will say that she is good at what she does but I will take her sisters any day. This was too much for an hour class. I had a damn date tonight. I might be cancelling that for real. I don't want to do anything but lie down and go to sleep. She done made me sweat out my wrap," Colleen expressed while she put her hair up in a ponytail.

"This was our first Sexercise class though. I mean, how many of us actually workout? We basically used muscles today that we normally do not use and never paid attention to. This is an eight week class ladies. Before it's all over with, we will be doing these moves with no problems, looking just as professional as Candice." Sandy said while she is stretched out on the floor with her eyes closed and her towel over her face.

"Well, Candice used to dance on the pole, so she has years of experience with this damn thing. She up there making this shit look all easy. Just like when I'm in her cardio class. Just jumping around and leaping in the air with little or no effort." Colleen emulates how Candice looks in the class to the girls. "Then these damn thick thighs of mine show me something totally different from what she showed. That's okay though, because I work at my own pace. Fuck that. I can hang but it's at my own pace. I won't be getting on nobody's pole any time soon. I'm not killing myself for her or any man that might feel I could stand to lose a few pounds. They can kiss my ass."

"I know that's right girl. I'm with you on that. Thank goodness I only have to worry about one man and he has no complaints. At least none that he has brought to my attention," Regina says then takes a few swallows of her water.

"Well, right, none that you know of. You know how they will tell it to their boys long before you hear it from them," BeLynda mentions and all the ladies shake their heads agreeing with her.

"*Shiit*, all that booty Regina toting around, I am sure Stan's complaints are minimal to none. And I doubt very seriously if he is talking about all of that ass to *any* of his friends. Hell, he won't have any friends if he did because they'd become his competition, coming over knocking on his door knowing damn well he ain't home. Y'all know he has a past life and it ain't one to play with," Sandy says and they all laugh.

BeLynda breaks out in a verse from the O'Jays *Back Stabbers:*

♪They smile in your face

All the time they wanna take your place

The Back Stabbers

Back Stabbers♪

The Ladies all laugh again.

"Okay, enough talk about her ass for one night, damn! Let's go, I'm tired. I need a long hot bath to soak these joints and muscles. I could smack Candice's boney ass. She must didn't understand when I said 'don't kill us tonight.' I have some contracts to write up tomorrow. I don't think I will be able to hold the damn pen to write." They all laugh at Colleen and head towards the door.

Regina is glad that they all parked side by side in the parking lot. She is feeling sort of uneasy. During class, she thought she had seen something or someone again at the door a few more times. She didn't know how long they had been there watching. Every time she would get back into the swing of the class, then decide to look back towards the door, there it was again. She thought it was strange that every time she would look towards the door, the figure would quickly move from the door. That made Regina believe whoever was there was watching her and no one else. That made her very uncomfortable the entire time they were in class. She can't figure out who was watching and why they wanted to. Then again, they were taking sexual enhancement classes. She thought maybe they were getting off just watching what they were doing. Whatever the reason gave her a distressed feeling.

"All right ladies, y'all have safe drives home," Regina says trying to sound normal opening her back door to put her gym bag on the floor. "Call me when you get home to let me know everything is all right. We are women and we can't be too content with our surroundings you know" Regina says getting in her lunar blue S550 Benz and starts it up.

"I know. You never know who the hell is up in the cut just waiting," BeLynda says looking around. "Okay, you do the same girlie, love you" BeLynda and Sandy says in unison as Sandy is pulling her red Camry out of the parking space. BeLynda rolls up the window. They are riding together. Even though Colleen lives closer to BeLynda, it had been arranged for Sandy to take BeLynda home due to Colleen having plans after class. So they are in three cars tonight instead of two.

"Regina, I'll call you when I get home. I doubt if I go anywhere except to bed. I am truly worn out girl. That nigga gonna have to take a raincheck." Colleen yawns and rubs her left arm while putting her gym bag in the trunk. She is moving in slow motion, dragging her feet towards the driver's side of her metallic beige 750Li BMW.

"Ha, ha, ha okay girl. I hear you. Stan will probably be in his office when I get there. I will go sit in the sauna for a few and then call it a night." Regina notices a black Charger with black tinted windows sitting on the other side of the parking lot. She could tell it was running but the lights weren't on. *Maybe that is Candice getting ready to pull off*, she thinks.

"Girl did you hear me? Where are you because you surely are not here in the conversation? I've been talking to myself apparently. Don't have me break in another O'Jays song," Colleen says.

"Oh, damn, I'm sorry. My mind was somewhere else. I didn't mean to be rude," Regina replies.

"Well, the place your mind just went doesn't seem like it was all that great. You look worried. What's wrong?"

"Oh, it's nothing. I thought I saw something, that's all. I'm just probably trippin' and I am not too fond of doing that."

"Well, what did you think you saw? You freakin' me out Girl. Don't keep shit like that to yourself. Fuck!! Especially after saying that shit about us being out here at night."

"Don't look right now but there is a Black Charger over there. Look at it on the sly. I know it is running but the lights not on. It's makin' me feel like whoever is in that car is watching me or us." Colleen plays it off then slowly looks over in the direction Regina is talking about to see what she is talking about. She sees the black Charger.

"Why you think they are watching you … or us?" Colleen is getting very concern. She's not liking what Regina is saying right now.

"It's probably just me being paranoid. You know how I can get." Regina tries to not alarm Colleen.

"Have you seen the car before? Who do you think it is? Is someone actually following you?"

"I'm not gonna say I've seen that one but … I will tell you about it later. I just want to get home to be safe in my home and know my baby is near."

"Okay, well let's pull off together. If you see another Charger and you're feeling uncomfortable, get the tag number so we can make sure if it's the same car or not." Colleen looks back over to the car and then back at Regina. *You'll talk about it later? What the hell is going on? I am not one to be looking over my shoulder.*

"Cool. I will call you when I get home." They pull out of the parking lot side by side. Regina goes left and Colleen goes right.

Some crazy shit has been happening tonight. I'm praying it is just my mind playing tricks on me. I may need to carry some mace or some heat with me. I don't know what is going on but I plan to be prepared for the bullshit. Regina thought as she turns on her CD player to listen to some Maysa to calm her nerves on her drive home. She looks through her rear view mirror to see if the car decided to pull off too. It hasn't. She calms down a little more.

Chapter Eighteen

18

"Good evening Senora Wooten. Te ves muy cansada (You look very tired). How was class," Maria asks Regina taking her gym bag and coat. "Is there anything I can get you before you go upstairs?"

"Hey Maria. Yes, I am very tired. Class was exhausting today. You can set the sauna up for me, thank you. I surely need it. Is Stan in his office," Regina says trying her best not to move her arms while handing Maria her bag and coat.

"Si Senora Wooten, Senor Wooten is in his office. It sounds like he is in a very heated discussion. He asked me to bring him ice cold beer and one of those small glasses. He already had the brown stuff sitting on the desk," Maria laughs. She knows when Stan gets frustrated with work he chases his drinks with beer to take the edge off.

"Really?! Oh Lord. Let me go tell him I'm home. Sounds like it's gonna be a long night for him. Especially if he has the bottle of Remy XO out on the desk." Then it becomes a long night for her to help relieve his stress. She surely didn't feel like it tonight. Her arms were killing her.

"Bueno (Good). He will be glad to see you. He's been in there fussing for two hours. I just shake my head. He works so hard Senora. I tell him all the time, 'No trabaje demasiado' (don't work so hard). He no listen to Maria," she chuckles.

"Yeah, well you know how he is. In his mind, he isn't working that hard until I point it out to him. I swear I don't know where he gets the energy from. One thing I can say is that he always has time for me, so I guess I really can't find anything wrong with it. But he does need to relax and stop getting so wired up on these calls and meetings."

"I know, I know, I told him. He just laughs at me and say, 'I love you too Maria.' He is so testarudo (stubborn)," Maria shakes her head as she walks down the hall towards the kitchen shaking her head. Before turning the corner, she says, "I cooked baked turkey wings, steamed seasoned broccoli, and cauliflower. Is that okay? Senor Wooten wanted to eat light for dinner."

"Oh he must've had a heavy lunch. Or he needed more energy for his yelling match," she laughs. "But I'm okay. I don't want to lift my arms for the next three hours. That includes lifting them to my mouth." They laugh.

Regina laughs and walks through the foyer in the opposite direction towards Stan's office. Before she knocks, she hears him yelling at someone. It made her jump a little bit because that tells her exactly how long her night is going to be. Thank goodness she doesn't work because she would have to call her supervisor to say she wasn't coming in just so she could recuperate. Her arms are already sore. The last thing she needs is for her coochy to be sore and swollen from the strenuous activity.

As she walks in, Stan is steady yelling, "Nah, fuck that!! That ain't how the damn plan is gonna go. The contract I gave those motherfuckas didn't say any of that shit. They signed it and that's what we are gonna go with. They can act like they are gonna back out and they will be sittin' under the jail when our attorney finishes with their asses!!" Stan takes off his tie and unbuttons his shirt and throws it on the plush leather couch.

Regina smiles and walks over to Stan to give him a kiss. She bends down to give him a kiss on the cheek, and he moves away, standing pacing back and forth shouting at whomever is on the speaker phone. She stands there shocked at what just happened. She puts her hands on her hips and looks at him as if he has three heads. *Did he just move away from me? I'm gonna give him a pass on that one. I am not a part of that damn meeting so I'm the last person that should be getting his pissed off attitude.*

Stan turns around and notices Regina's expression with her hands on her hips. He smiles, blows her a kiss and motions for her to come to him. She doesn't move. Stan is still yelling at the speaker phone going from smiling at Regina to frowning and screaming at the phone. Regina jumps a few times at his yelling. He finally gets over to Regina and gives her a big hug and a kiss on both cheeks and her lips. He moves his lips saying "I'm sorry." Regina gives him a faint smile and hugs him back but she is still a little salty at how he brushed past her a few minutes ago. She moves her lips to say "I'm going in the sauna for a little bit. I'm tired." He shakes his head okay and resumes his yelling match on the phone, never missing a beat.

Walking out of Stan's office, she walks into Maria. "I have set the temp to eighty-five degrees on the sauna room for you. By the time you get undressed, it should be ready for you," Maria told her as she hands her a glass of Merlot.

"Thank you Maria. I think I want a glass of Sauvignon Blanc instead. I need something cold right now. The red is going to put me to sleep. I'm sorry Maria."

"No problem Senora Wooten. Didn't know you would take since your arms hurt. Would you like bottle and some fruit or cheese?"

"Yea, my arms do hurt but you knew I would take this glass of wine. You know I don't turn down my favorite pastime," Regina laughs. "Fruit will be fine. I appreciate that, thank you so much." Regina gives her a faint tired smile.

"My pleasure." Maria walks off back to the kitchen

Regina goes up to her room and sits down at her vanity looking in the mirror. She couldn't stop thinking about the strange things that had been happening. First it was the black Charger outside their house looking like someone was taking pictures. Then it was the craziness that happened when she and Stan were in the Poconos. Tonight at class, the figure that kept appearing at the door, and the black Charger sitting in the parking lot running with the lights off. *What was it all about?*

She thought it was the instructor getting ready to leave but once she got home, she could feel someone watching her. Before she entered the house, she turned around and saw the black Charger driving by. It wasn't moving slow as if on the creep. Maybe it was someone in the neighborhood and it was just a coincidence that it was driving by. *Maybe I am just tripping but I don't know why,* Regina says to herself.

Regina removes her clothes and stares at herself in the mirror. She turns to the side and look at herself. Stomach is nice and flat still showing her four pack. She is always checking to make sure the body and the scale stay looking the same. She laughs because she knows Colleen is always talking about the models in the magazines having their six pack abs airbrushed to give it the appearance of them being in shape. *Mmmp, she needs to see mine and I want her to say some crazy shit like that about mine being make-up and not the real thing.*

Then her smile slowly leaves her face. She is remembering the trainer she had. She had to fire him because he started acting strange. At first, she thought it was her imagination. His touch when he would spot her would feel uncomfortable. When he flirted with her, she didn't pay it any mind because that's what some men do. Once he started asking her to go out with him she knew he had other thoughts. He was saying things like "your husband won't know," "I want to show you a good time," and "I'm really digging you." She cursed him out and told him that they were strictly business. That wasn't clear enough for him.

The day he tried to kiss her and wouldn't let her go, she smacked him and told him his services were longer needed. She never told Stan. He was the one that found the trainer for her. She knew that the man wouldn't be breathing too much longer had she told Stan about his fucked up choice in a trainer. She didn't need for that switch in Stan's head to go flip on. If it did, things were going to be so wrong.

Stan has a tainted past and the last thing she wants is for her husband to get into any trouble that required jail time or being on the run. All he worked for would've gone down the drain. But she knows if these mishaps continue to occur, she would have to inform him so he won't be caught off guard if something or someone came to him on some bullshit tip.

She changes into her robe and walks out her room to go downstairs to the sauna room. Outside of the sauna, Maria has placed a tray with the Crane Lake Sauvignon Blanc, a glass, and a plate of sliced honey crisp apples, pears, and New York Aged Cheddar. This is Regina's perfect tray of goodies to go with her white wine. *My girl. She knew to put cheese on the tray anyway. She's knows me like I'm her child.* She grabs the tray and enters the sauna. It feels so good inside and she's thankful that Maria knew just the exact temperature to set on the thermostat.

Sitting the tray on the bench, Regina realizes she forgot to get her music. She leaves out to go in the entertainment room to choose a CD from the shelf. Once she has what she wants to hear, she goes back to the sauna, placing the CD into the system outside the door, presses play and enters the sauna. Removing her robe, she lets out a sigh getting ready to relax her aching limbs. As she pours a glass of wine, Phyllis Hyman croons through the speakers. She takes a sip and closes her eyes enjoying the wine go down her throat.

♪*Meet me on the moon*

As soon as you can

In the middle of the sky

Just you and I

Riding on a cloud

Soft as you please

We can sail upon the breeze

To the everlasting moment of love

Oh I feel your symphony

So strong and so pure

It echos on through me

I am so sure

That we were meant to be

Sharing this love

We share ♪

The wine feels so good going down and throughout her body giving her the feeling she needs. She closes her eyes enjoying the hot steamy room, her wine, and singing along with Phyllis. *Damn Phyllis is singing the hell out of this song. Gone too damn soon. She is surely missed,* Regina thinks to herself. This is taking her mind off of the spooky events that were going on around her and she needs this moment.

By the time Phyllis is on her fifth song, Regina is half way done with the fruit and cheese, has finished the bottle of wine and is feeling right nice. She is rocking back and forth and is singing right along with the song.

♪*When I give my love*

This time

I'm gonna make it last forever

And when I give my love this time

I'm gonna give it all I got for sure

No more mistakes that's my resolution

Lord knows I've been through so many changes

Stick to the path that's the solution

It's for sure I won't go wrong

At last I've found someone

Someone that I can trust

Feel good about myself

Feel like nobody else ♪

That's how she feels about her relationship and marriage to Stan. She had been through so much bullshit before they got together, she was about to say fuck a relationship. When he came along, she didn't know if he was being true and if it would change for the worse. So far, it hasn't and she is thankful to God for that. He has been so good to her and she has reciprocated. There is no way she is going to mess up what they have. That trainer was fine but he could kiss her ass. She could have hooked him up with one of her girls since they are single.

She wouldn't even have a reason to step out on Stan. Even if she did, she made a commitment to her man and that is that. She has no major complaints. The little ones aren't even big enough to even state them. No one is perfect and the little things are his flaws. Thank goodness, there aren't too many of them. If she had to count them, they could be counted on one hand. There was more than that when they first got together but over the years, he has worked on eliminating more than half of them. She made sure she did the same.

Regina and Stan do want children. She wants a girl and a boy but Stan wants a damn basketball team. She wasn't going to agree to that. She is the one that has to carry all of those babies and push them out. All he has to do is walk around being the proud father. They haven't been trying but a few times she did think she was pregnant. Stan seemed happy when she told him she thought she was pregnant. When they found out they were false alarms, she couldn't figure out his expressions. It was hard to tell if he was disappointed or happy that she wasn't pregnant. He did say that they could keep trying.

When the CD finished playing, she wanted to put in another CD but she had only took one off the shelf and she didn't feel like walking down the hall to get another. She is in the mood for some old tunes. The Isley Brothers or Barry White would have been nice, but she knows once she leaves the sauna, she wasn't coming back. Maybe she would go get them anyway and take them upstairs to listen to while she is in the tub.

Regina is nice and wet with sweat beads all over her body. Her face is so wet she thinks she is back in the sexercise class. Lord knows she is glad that is over for the week. *Maybe next week won't be too bad*, she is hoping. She puts her plush pink robe on, slips her feet into her Daniel Green slippers and goes to get the CDs.

She walks down the hall to see if Stan is still in his office. He is and he is no longer yelling into the phone. Actually, he isn't on the phone at all. When Regina peeps her head in the door, he is listening to Average White Band *A Love of Your Own*, has the television on CNN, and is going over some papers he has spread all over the desk.

"Hey baby, what you doing" Regina coos to him entering his office.

"Hey you. How are you? Where you been, in the sauna," Stan asks yawning, stretching, and scratching his head.

"I'm fine. Yeah, I was in the sauna with a bottle of wine. I needed to relax. Today was sort of stressful."

"Oh okay. Well, that's why we have a sauna. For days like this. Did you need something," he asks turning down the music and muting the television giving Regina his undivided attention.

"Oh, nah, I'm okay. I was just checking to see if you were still yelling at someone. You were in rare form when I came in here an hour ago. Is everything all right? Is there a problem with one of the companies?"

"Oh yeah, sorry about that. I didn't mean to snatch away from you like that. Everything is fine though. You know how people are sometimes. Always tryin' a nigga. They should know by now, I am not the one to try with the bullshit. So you know I got that straight with the quickness," Stan laughs and takes a sip of his beer.

"I know that's right. That's why you are who you are and very good at what you do. They don't want to see the other Stan come out. How long you gonna be in here Mr. Wooten?"

"I know, right? He's been buried deep. Don't want to bring him out for no bullshit. But, babe, I'm not even sure how long I'll be here. Got a few phone calls to make. I know it's late and they ain't gonna be too happy with me ringing their phones. But they will know that they'd need to answer. Go 'head and do whatever you want to do. I might be sort of late. If you're sleep, you know I will wake you," he gives her a wink.

She was hoping he didn't say that, not tonight anyway. She wants to just chill. She wouldn't even be focused and that would piss him off. "Okay. Let me leave so you can make your calls. Well, I'm gonna go on upstairs and take a bath. The jets need to massage these arms. They are kind of tight."

"Really? Your arms? Tight from what? They working you that hard in class? What, you had to do a lot of writing today? Normally you come home happy and half the time you have the crew with you. But tonight, you're alone and have sore arms. Poor baby. You need me to do anything for you?"

"Mmm - hmmm, yeah, something like that. I need to clean out my bag. It's getting mighty heavy with all that class stuff in it. *If you only knew what they had me doing in class today.* Regina has to laugh to herself. "Oh, no, go 'head and make your calls. I'ma big girl. I'll be fine."

"Aiight. Damn, they working my baby for real, huh? Well, I know you got it all under control. You're not Mrs. Wooten for nothing," Stan says smacking her on the ass, watching it jiggle like a tight bowl of jello. Regina jumps back trying to wave his hand away. That is the wrong move because she almost screams at the pain in her arm. Stan doesn't notice because he is too busy watching her ass.

"Damn, baby. Come here. Let me see somethin'," Stan motions for her while watching the melons in the back of her robe wanting them to keep moving.

"What you want Stan? You know that didn't feel good. That was too hard. Just in case you haven't noticed, it is attached to my body and it does have feeling in it," Regina whines rubbing her left cheek. He can be so heavy handed sometimes.

"Oh, I'm sorry but it sure looked damn good when it reacted to my smack. You didn't see the view I had. Let me do it one more time. I won't be so hard this time. Come on, come back over here.

Pull your robe up so I can see." Stan is looking at her like he want to push everything off of the desk and bend her over it.

Regina walks back over to him unenthusiastically and he palms her right cheek like a basketball. She lifts her robe up for him to get a full view of her damp derriere. "Now, that's what you call a firm ass. It ain't all sloppy. Ain't no jelly or jam up in this right here. My baby takes care of her body," Stan brags. He smacks it but more gentle this time. He doesn't get the same effect he got when he popped the left cheek but it still dances for him.

"Yeah, you go ahead and take a nap or whatever it is you were gonna do," he run his fingers up the crack of her cheeks. She rolls her eyes blushing at the same time. "I will see you in a few hours. All you need is your birthday suit. I know you're tired. I promise I won't be all night. Just for you aiight?" He gives her a devilish smile while rubbing her back.

"Yeah, yeah, that's what you always say. And then you think you're supposed to do a marathon or something. You don't know what a quickie is. I'm really tired though so hopefully this time you keep your word. I don't feel like all *that* tonight. I told you my arms are sore," Regina says lifting her arm slowly to run her fingers through his hair.

"Okay, okay, wow. Listen to you. My baby really is tired and sore. I ain't ever heard you sound like this. Maybe I need to go talk to your teacher and tell her or him to not work you so hard. But I promise I will be quick. Your arms will be fine, you won't need them for what I want to do," Stan laughs. Regina isn't seeing the humor.

"Yeah, we'll see Mr. Wooten. How many times has your wife heard that?" Regina slowly walks towards the door and Stan calls out to her.

"Hey, Gee Gee!!" She turns around to see what he wants.

"Yes, baby. What's up?"

"You did hear me when I apologized for snatching away from you earlier didn't you? I really didn't mean to do that. I was in the heat of the moment. Wasn't anything towards you at all," Stan is looking serious and Regina can tell he genuinely means it.

"Oh, yes, I heard you, thank you baby. Don't worry about it. You're fine. I understand that it wasn't directed at me. I was coming to get a kiss while you were in the middle of a very intense conversation. Just make sure it doesn't happen again," Regina gives him a wink and smile and turns back around to head out the door.

Stan smiles and leans back in his chair watching her and her melons walk out of his office. *That's my baby right there.* He says to himself and gets back to work picking up the phone to make his first call.

"Hello," Regina says answering her phone. It's Sandy calling her. She did notice she had five missed calls from the girls. She was in a so much of a hurry to go in the sauna, she had forgotten about telling the girls to call her when they got home. With all the missed calls, she knows they were worried.

"Damn girl!! You aiight?! Everything okay over there? This is my third time calling you. Me and Bee were starting to get worried. Where were you," Sandy asks with concern in her voice.

"Hey girl. I'm sorry. When I got here, I had Maria to set up the sauna room for me and bring me a bottle of wine. I just left from

Stan's office and came upstairs. Y'all calling slipped my mind. My phone was upstairs in my purse," Regina says while running her bath water.

"Damn, I could've used the sauna room myself. I think we all just wanted to get the hell home to our beds. Well, I'm glad you are home and okay. I was starting to think I might have to come over there to check for your car in the driveway. Have you heard from Colleen," Sandy asks.

"I've not talk to her but she did call twice. She called from her cell instead of the house. I need to make sure she is home. I will call her in a few minutes. Hey, you call Colleen. I don't want to wait until after I finish to know she is home," Regina bends over to test the water.

"Oh okay, aiight, I can do that. I'm not gonna hold you. It sounds like you are getting ready to take a bath. I will tell Bee I spoke with you."

"Yeah, I am ready to be in it right now. I guess I'll set up my ambience while I'm waiting. I need the full effect tonight. A sista is beat down." They both laugh and say their good nights. *click*

Regina gets in the tub, with the jets on full force. The water feels so good against her body, especially her arms. She lets out a huge sigh and sinks into the water. She has her head laid back against the pillow, eyes closed, listening to The Isley Brothers' *Make Me Say It Again*, enjoying the bath and ambience. *I can stay here all night if the water would stay hot.*

An hour later, she awakens, the water is quite chilly, yet she is feeling so much better. She gets out the tub and dries off while looking at herself in the mirror. Regina laughs at what Sandy was saying in class, turns to the side and does her version of the romp shaker dance. Smiling, she shuts down the ambience she has going and enters the bedroom. Stopping in her tracks, she sees Stan is already in the bed and snoring loudly.

Aww, he was tired too. Good!! I will see him in the morning.

Chapter Nineteen

19

Oooh, I'm so glad this day is over. I can't wait to get home and pour me a glass of wine and meditate. This has been a very trying day for me. If I had to sit in Clarice's office any longer correcting her mess, I think I would have had to beat her ass. She's so smart until she's literally dumb. I don't even know why she is still employed with the company. Hell, demote her ass and give me the position. I didn't come on board to be the cleanup woman and not get paid for it. I didn't get my degree to be doing "busy" work.

Sandy is sitting in her car taking deep breaths, trying to relax and ease her stress level. Working on starting her own business is sounding more and more like the answer for her these days. She really thinks that she isn't too far from telling Clarice what she actually thinks of her ending it with a punch in the face. She is just sick of the bullshit. If the shoe was on the other foot, they probably would have been giving her a warning letter. *I swear she must be one of the supervisor's relatives or something.*

Sandy thumbs through her CDs in her console to figure out which one she wants to hear right now. She already has five CDs in the changer but she doesn't want to hear any of those this evening. She decides on Gota Yashiki, inserts it into the sixth space in the changer and pushes the track button for the third song *European Comfort.* When it starts, Sandy closes her eyes and starts swaying to the jazz beat getting into the groove. She can listen to this jazz piece all day. Her groove is interrupted by the ringing of her cell phone.

Sandy opens her eyes, picks up the phone and flips it opens to see who it is. She doesn't recognize the number. Normally, she will ignore unknown numbers, but something tells her to answer it. She lets it ring one more time before she pushes the Bluetooth in her ear.

"Hello," Sandy answers in the tone of "who is this and why are you calling me?"

"Hello, may I speak to Sandy please," a strong baritone voice booms through her ear. Sandy gets wide-eyed because she has no idea who this is calling her. She knows damn well it is not a bill collector sounding this sexy and good. Besides, the caller asked for her by Sandy, and not Sandra. *Who could this be?* There was only one way for her to found out.

"This is Sandy. To whom am I speaking to?"

"Well, hello Sandy. This is Ray Daniels. We met at the club a few weekends ago. How are you doing today," the strong baritone voice responds into the phone.

Oh my!! He finally calls!! Sandy is focused. "Hi Ray. Yes, I do remember us meeting at the club. I'm not in the habit of giving out my number to any and everybody. Plus, I do recall I had to call you first in order for you to be returning my call. Remember, you didn't ask for my number. However, I am doing fine, thanks. How are you doing?" Sandy is too tickled but she dares not let him hear it in her voice.

"Oh, that's a good thing. That makes me feel quite special to be one of the few chosen. I will make sure that I use it wisely. I am glad to hear that you are doing fine," Ray chuckles. "That is always a great thing to hear. I did see that you had called me and I listened to your message. I listened to it a few times to be honest. I've been somewhat busy with a few things but other than that, I can't complain about anything. Now that I am free, I called to hear your voice. Were you busy?"

So, you've been busy huh? With what? With whom? Video games? Another woman? "Oh okay, I was wondering if you had given me the wrong number. Your greeting doesn't mention your name. So you've been keeping yourself busy, huh. There is nothing wrong with that. It keeps you out of trouble. Right, now, no, I am not busy. As a matter of fact, I am actually just leaving work. Now … what do I owe this pleasure of receiving a call from you? I am sure it isn't just to hear my voice, really."

She's funny. I can imagine how sexy she is looking when saying that. "Oh, well I see I caught you at the perfect time. I know I haven't spoken with you since we met and yes, I am glad to be hearing your voice. But I was also wondering if you wouldn't mind joining me for dinner this evening? Nothing fancy. Just the two of us meeting up, getting something to eat, and enjoying each other's company and conversation. Would that be a problem?"

Dammit!! Of all days, he calls today and wants to meet up. My hair is a mess and I am not dressed to have dinner with a man today!! "Dinner? This evening? What time were you thinking about? I would need to go home and change. I didn't dress for possible dinner dates today." They both laugh.

"I was actually thinking about six this evening. Remember I said nothing fancy. I am casually dressed too. Oh, I am quite sure it is hard for you to look a mess. What you have on doesn't matter. As long as I am sitting across the table from you eating my dinner, I will have a big smile on my face the entire time. Sooo, what do you say Ms. Robertson?"

Oh he remembers my last name too. Well, come to think of it, I did say it in the voicemail I left on his phone. "Are you sure? I don't want to you telling your friends that I was looking jacked up when you saw me." Ray laughs at her statement.

"Trust me. I wouldn't do that at all. I said I wanted to see you in another setting. So, if you are not dressed for a dinner date, that's perfect. I don't need thrills and frills. Let's say this is a come as you are date. I'm a simple man. Does that put you a little more ease with seeing me this evening?"

"Well, okay, since you put it that way, sure I would love to meet you for dinner this evening Ray. I mean, I was pleased with how I looked when I left for work this morning." Sandy blushes through the phone.

"Good!! Since you are already in your car driving, would you mind meeting me at Old Ebbitt Grill? Do you know where that is? Or would you rather I pick you up from work, we ride together, and then I take you back to your car? Either one is fine with me."

"Old Ebbitt Grill? Okay. Yes, I do know where that is. I used to work downtown DC. I am fine with driving, thank you for offering. I won't make it there by six though. I won't get there until about six fifteen. Is that fine," Sandy asks checking her hair in the mirror to see if she needs to do something with it.

"No problem at all pretty lady. I will already be there. Is there anything you would like for me to order for you before you get there? I can have them bring it out at six fifteen for you."

"Oh, no that is okay, Ray. You don't have to do that. I can order when I get there, thanks for asking though." *Hell, what does he think this is? Who does he think I am? He expects to order me a drink or food while I am not there so he can put something in it? We are not on those terms yet Boo.*

"Of course. I am just checkin'. I don't know how hungry you are. I am just trying to make sure I have you covered. So, I will see you at six fifteen Sandy."

"Okay, Ray. No problem. I appreciate that. Talk to you when I get there." They both push "end" on their phones.

✱ ✱ ✱ ✱

Sandy's cell rings again but this time she knows it is BeLynda calling her. She gave her the ringtone of Vivian Greene *Rollercoaster*. That was when BeLynda was going through all those changes with her ex-husband. Sandy has been meaning to change it long before now but she never got around to it.

'Hey, what's up Bee," Sandy says after pushing the Bluetooth on in her ear again.

"Hey girlie, ain't nothing much going on. What's up with you? You still at work or you've left already? You know sometimes I think you spend the night there. You sure you don't have an inflatable bed in the office? C'mon, you can tell me." BeLynda laughs.

"Please, I was not about to give them another minute of my time today. I swear I need to find me another job, start my own business, hit the lottery, or find me a man to take me away from all that madness. I'm really starting to dislike the people I have to deal with at that place." Sandy fumbles around in her black B. Makowski handbag looking for her Coach shades.

"I know that's right. I told you a long time ago to start your own business. You have too many talents to be wasting time working with and for people that do nothing for your peace of mind. Work shouldn't be stressful. Life is too short Girl. Put one or two of your talents to work for you."

"Yea, I know girl. I have heard it over and over again. I'm gonna get it together and figure something out. I need money for starting a business though. And I am not trying to be a failure at whatever I decide to do and then still have to pay that damn money back. Nah, I need a business plan that is concrete and covers all 'what ifs' in the business of competition. *But moving on*, what's going on with you? You sounded like you called for something since you asked if I was still at work." Sandy says her piece and changes the subject. Today is not the day to get into business talk. She has a date to get to and she expects to arrive with a clear mind.

"Oh, I didn't want anything in particular. I was just checking in with you. You know, just to holla at you for a minute. Hey, did you ever hear from Mr. Ray from the club? It's been a minute and the last time we saw each other, you still hadn't heard from him. I know you called him once and left a message but I didn't know whether or not he ever returned your phone call. Or if you had decided to call him again. Shit, you ain't call him again, he ain't call you back. What are y'all waiting on? I know I'm ready for some juicy-juicy." They both laugh.

"Heifer, what you got ESP or something? I just got off the phone with him. Yes, he finally returned my call. Oh, I wasn't calling him again. I called once and left a message and if he had given me the right number, then he got my message. So the ball was in his court and he finally decided to take charge of the ball. He said he had been busy. We didn't get all into exactly what he had been busy with but I took him at his word," Sandy responds with her smile stretched from ear to ear.

"Really? This is the first time you have heard from him and I just so happen to ask about him a few minutes after y'all spoke? That is too funny. See, he knew that I was gonna ask you and he wanted you to be able to say 'yes' you've heard from him. But I can see him being busy. I mean a video game designer. That sounds like a lot of tedious work and the need for complete concentration. Being mixed up in your conversation would have had him fucking up something," BeLynda and Sandy laugh.

"Yea, that is crazy. He sounds so good on the phone too, girl!! All sexy and shit, had me melting in my seat. He said he called to hear my voice."

"Oh he did, did he? That's so original. But I guess the handsome nerd is a little rusty in the mackin' game," BeLynda says sarcastically.

"Yea, that's what I said. But the way his voice was sounding, I wanted to believe everything he was saying," Sandy and BeLynda laugh. "As a matter of fact, I am on my way to have dinner with him now. I told him I'm not dressed for dinner but he said he is casually dressed too. So I am meeting him at Old Ebbitt Grill downtown."

"What?! Wait a minute? Hold … up! A date? For dinner? At Old Ebbitt Grill? Really? Just like that huh? No talking on the phone to get to know each other first. Isn't that going against Sandra Robertson's Dating Rules," BeLynda asks laughing.

"Yes ma'am!! A dinner date, just like that. We can get to know each other over several dinners. Rules are meant to be broken from time-to-time," Sandy laughs. "You know I am not too fond of driving downtown either but he is paying and I already checked out the menu online. It seems pretty nice and not that expensive. So I am going to get my fried oysters."

"Not that expensive? Oh right, that's when you're not paying," they both laugh again. "Oh I hear you Big Girl. Well, I'm not gonna hold you. I know you have to get mentally prepared for your date, just in case he's not wrapped too tight," BeLynda laughs out loud.

"Oooh, Girl!! Don't even say that. I will turn this car around right now and go the hell home. Or hit him over the head with the damn plate of oysters," Sandy and BeLynda laugh.

"Unh-unh, girl, don't do that, eat *all* of them. Don't spare *any* of those. Eat your expensive meal. Now maybe a glass of red wine or a Bloody Mary could be poured on his ass to fuck up his outfit but never the oysters. He pays for them and then if he's crazy, go home and let Larry enjoy you!! You know what they say about oysters. That's how you do the crazy motherfuckas." They both are laughing out loud by now.

"Girl you are so crazy. Listen to you ... bye, love you," Sandy says to BeLynda and then ends the call *click*.

Walking in the restaurant, I feel a little uncomfortable with my outfit. Not that I am under dressed, I'm just not used to being dressed like this for a date. I look around for a minute to see where Ray is seated. I don't see him. Did he stand me up? Well it is six thirty and I told him I would be here at six fifteen. I was in the area but I had to find parking and then walk here. That's one thing I hate about downtown. I hope he didn't think that I stood him up instead. Just then a gentleman walks up to Sandy.

"Good evening Madam, welcome to Old Ebbitt Grill. Are you meeting someone or a party? Do you need a table or would you like a booth," the gentleman asks.

"Good evening, I am here to meet Mr. Ray Daniels. Has he arrived yet," I ask the gentleman.

"Ah yes!! Mr. Daniels. You must be Ms. Robertson. Yes, he has arrived and instructed me to bring you back to where you will be having dinner. Follow me this way young lady," the gentleman smiles with a slight head bow with his hands behind his back.

All righty then. Ray has it like that, huh? The gentleman walks me through the occupied tables to a nice secluded booth in the back of the restaurant. I see Ray seated paying attention to his phone. Ray is looking handsome as ever. His caramel brown complexion complements his tapered haircut and well-groomed beard and mustache. His lips are so inviting. I am not sure what kind of dark jeans he has on but they look nice with the black Nike boots and red polo sweater he is wearing. Even though he is casual, he still looks like he is dressed up a little.

As I get closer to the booth, I notice will be the only ones seated in this area. From a distance, Ray appears lonely. However, I realize we're actually having a private dinner date. Awww, now, I really have something to talk about to the girls!! Colleen is going to have something rude to say to my story.

The gentleman and I arrive at the booth. Ray still has his head down engrossed into something on his phone. It must be work because it looks like he is checking his email. "Excuse me, Mr. Daniels, your dinner date has arrived. Enjoy your meal." He turns around and leaves us to get acquainted with each other.

Ray looks up from his phone. His mouth is open and his eyes are slowly looking at me from head to toe. He closes his phone and places it back on his right hip. *I am not sure if his look is that of a satisfied or disappointed man. So he needs to say something fast before I make an about-face and walk up out of here. At that moment, Ray stands with a smile on his face. It is the prettiest smile I have ever seen on a man. Is it phony though? I mean, is he just smiling because he figures he has to and doesn't want to hurt my feelings?*

"Sandy? Oh my goodness!! Wow!! You look beautiful. I'm so glad you could make it." Ray holds his right hand out towards me. I give him my right hand and he kisses the back of it. *Damn those lips feel so good.* Then he gestures for me to have a seat across from him in the booth. I smile and gladly slide into the booth taking my jacket off and placing it on the seat next to my handbag. Ray is still smiling at me with his hands clasped together. *Well groomed big hands, hmmmm.*

"Good evening Ray. It's nice to see you again. You look very handsome today. Now, did you follow me today? Our outfits look like this dinner was planned way ahead of time. Like we verified what we will have on to make it easier to locate each other." *I have on jeans, my black Via Spiga boots and a red cashmere and cotton blend sweater. I even notice that the leather jacket he has with him is black. Mine is black too. Coincidence?*

"It is very nice to see you too Ms. Sandy. Seeing you standing at the booth made me realize that it has been too long since

I last seen or spoke to you. Yes, our outfits do match, huh? I wonder if that means something. Oh, and no I didn't follow you today, I swear," Ray chuckles holding his left hand up.

"Oh ok. I was just checking. Someone might think we are lovebirds or something up in here all matchy - matchy." I smile giving Ray the side-eye. "But hey, as long as our under clothes don't match, I'm fine with the coincidence. And I don't think it is my fault that we're just seeing each other again."

"You are absolutely right about that. It is not. However, would there be something wrong with us being labeled as lovebirds? I don't see anything wrong with it. And just in case you want to check, my socks are green argyle, my wife beater is black, and it matches my drawers," Ray says raising his left eyebrow with the anticipation of my response.

I start laughing. "Okay, wait … green argyle socks?! Really? What do they match with? Or do they stand for something?" *I'm hoping it stands for how colorful his money is so he can pay for this dinner.*

"Hey, why you laugh, I have on boots. No one can or will see my socks but my dogs when I get home and take my boots off." We both laugh out loud. *Damn he has a beautiful smile.*

The waiter came to take our orders. We're still laughing at the topic of conversation. "Hello Mr. Daniels. What can I start you and the pretty lady off with this evening?" *Damn, is this his regular spot? The waiter knows his name too?*

Ray looks at me, "What would you like to drink? Or do you want an appetizer? Hell, would you like both? You haven't had a chance to look at the menu, have you?" *I just melt all in his mouth. I haven't been on a date like this in a minute and never to a place like this.*

I clear my throat as I close my mouth before I start drooling. "I will take a glass of water with lemon and lime in it, please. I also would like a glass of the dry Riesling. Um, as for an appetizer, I would like to have the Seafood Sauté. The description sounds good," I say and then look up at Ray. "I did check out the menu online before I got here. I figure we could share the appetizer. Is that all right with you Ray?"

He smiles at me and I try to do something else like look in my purse pretending I am looking for something, anything to keep from staring into his smile. I think I am getting a little moist between my legs. Ray looks at the waiter making sure he is writing down my requests. Then he looks at me and says, "That's all you want right now? Don't be shy. Get whatever you want. You don't eat like a bird do you," Ray says to me winking.

"Yes, this is enough for me right now. I'm fine. I want to make sure I have room for dinner. And no … I do not eat like a bird. I pace myself," I respond. *I mean, I thought I was doing something by ordering what I did but I guess not.*

"You pace yourself. Oh okay," he smiles looking at me and then turns to look at the waiter again. "You can bring us the bottle, thank you. And yes, we will share the appetizer." Looking at me again, he asks, "Did you want to try another appetizer? The crab and artichoke dip is pretty good."

He actually has me stumped at requesting the bottle of wine. The menu says the bottle is twenty-seven dollars. Hell, a glass of the wine is eight dollars. That's more than the bottle of wines I am used to drinking over at Regina's house. I went along with the suggestion though. I did not mind Mr. Daniels treating me to a nice evening that didn't require me to add up how much I was gonna pay for my meal.

"Oh, that's fine, I don't mind. I will try their crab and artichoke dip too since you say it's pretty good. I will trust you on this Ray." He smiles and I blush pulling on the cuffs of my sweater.

The waiter jots down our orders and says he'd be back with our drinks in a few minutes. Ray hands him our menus before he leaves.

I notice he is very much into watches. I am sure the Tag Heuer that he is wearing is at least four thousand dollars. I saw one in Macy's once and it was four thousand and nine hundred dollars. I know what kind of watch it is because Samuel L. Jackson and Leonardo DiCaprio wear them and I am fans of both.

Oh shit!! Ray might be out of my league. He has a ring on the ring finger of his right hand full of baguettes and black diamonds. I can tell that is not a cheap piece of jewelry. There is no shadow on his left ring finger to insinuate that maybe that ring actually belongs on the left finger instead.

"So, where were we before we were interrupted? Ah yes, we were trying to see if our under garments match as well. But I do bet one thing ... I bet that is one thing we are not matching in and that is our socks," he winks at me and we both laugh. *I am really having a good time so far. He is so refreshing and I am glad that I decided to meet him for dinner this evening.*

"You are absolutely correct on that one." I touch my left earring and run my fingers through a few of my curls. "Well, I have on knee socks and they are red. My underclothes are black trimmed in red," I say this but I am not looking at him when I say it. *Silence.* I can feel his eyes on me burning a hole in my face. When I finally look up at him, he is now leaning back in the booth with both of his arms stretched out on top of the seat backing, just staring at me, smiling showing all of his beautiful teeth. I smile back at him, lean my head to the right and ask, "What? What's the matter? Why you look at me like that?"

"Well ... I am looking at you because you're so beautiful. And I'm just sitting here soaking in what you just said. You have on a matching bra and panty set that is black. Mine isn't a set but it is matching and just so happens they are black. Your socks match your sweater, but ... is that why you chose red socks?" He is now leaning closer to me with his arms on the table, hands intertwined. He wants to hear what I have to say.

"Is there something wrong with my bra and panties matching? I mean, Vicky's does sell sets to make sure us women match. They may not be placed together on the same rack or table but they are there for us to create sets if we want to." They both share a laugh. Sandy rubs her hands across her right earring out of nervousness yet she really isn't nervous.

"Ah, Vicky, huh? As in Victoria's Secret? A nice place to choose your undergarments. Very sexy and feminine and good taste. I like that in a woman."

"Oh, was I supposed to go to JC Penney's or Hecht's? I don't think so. They may sell those items but they do not specialize in them. Plus, I'm into matching, remember?"

"That's right. How could I forget that fast? So let me hear this story about why you chose red socks when you have on pants and knee-high boots."

"Well, I chose red because, that is my favorite color for one. For two, they are long enough to wear with my boots helping to keep my legs warm. And for three, if I needed to take my boots off for any reason, I will still be matching." Sandy and Ray both get a big laugh out of that.

"Now, that is classic. I will have to remember that. Maybe I will use your third reason tomorrow when I get dressed. Oh, Ms. Robertson … I see I am going to enjoy spending time with you pretty Lady. That is what they have been calling you since you got here, right? I most definitely agree with them."

Damn, this man sure knows how to make me blush.

Chapter Twenty

20

"Well, Mr. Daniels, I can say that I have enjoyed you and our dinner date. I am extremely stuffed. Everything was exceptionally delicious. I don't think I can walk. Maybe when I stand up, some of it will go down because right now, it feels like I'm about five months pregnant. I am going to have work extra hard on my workout," Sandy leans back into the back of the booth seat and rubs her stomach.

"Okay, Ms. Robertson, I am glad that you enjoyed me and our dinner date. I do aim to please. Yes, this is one of my favorite places to come eat. I am just glad that I didn't have to eat alone this evening. Maybe we can do this a little more often. Let's say twice a week? Is that too much to ask," Ray grabs both of Sandy's hands and caresses them gently. She has her eyes closed enjoying the feeling.

"Oh, I'm sure that can be arranged. What days are good for you?' Sandy is liking the two-nights-a-week dinner invite. That means she doesn't have to cook that much, grocery bill will decrease and so will the gas bill.

"Oh my days are clear after three thirty in the afternoon, baby. I won't even have to pencil you in. So whatever days and time that you choose are the days and time I will be spending with you looking into your beautiful face," Ray is looking serious right now. *WOW, he is really serious and means it. Let me try this and see what happens.*

"Okay, it's like that?" Ray nods his head "yes" staring into her hazel brown eyes. "All right, then. Let's meet for dinner on Tuesdays, Wednesdays, and Saturdays. How does that sound?" *I want to see just how free his calendar is since he claims to be done with business at 3:30 every day and making me feel as if I have no other woman to worry about.*

Ray's eyes get wide and he smiles. "Oh, I get three days with the lovely Sandra? Really? I am honored and I humbly accept," he puts his hand on his chest, bowing his head, with eyes closed, and a huge smile.

I am shocked!! I thought he was going to make up some excuse as to why it had to only be two days. I mean he did mention two days and not three or four. I wonder what would have happen if I had said we could meet every day. Hell, I would have had to object to that one though. That runs into my girlfriend time. Not to mention, I am feeling him but I always take it slow when it comes to giving up my goodies. Too much time together will eventually lead to him wanting to be inside of me.

The waiter brought the bill and laid it on the table. I didn't see how much it was but when he pulled out a White Card, I tried not to seem like I've not been around that type of money before. *To* *be honest, other than Regina and Stan, I hadn't. Regina carries around a Black card and told me the card has a four hundred and ninety-five dollars annual fee. Hell, my cards need to have a $0 annual fee. Could I be on my way to Regina's status? I will ask Regina later if she knows about the White Card.*

Ray stands up and helps me with my jacket. Damn he smells so good. I want to ask him what is he wearing but I will wait. I don't want him to think I am in to him too much too soon.

Afterwards, Ray walks Sandy to her car. They are engrossed in a great conversation. They are laughing and seeing how much they have in common. The evening is still going great. Neither of them really wants it to end. Once they arrive at Sandy's car, Ray gives her the money to pay for parking. It is more than she expects and she doesn't accept all of it. *Hell, I am not your woman yet and I won't have you thinking that I am a gold digger because I am not.* Ray smiles and insists several times for her to keep it until Sandy stuffs it in his jacket pocket. Ray opens the door for her and waits for Sandy to get in the car.

"All right pretty lady. Until we meet again in a few days." He leans into her car and gives Sandy the nicest warmest kiss on the cheek. She wants to turn her face to him and have that feeling on her lips but, she must be a lady at all times … well, until it is time for her to be something else. He closes her door and says, "Drive safe. Good night Ms. Robertson."

Sandy pulls off and Ray stands there watching her sitting at the red light until the light turns green. She watches him in her rearview mirror until she sees him walk away back towards the restaurant. *Is he going back inside? Maybe they have parking underground. I guess he is going to get his car and go home. I wonder what he is driving. At least I hope home is his destination,* Sandy says to herself.

Ring! Ring!

"Yea, what's up," the male voice said on the other end.

"Hey, it's me. She just left. I'm in my car now heading home from Old Ebbitt Grill," Ray says dryly to the man on the other end of the phone.

"How did it go? Will there be another date with the bitch? Or did you fuck that up?"

"It went fine, so chill. We will meet three days a week for dinner to start."

"Good, good … *real* good. Yes, that is a great start. I see your charm really does work, huh? I thought I was going to have to send someone else in to get the plan rolling. I already have that other chick on standby if you fucked this up."

"Charm? What charm? This is all me bruh. I don't have to pretend. Your charm would work too if you knew how to choose them and went about it the right way. Let me take that back because charm will never be a part of you. And what other chick? What the fuck are you doing?!"

"Kiss my ass nigga!! I chose who I wanted but she wanted to play hard to get and humiliate a muhfucka!! So, I'm gonna show her how to play the fucking game. She wants to take those damn ho ass classes to impress her man, she will be showing me all those muhfuckin' moves too and very soon!! And don't worry about what other chick. This is my shit, nigga!! Oh let me get this straight. You're not pretending? Are you digging this bitch?!"

"No, I'm not digging her. I was just saying that I don't have to act or pretend for no muhfuckin' body. I keeps it one hunnid." *Damn, this nigga got me talking like his ass and shit. I worked too damn hard to sound and be intelligent and he always seems to take me there.* "Hey, I was there the other night. The classes don't look that bad! Fuck, I think she may have seen me at the door watching. Look, I said that I would help but I think this is starting to sound like you're on some other shit … again. I don't want no parts of any grimy bullshit. I have a business to run and a name that means something in this town. I'm not gonna lose my shit fuckin' witchu! I don't know why you dragged me into this one anyway!!"

"Fuck that!! You're my brother and you owe me Mr. One Hunnid!! You're already into this grimy bullshit. You done jumped in bed with me on this one Ray!! You said that you would get close enough to one of her girlfriends so that I would be able to corner Regina's uppity ass. I'm gonna show that ho how it feels to get smacked, rejected, and humiliated. I lost three clients behind her ass once they saw she stopped fuckin' with me!! Nobody fucks with my money, my business, or my heart!" Ray's brother was livid at this point.

"Oh so now she's a ho?! Why is that?! And nigga how she fuck with your heart?! No one told you to fall for her knowing she is happily married. I've seen her, bruh. She doesn't even seem like the type to be stepping out on her man. And that house they live in, all them expensive cars, and a damn maid … nigga you can't compete with that!! Let it go! Oh, and I don't owe you shit! You're not gonna keep holding shit over my head." Ray is getting heated. He is tired of his brother's bullshit.

"What you mean I 'can't compete with that'? So what you tryin' to say Ray?! I gotta a dick just like her damn bougie ass husband and mine might be bigger and better!! She gotta be taking those damn freak ass classes for some reason and I am gonna find out ... *MY WAY*!! She'll be begging to be with me when I'm done with her ass! If not, she'll be burying that muhfuckin' husband of hers! I play for keeps my nigga!!"

"What kind of shit you on bruh? Stop watching so much damn TV. You ain't really gangsta wit yo shit!! Look, I gotta go. I'm done with this muhfuckin' conversation," Ray pushes the end button on his cell.

Ray slams his hands down on his steering wheel. *Why did I even agree to help his ass before I knew what he was planning? He is always on some grimy shit and trying to pull all of us into his crap. I was okay with this shit all the way up to when I met Sandra at the club and danced with her. He didn't tell me all the details until right before I was to meet with her this evening. Dammit!! I should've known. Now that I have had dinner with her and the conversation was off the chain, and she is one of the most beautiful women I've ever met, I want to get to know her for me. Not to lose her because his ass wants to do harm to someone she is so close to. I am not sure how I am going to work this out but I need to figure it out fast. I am not feeling his ass at all on this shit but I am feeling Sandy!!*

When Ray gets home, he pulls into the garage and sits there for a minute. His head is aching and he is tense from that conversation with his brother. He doesn't know what to do. He can hear his dogs barking at the door waiting for him to come in. He looks at his phone and sees that it is only eight-thirty. He really enjoyed himself with Sandy this evening. It has been a long time since he has been able to say that. He lets out a big sigh and heads towards the door.

He opens the door and both of his male Rottweilers come charging at him, wagging their little nubs of a tail jumping up at him almost to knock him down. Normally, he would play around with them for a few minutes but not tonight. His mind is somewhere else and he isn't in the mood. *Hmmp, where are my bitches?*

Walking through the grand foyer, he could smell something delicious being cooked. *Mmm, let me peep my head in and see what is that I'm smelling.* Passing the water fountain in his grand foyer and the library, he bends the corner to the right and enters the kitchen. He sees Rachel, his mother cooking a big meal. She has her apron on with the music blaring through the surround sounds humming while she is cooking. He told her she doesn't have to do all of that but she insists. That explains why he didn't see his female Rotties. She always lock them up when she is there because the males are always chasing them around trying to fuck and that turns into a bunch of barking and fighting. That gets on her nerves.

He walks up behind her and greets her with a kiss on the cheek. "Hey Ma. What you doing," Ray asks. She is always coming over to cook for him.

"What does it look like I'm doing? I'm cooking my baby something to eat. I have a turkey breast and a ham in the ovens over here. The greens and green beans are on the stove over here too. I put the yams, mac 'n cheese and corn pudding in the oven over there. I put the cornbread sausage stuffing that was leftover in the freezer, instead of cooking it. I've fixed you enough bad carbs for the moment," she laughs and leans in for another kiss.

Then she turns around with her left hand on her hip and a disappointed look and says, "Let me guess, you ate already. Awww, Ray, I done told you time and time again to stop all that eating out. It's not good for you. You don't know what they putting in their products and how they are preparing that shit you keep putting in your system. You gone hear me one day and hopefully it is not after the doctor announces you have a clogged artery or you have to take meds for high blood pressure or diabetes."

Now here she go with that again!! Ray says to himself. *How old am I and she still wants to tell me about eating. Sigh. But I love her to death though. That's my Mama.*

"C'mon ma, not now, not today. I've eaten already and that's that. There's only two ways to get it out of my system at this point and one of them I don't plan on doing. And I didn't eat alone. I had a date. Had I known you were going to be here cooking, I probably would have brought her here." Ray says and Rachel puts down her fork and turns around to face him again.

This time, she has a surprised look on her face. "Did you say you had a date? With whom Ray?! And you would've bought her here? You wanted your Mama to meet her already? Tell me all about her. Is she nice? Pretty? Intelligent? Black? White? Hispanic? You know I prefer black but right now, I will take seeing you with any woman. It's been how many years? You have got let it go Ray."

"Slow down ma!! Her name is Sandra Robertson. Yes, she is very pretty, nice, and intelligent and she is black. Don't worry, I love my sistas. And before you ask, she has her own place, she does not have any children, she is very shapely, seems to have her own money, the few times that I have seen her she was well dressed, and yes I will be seeing her again," Ray dryly says rolling his eyes to the ceiling as he is getting a glass of water. He hops up onto the marbled island taking a big gulp of the water.

"Oh okay, that sounds like a winner so far, son. Maybe I can finally get some grandbabies from you to spoil. You know we have to share all of this luxury with some little ones, right? You have too much house and money to be living here with four damn dogs. And get off that island. It wasn't made for asses," Rachel says while swinging the dish towel at Ray's leg. "But, wait a minute, you said that so dry. Why? What's going on? What is wrong with you?

You said that you would be seeing her again, so why aren't you smiling or sounding excited or upbeat" Rachel asks her son looking at him side-eyed. She knows her sons and they can be up to some no good shit sometimes.

"Nothing ma. Everything is fine. I am fine. Nothing is going on." Ray jumps down off the island and takes the last swallow of his water. "Hey, I am glad that you've cooked ma. I really appreciate it. Seriously. Maybe Sandy can come over here and help me eat it. If not, I'm sure most of it will go to waste. I might take a plate to her tomorrow. But right now, I need to go shoot some pool to clear my head and do some thinking," Ray kisses his mother on the cheek again and gives her a big hug.

Rachel looks at him suspiciously as he heads towards the second set of stairs down the hall to the pool room. *Mmm-hmmm, he still thinks I am crazy. After all this time, he finally meets someone that he is interested in and he talks about her with a depressing tone and a sour-puss face? I'm a long ways off from being senile. The only time he acts like that is when that damn son of mine, Rennie, has him mixed up in some bullshit. Oh I will get to the bottom of this. They can count on Mama Rachel doing just that. I will call Rone as soon as I get home. He may not be involved but I am sure he has an idea as to what is going on.*

Rone is Rachel's youngest son. He seems to stay out of trouble more than her other four boys. The reason for that seems to be because he is married and has a strong woman beside him making sure that he doesn't fuck up what they have built. Rachel loves that and is waiting for the day that the rest of the crew finds the same thing. As long as Rennie, Ray, Rick, and Rufus are single and have no one to positively occupy their minds, they tend to get caught up in some bullshit. Most of the time Rennie is leading the pack.

Rachel pushes the intercom button for the driver that Ray got her. "Hello, where would you like to go," says the driver. "Hello Carl, I will be ready to leave in about forty-five minutes," Rachel says while wiping her hands and taking off her apron. "Yes, Mrs. Daniels. I will get the car and bring it around front. I will be waiting."

"Thank you Carl," she releases the intercom button and heads upstairs to The Mother's Quarters to get her things ready to go. She is shaking her head talking in her head about Ray's behavior. She puts on her mink poncho, steps into her Christian Louboutins, and grabs her Marc Cross handbag off of the leather ottoman heading for the door.

Your ass is hiding something. I don't know what it is but I will find out. I have a few phones calls to make and they better give me the answers I am looking for or else.

Ring!! Ring!!

Ray's phone is ringing. He starts not to answer it thinking that it is his brother Rennie. He had had enough of his foolishness for the rest of the month. When he looks at the screen, he sees that it is Sandy. He hurries to answers it before it went to voicemail. He is thinking about giving her the ringtone Floetry *Say Yes*. All she has to do is say "yes" and it is a wrap!!

With a smile, he says, "Hey gorgeous. I can get used to hearing my phone ring and it is you calling me. What are you doing Miss Lady? What's up? Is everything all right?" *Damn, maybe I shouldn't have asked her if everything is all right. My tone may have her getting suspicious. I know where she lives, and I'm not supposed to ... yet. I know how long it would take her to get home and she isn't home yet. Shit, I'm getting paranoid about Rennie and his damn plan. Calm down Ray,* he says to himself.

"Is that right? That's good to know. Oh, nothing is up. Everything is fine, thanks for asking. I'm on my way home, I'm still in the car. I have about fifteen more minutes to go." Ray knows that. "I just wanted to call and tell you again that I really enjoyed myself with you and dinner this evening. I haven't been out in a very long time and I will say that my waiting wasn't in vain. Thank you Ray. It was a pleasure joining you this evening. Oh, I'm sorry, I'm just running my mouth. Did I interrupt you?"

"Nah, you cool, I was just getting ready to shoot some pool. Nothing important. That can wait. I am glad you enjoyed yourself. I do aim to please when I am interested. I appreciate me being your choice since it been a long time."

"Shoot pool? Oh you made a stop on your way home, huh?" *With some bitch leaned over the table so you can watch her ass?* "Oh, I'm sorry. I will let you go. I didn't mean to interrupt. I'm just running my mouth and never thought to ask you if you were occupied. Again, I just wanted to say thank you for this evening. I'm really looking forward to our dinner dates." *Damn, should I have said that? Did I sound too pressed for him?*

Ray laughs out loud. "Oh, you didn't interrupt. Occupied? With who? After my wonderful dinner with Sandy Robertson? Why would I do that? I am home. I'm just in my Billiards Room. I'm not on a time schedule to get started. I got all night. This doesn't close down at a certain time. This table, sticks, and balls are not going anywhere." *Damn, that didn't come out right Ray. It's been a minute since you've spoken to a woman. Work on not sounding so crass. Maybe she didn't think I was being crass.*

Sandy takes the phone from her ear and looks at it saying to herself, *Damn, he got a Billiards Room in his damn house? Where he live at? What does he live in? A big ass house or mansion? What the fuck I have to offer him other than some pussy?* She puts the cell phone back to her ear.

"Billiards Room, huh? I hear you Mr. Daniels. You must have a large basement. I have seen pool tables and played on a few. So I know they take up a lot of room."

Ray hesitates to respond. Should he have told her that? He doesn't want to run her off. He can tell by her apprehensive response that she is feeling uncomfortable. He will work on her uneasiness as time goes on. Ray is really digging Sandy. He would like to invite her over to his house but he doesn't want to scare her off. She doesn't appear to be like the other women he has taken out or his brothers have introduced him to. Hell, his mother didn't even like any of the other women. He has a strong feeling she is going to like Sandy.

He thinks she has a very sexy voice too and it sounds even better over the phone. Makes him feel like she is whispering in his ear. It is making him horny. It surely has been a minute since he has been in some pussy. That has been by choice because he knows he is a handsome man and can have the pick of the litter. He can tell that Sandy is a real woman. He knows it is going to take some time before he get in between her sexy thighs. Ray is willing to wait too. Hell, he has waited all this time, a little longer won't hurt.

"Yes, I have one of those rooms and it is not in my basement." Sandy's eyes open wide and her mouth falls open. She is almost drifting into another lane listening to him. Ray continues. "No need to thank me Sandy. However, you are quite welcome. I will say that I haven't been out in a long time either. So that's another similarity for us to add to the list, huh? I can say that most of the previous potential dates let it be known through slick comments that they were looking for someone to take care of them. When and if I choose to take care of a woman, it will be because I choose to and not because that is what she is expecting me to do. So I just decided that I would take a break from the dating scene." Ray is now leaning on the pool table holding on to the pool stick.

"Really?! That is very surprising to hear but okay, Mr. Daniels. We will add that to the list of commonalities. Wow, women are that forward nowadays, huh? Well, I guess they don't think there is anything wrong with their forwardness. Men do it all the time, especially when they want to sleep with us. But I know what you mean. Trust me, I do understand.

I wonder how many women I know that actually think like that? I mean I would love to have a man with a six figures salary but I wouldn't necessarily expect him to take care of me right from the start. I just want to live comfortably, without having to worry about anything. And he must have it going on for the women to think that. "I have gone out on a few dates but I guess I actually must've been in a cave for a few years to have missed all that. I mean how does a woman expect that on first meeting a man?" Sandy says almost arriving to her neighborhood.

Ray gets very quiet in the midst of listening to Sandy. *Dammit Rennie!! I really can't go through with this bullshit!! I've gotta get out of this bullshit and FAST!! I can't lose her over this ... I've finally found her!! I know she is the one!!* Ray closes his eyes showing much sorrow. He knows at this point, all bets are off with going through with his brother's plan.

All the while, Rachel is standing at the entrance to the room listening to her son's conversation and watching his face. *Mmm-*

hmmm, something is definitely up. You sounding all sexy on the phone talking to her yet looking like you are constipated about to break that damn pool stick. Oh don't you worry baby. I'm about to be the laxative you need. You'll be with her, fall in love, get married, and have some kids. Believe that. I've got some work to do. She walks off headed to the car to go home.

Walking outside, she sees her car waiting for her. The driver takes her bags and places them in the trunk. He opens the back door for her and she gets inside. Pulling out her cell phone, she dials her son Rone's home number waiting for someone to answer.

Ring!! Ring!!

"Hey, Mama! What's up? I'm surprise to hear from you. It's nine – thirty."

"Hello baby. How are you? I know what time it is. How is my daughter-in-law and my grandbabies?"

"We are all fine Mama. Now, what's up? I know you didn't call this time of night to ask how we are doing. Spill it. Where you coming from? I can tell you are in the car."

"I just left Ray's house. Something ain't right and I need to check with you to find out what is going on. I know you know. So I need to meet up with you pronto!! If Rennie is on some bullshit again, I'ma slap his ass!"

"Uh, I ain't sure what's goin' on with Rennie but I can find out." Rone says nervously.

"You do that. Let me get off this phone. There's another set of ears in this car. I'll be waiting to hear from my last born."

"Aight Ma, goodnight." *Damn!! His ass is actually going after that Lady. And Ray always gets caught up in that nigga's shit!!*

Private Classes 2 is ready for you to continue with this hot steamy saga!!

Before you get started on the next book, it would greatly be appreciated if you write a review/comment on Amazon about this first installment to the *Private Classes* serial novel.

www.ingramcontent.com/pod-product-compliance
Lightning Source LLC
Chambersburg PA
CBHW030026180626
46810CB00001B/232